Fetish for a

Blue Skyy

Fetish for a Blue Skyy

LaKesa Cox

authorHOUSE®

AuthorHouse™
1663 Liberty Drive
Bloomington, IN 47403
www.authorhouse.com
Phone: 1-800-839-8640

First published by AuthorHouse   08/20/2011

ISBN: 978-1-4634-2735-1 (sc)
ISBN: 978-1-4634-2734-4 (hc)
ISBN: 978-1-4634-2733-7 (ebk)

Library of Congress Control Number: 2011910634

Printed in the United States of America

Also by *LaKesa Cox*

- *After the Storm*
- *Water in My Eyes*

Anthologies

- *Nikki Turner Presents: Street Chronicles—Girls in the Game*
  (Contributing author)

- *Nikki Turner Presents: Street Chronicles—A Woman's Work*
  (Contributing author)

Dedication

For Almeda Crossin—
3-19-32 through 4-25-10

I miss you Granny.

Acknowledgements

I have to give thanks to the heavenly Father for continuing to bless me and for guiding me in the right direction in this thing we call life. To my husband, thanks for being able to sleep through the sound of keys clicking on my laptop as I stayed up night after night pushing this baby to its birth. Yeah I know it probably felt like I was having an affair with HP Compaq but really, it was just work! A special thanks to my children and the rest of my family for always supporting me and being my biggest fans. To my "unofficial" editor, fellow author and friend Denise Johnson, thanks for reading this before anyone else and for pushing me to give you more and more of Skyy which in return motivated me to finish telling her story (even though you don't like her very much lol). Your feedback and critique was invaluable and I appreciate you for that. Now, the ball is in your court—are you finished yet??? To my "official" editor, Ms. Carla Dean of U Can Mark My Word, thanks for cleaning this baby up, giving it a more polished and professional look. You are great at what you do. I'm still waiting on you to put on that literary agent's hat ☺. Dashawn Taylor with hotbookcovers.com, you are the best! I fell in love with the cover from the moment I saw it. I appreciate your professionalism and how expeditious you were in getting the cover and the rest of my marketing materials completed. Your work truly speaks for itself. Finally, for everyone who purchased *After the Storm* and *Water in my Eyes*, I would like to thank you for all of your support. I hope you enjoy this story as much as I enjoyed writing it.

I encourage your feedback—hit me up on Facebook (www.facebook.com/lakesacox), Twitter (@IamLakesa) or sign my guestbook at www.lakesacox.com.

Truly,
LaKesa

Prologue

"Please, this is not right! Please don't do this!" Skyy shrieked.

Tears mixed with mascara streamed down her face, looking as if someone had thrown black watercolor paint on her. She squirmed a bit, trying to loosen her hands that were taped behind her. Her feet were duct-taped to the legs of an oversized dining room chair that belonged to the oversized oak table she had received as a gift. The tag, which was still attached to the brand-new Thomasville set, scratched her bare leg as she struggled for freedom. Ironically, Skyy had bigger worries than the tag on the chair.

"Don't do this? Don't do this? You started this! What made you think you could just play me like this? Huh? Huh? You think this is a joke? This is not a fucking joke!" the man said, waving his .38 semi-automatic in Skyy's face.

"I'm sorry! I'm so sorry!" Skyy cried.

"You're not sorry. You're scared. If I didn't have this gun in my hand, you would be singing another tune. What was that you told me? Leave you the fuck alone? Was that it? You think you can go and put a restraining order on me?" He rubbed the barrel of the gun around the outline of Skyy's mouth. "You think you can leave me? You can't fuckin' leave me. You owe me. If I can't have you, nobody can."

"What do you want from me? I'm sorry. I'll do what you want me to do. Just please, please put the gun down, and let's talk about it."

"Oh no, you're not sorry, but it don't matter 'cause you fuckin' owe me. You don't care about me. You've never cared about me. Your whole life you've walked around like you're the shit, queen of the fuckin' world. But guess what? Tonight . . . tonight, you're gonna pay for everything. Everything!" he yelled.

"Fetish—(fet'ish)—An abnormally obsessive preoccupation or attachment; a fixation"

Chapter 1—(8 Months Earlier)

"It's a beautiful day here at Blue Skyy's Hair and Nail Salon. This is Coco. How can I help youuu," sang Coco, a twenty-six-year-old, overexuberant, homosexual hairstylist that worked in the small downtown salon.

Situated in the heart of Richmond, Virginia, a stone's throw away from historic Jackson Ward, the hair salon took up space in a refurbished building that once housed the old Army Navy Surplus Store back in the seventies. Sitting between a tattoo parlor and beauty supply store, Blue Skyy's Hair Salon was an eccentric salon filled with vibrant and chic colors, hues of cinnamon, bright red, chocolate brown, and bright yellow. All of the furniture was chocolate brown leather, from the sofas in the waiting area to the salon chairs at each station. Four identical stylist stations lined the area to the right of the salon, which was the area behind the receptionist desk and waiting area. Six dryers lined the wall to the left, and there were flat-screen TVs mounted in three corners of the salon. The shampoo area was nestled in the back of the salon, adjacent to the breakroom/kitchen area and the bathroom. Beyond the bathroom was a small office where Skyy, the owner, took care of the business.

Coco, a tall, thin, Naomi Campbell wannabe, held the cordless phone to his left ear with one hand, while using his other hand to write a message on a piece of paper.

"Okay, I'll give Skyy the message. Thanks for calling," he sang before hanging up. He then took the message and put it in a pile on top of the check-in counter.

Niya, the unreliable, eighteen-year-old receptionist, who was also the younger sister of Tiffany, the nail technician, had neglected to show up for work. So, Coco was working double duty as a stylist and a receptionist.

1

"Okay, for real, if Ms. Thang don't hurry up and get her ass in here, I'm calling Skyy, because this is ridiculous," Coco said, sashaying his six-foot, skinny frame across the floor in his tight, size 29, True Religion low-rise jeans.

Coco lived up to his name with skin the color of Hershey's cocoa powder. He wore his platinum-colored hair cut really low and occasionally changed the color to fit his mood. He topped his flamboyant aura off with light blue contact lenses. And it didn't stop there. Coco kept up with every style known to women. Every designer jean, designer handbag, and even designer shoes, Coco had them. He was the shop gossiper as well as the shop tattletale. If there was tea to be spilled, Coco spilled it. At the same time, Coco acted like a little girl whenever things didn't go his way. He was famous for running to Skyy every time there were problems in the salon. He was truly a drama queen, which Skyy made mention of at least once a day. But, don't get it twisted. Piss Ms. Coco off, and he would kick a bitch's ass if need be.

It was Tuesday, and coming off of a weekend, Skyy hadn't made it into the salon yet. More than likely, she didn't have any early appointments since weekends were the times she did her socializing. She never scheduled early appointments on Tuesdays particularly for that reason. Besides, it wasn't Skyy's job to be there to answer the phone and greet the customers; it was Niya's, who was now officially two hours late. Coco, whose clientele surpassed everyone's in the salon, was always in early, Tuesday through Saturday.

"I wonder where Ms. Skyy went gallivanting off to this weekend," said Coco, as he used his Chi flat iron to slightly bend his customer's hair.

He was talking to Debi, the thirty-something stylist who'd just come in. Her station was located next to Coco's. Debi was average looking, wore expensive lace front wigs, and was fighting to lose those last fifteen pounds of baby fat she gained while pregnant with her now one-year-old son. Her clothes were always two sizes too tight, probably because they were always junior-sized clothes that she wore.

Today, Debi was running late, as usual, and had a customer in the waiting area. Ever since she had her son, she could never seem to get to work on time, and her customers were starting to complain. As she slipped off her wedge sandals and replaced them with a pair of navy blue Crocs, she motioned for her ten o'clock appointment to come to her chair. Next, she grabbed her chocolate brown smock from the hook on the oval mirror at her station, tied it around her waist, then slipped her purse and other belongings in her drawer.

"I'm so sorry I'm late. My baby was up with a fever all night. I'll give you a discount today, okay?"

Her customer nodded in agreement before saying, "I think I need a relaxer."

"Chile, from where I'm standing, there's nothing to think about, okayyyyy?" Coco replied.

"Coco, don't start with my customers."

"I'm just saying, Ms. Thang knows good and well it's time for a touch-up."

"Don't listen to him. Be quiet, Coco."

"Honey chile, listen to me. A relaxer can be your friend." Two of Coco's customers that were sitting in the waiting area chuckled, as did the customer sitting in his chair.

"Coco, shut up! I'll give *you* a touch-up." Debi threatened, while grabbing a brown plastic cape and fastening it around her customer's neck. She combed and parted her customer's hair carefully before applying the relaxer.

"For real, Debi, I think I need to call Skyy. I can't believe Niya is not here yet. Every Tuesday she comes in late."

As if on cue, in walked Skyy, a five-foot, two-inch LisaRaye lookalike, with sun-dipped caramel skin and long sandy-colored hair kissed by blonde highlights.

"What's going on, divas *and* Coco?" she said coyly, pushing her Chanel sunglasses from her face up to the top of her head.

Her black, oversized Tory Burch totebag matched her Tory Burch thong sandals, and her size 28 Rock and Republic skinny jeans hugged her booty tight. Her 38 double D's moved freely in her striped red and black tube top, and it was apparent she was not wearing a bra. As she threw her totebag and keys on the counter to grab her messages, sterling David Yurman bangles jingled on her wrist. It was evident by all who knew her that Skyy had great taste when it came to fashion, and Coco was always trying to compete with Skyy in that department—friendly competition, of course. Whether

3

she was just kicking it around in the shop or stepping out on the town, Skyy always wore designer brands. Nordstrom and Saks Fifth Avenue were the only two department stores in Richmond that catered to her taste.

For a thirty-seven-year-old, Skyy was doing pretty good for herself—a successful business owner, had her own home, and shopped and travelled all across the country. However, all of this was not by way of her hefty clientele or business profits. It was by way of her personal life. See, Skyy had a fetish. For those who didn't know her, they might think her fetish was shoes, clothes, designer bags, or maybe even jewelry. But, that wasn't it. Skyy had a fetish for men—married men. Currently, she was in a relationship with three different married men.

First, there was Kyle, a general manager of one of the most popular Toyota dealerships in the city. Kyle, married for five years, found his wife undesirable after she gained sixty pounds while pregnant with their son. So, he was no longer attracted to her.

Then there was Davin, married for ten years, who owned his own mortgage company. He was married to a woman who spent more time at work than with him. He loved his wife and wanted to spend time with her, but all she wanted to do was bring her boardroom to the bedroom, treating Davin like one of her subordinates.

The music mogul, a.k.a. the Mystery Man affectionately called "J", lived in Atlanta and had been married for twenty years to his high school sweetheart. He was truly unhappy in his marriage. He could afford to leave his wife, but since he didn't sign a prenup, he selfishly refused to do so because she would be entitled to half of everything he owned. Therefore, he cheated to stay sane.

Skyy dated all of these men with the understanding that they would stay with their wives. Unlike other mistresses who plotted and schemed to make the wife the ex, Skyy was the complete opposite. She didn't want the commitment. She liked being single, while giving those men what they were missing at home. If a man approached her and he was not married, Skyy quickly turned him away.

"Awww, look at you all relaxed and well rested. So where did you go this weekend? Jamaica? Bahamas? Vegas?" Coco asked.

Skyy thumbed through her messages while checking her Movado watch, trying to ensure that she stayed on top of her upcoming appointments as well as her business callbacks.

"Vegas, honey. Stayed at the Bellagio Hotel. You know my men know how to treat me."

"And who was it this time? Kyle, Davin, or Mr. Music Mogul?"

"Coco, mind your business. Mind your business," Skyy teased.

"If you were flown out to Vegas and stayed in the Bellagio, I would put my money on Mr. Music Mogul. Okay, so what did you get? I know you can't wait to tell it."

Coco and Skyy were tight. In fact, Coco was the first stylist that Skyy hired when her salon opened five years ago. Prior to that, they'd both worked together at the Hair Cuttery on Brook Road for four years. So, their friendship spanned almost a decade, and they were loyal to one another. Skyy wasn't afraid to tell Coco what was on her mind, whether it was right, wrong, or indifferent, and vice versa. They had that sort of relationship.

"A Gucci Guccisima Pelham tote, a pair of Gucci wedge sandals, and a Louis Vuitton Damier-print Speedy Bag."

"And you know I will be borrowing it all. Heyyyyyy," sang Coco, as he snapped his fingers.

"Yes, diva, I will be more than happy to let you borrow them … after I wear them first."

"How much does all that stuff cost?" Debi asked.

"Shit, that Pelham bag alone is almost two thousand," bragged Coco, as if the stuff was his.

"You let him spend all that money on materialistic stuff? Hell, I would've rather had the money," Debi said in a narcissistic tone.

Coco and Skyy looked at each other because they knew Debi was probably thinking of her own money problems. Unlike Coco and Skyy, who had men that basically supplemented their lifestyles financially, Debi and her husband had financial issues. Debi paid all the bills and took care of their son, while her husband, Eric, spent his time in between odd jobs while collecting unemployment. When they first got married, Eric had a decent job working for Dupont as a floor supervisor, but he was laid off six months ago. Even while Eric worked, he still had a problem managing his money, which resulted in Debi carrying the bulk of the financial load. After him being laid off, things got much worse, and at this point, Debi started feeling the pressure of being the sole breadwinner; it was taking a toll on her.

Skyy tried to switch gears a bit by scanning the salon. "Where's Niya?" she asked.

"Hmph, have you seen her? Because I sure haven't," Coco replied.

"She hasn't come in yet? It's after ten o'clock. Anybody called her yet?"

"No, I just got here myself," Debi said, while working the relaxer into her customer's hair. "You burning yet?" she asked her customer.

The customer shook her head, wanting to sustain as long as she could before having the relaxer rinsed from her hair. She knew the longer she let it stay on her hair, the straighter her hair would be.

"Coco, why didn't you call Niya?" Skyy asked, grabbing her BlackBerry.

"Because I can't be the momma, the daddy, and the baby up in here. Hell, I had three early customers this morning trying to get to work. I am too fabulous to be playing all these roles."

Skyy shook her head and laughed at her friend. She then looked over at Debi, who had a look of angst on her face. She made a mental note to be sure to tell Debi later on that if she needed to borrow some money, she had her back. Skyy dialed several numbers, listened to the recorded voicemail, and left a message for Niya.

"Niya, if you're not here by eleven, don't bother coming in at all. I cannot run a business like this, honey. Please call and let me know what's going on."

Skyy went to her station, which was the first in line, right next to Coco's. She grabbed the remote for the radio/cd player and turned the radio on.

"I'm going to my office. If my ten-thirty comes in, holler and let me know."

Before going to her office, Skyy watched as Debi took her client to the shampoo bowl. She mouthed to Coco, *Was she late again*, referring to Debi's tardiness. Coco tried nodding slyly, hoping Debi didn't catch a glimpse of him and Skyy talking about her. Skyy straightened the envelopes in her hands and disappeared to her office.

Chapter 2

"So I told him, 'Honey, you're a BMW, and I don't like BMW's'."

"BMW? What does that mean, Coco?" Debi asked.

"Body Made Wrong. Honey, he had a muffin top, muffin middle, and a muffin bottom," Coco said jokingly.

The women in the salon roared with laughter. Debi and Skyy still had customers. Having finished all of his customers for the day, Coco was sitting in his chair. Tiffany, the nail technician, was sitting at her table doing a fill-in for Niya, the receptionist that finally showed up.

"Coco, you are so crazy," said Skyy.

"What's crazy about that? Hmph, don't hate me 'cause I like what I like. Do I look like I want to be parading around with somebody named Dunlap?"

"I thought you said his name was Landon."

"I call him Dunlap 'cause his stomach done rolled way over in his lap."

The ladies were cracking up as Coco continued to entertain them like he usually did all day. He kept a certain energy going in the salon. Not only did he keep things lively between the stylists, but the customers enjoyed him as well.

"Well, Ms. Coco, you better watch your step, or you're gonna have a love triangle on your hands. Oh wait! That's not you; that's Skyy," said Niya.

"Little girl, stay in your place and out of grown folks' business," said Skyy.

"Look, honey, don't compare me to Skyy. I don't eat M&M's, okayyyy," Coco sang.

"M&M's? Coco, what are you talking about?" Niya asked.

"Married men. I likes my men single and free and all for me."

"I heard that!" came from the customer sitting in Skyy's chair.

"Wait! Why y'all hating on me? I'm not trying to take anybody's man away from them, not trying to break up no families or anything like that. So, why y'all getting all testy with me? Every week we have the same conversation," said Skyy.

"Well, morally, it's just wrong and not fair to the wife, even if the wife and the husband are having problems," Debi said.

"Chile, please! You don't even want to sleep with your husband, so why the hell do you even care?" Coco blurted.

Debi gave Coco one of her 'I know you didn't just go there' looks. She didn't appreciate Coco putting her business in the street like that. Even if it were true, it was not Coco's place to blurt it out and tell everyone.

"Shut the hell up, Coco. Damn, you have the biggest mouth!"

"Mmm-hmmm, that's what my boo-boo told me last night."

More laughter erupted in the salon.

"Okay, okay. Coco, that was not fair. Now apologize to Debi," Skyy said, trying to play mediator.

"Don't try and change the subject, Skyy. You know this all points back to you and all your M&M's."

"Why are we having this discussion again? You want everybody in the shop to start judging me, is that it?"

"No, I want folks to understand why you do what you do, especially the married ones. Maybe they would consider screwing their husbands once in a while if they could hear from the one that does."

Coco and Skyy went tit for tat, as they normally did. Sometimes the conversation in the salon would go too far, especially when it involved others, like tonight with Debi. It was okay for Coco and Skyy to go at it. That was just the way their relationship worked. Skyy never took offense to Coco's innuendoes. However, she never thought it was cool for Coco to put anybody else's business out there, especially Debi's. Most of the time, when Debi confided in the stylists in the salon, she didn't expect them to blab their mouths about it while customers were there.

"So, Coco, it's okay for you to go sleeping around with all these men who are on the DL, but I sleep with someone else's husband and I'm the bad guy."

"Oh no, you didn't go there."

"You know I'm right. Some of the men you sleep with are living double lives, too. Think about that."

All the women in the shop started nodding in agreement.

"The only difference between the men you date and the men I date is the men I date wear wedding rings," Skyy argued.

"All of the men I date are not on the DL, though, Skyy," Coco retorted.

The conversation continued to fill up the afternoon as the last few customers left the salon. They debated the difference between DL brothers versus married men. Coco tried to make his case about the men who were living double lives dating him and dating women at the same time. He argued how society forced these men into living double lives because the lawyers, doctors, and athletes that he tended to date would not be able to live as openly gay men without being chastised and ridiculed in their professions.

"Think about it. If the quarterback of your favorite NFL team went on national television and said he was one of the kids, what do you think the men in this country would do to him? What about his teammates? Same with lawyers. How many people in their profession would take them seriously if they confessed to being gay?"

"But, Coco, it's not fair to women like me who are out there dating these men and thinking they are heterosexual, but all the while they are sleeping with men, too," Tiffany, the nail technician, honed in.

Even though she was only twenty-four, Tiffany had her share of men problems already. Between having a baby daddy that was fresh out of jail and an ex-fiancé, Tiffany had had enough men drama over the last two years to last a lifetime. However, she was on the market for a good man to help her raise her two-year-old son, and it sickened her to think she could potentially fall prey to one of the DL men that Coco always spoke about.

"See, Coco," Skyy said.

"See *Coco* nothing. Skyy, you just dead wrong. That mess is gonna come back to haunt you one day," Coco replied.

"Yeah, Skyy. One of these days, you're gonna be ready to commit, settle down, and have a family. How will you manage to do that after being the other woman for so long?" Debi asked.

"Easy. I'm not trying to be anybody's wife. Not now or ever. And I definitely don't want any kids. Men are not reliable enough for me to commit to permanently. I've never thought about settling down. Uh-uh, not me. That's just not my thing."

"That's so sad. You're gonna be the old lady with a house full of cats, growing old all by yourself."

"No, I won't. I'll be living with you, Coco."

Tiffany and Niya erupted with laughter along with the two remaining customers. Debi was the only one who wasn't laughing. She seemed to be off in another place, barely concentrating on her customer's hair.

*   *   *

When Niya closed and locked the door behind the last customer, Skyy, Debi, and Coco swept the floor around their workstations, while Tiffany cleaned her area. When Skyy was done, she gave her station a look-over one last time to make sure it was clean before heading to her office.

"Hey, Debi, can I see you for a minute in my office?"

Debi reluctantly propped her broom against her station and followed Skyy to her office. Skyy took a seat behind the mahogany desk in her therapeutic office chair as Debi shut the door behind them. Debi stood at the edge of the desk, concentrating on the time because she had to get to the daycare by six o'clock to pick up her son.

"What is it, Skyy?" she asked.

"Sit down, Debi."

Debi moved slowly, hoping Skyy was not going to fire her for constantly being late.

"Debi, are you having problems at home that you need some help with? I'm not trying to get in your business or anything, but I noticed you've been coming in late every day. You seem disoriented, can't concentrate, and have even forgotten about a couple of your appointments. That's not like you."

Debi put her face in her hands and began to sob. Skyy watched Debi's shoulders move up and down with each sound she made. She sat there crying for several minutes before gaining her composure.

"I hate him. I can't stand my husband. And the more I think I'm going through a phase, the more I realize how much I don't want to be married to him anymore. He's lazy, selfish, and inconsiderate. I just don't want to be with him anymore." Debi started crying again.

Skyy was unsure of how to console her because she wasn't expecting that from Debi. She was thinking maybe Debi was going to say they were about to lose their house or car or something like that, but Skyy never thought Debi would express being ready to give up on her marriage.

"Debi, you don't mean that. You and Eric are perfect for each other."

"No. No, we're not. I get up, get the baby ready for daycare, drop him off, come to work, and stand on my feet all fucking day. Then I turn around, pick up the baby, go home, and when I get there, that lazy bastard is sitting on the couch watching TV or sitting in front of the computer. If I ask if he's been out looking for a job, he tells me yes, but I know he's lying. Since he's been laid off, he doesn't cook or clean. He doesn't do anything but sit around and wait for me to do it all. I'm tired, Skyy. I'm so tired of doing it all by myself. I just wish he would leave. I hate him."

Skyy walked over to hug Debi.

"I'm just so tired of being married to him. I don't want to do it anymore, Skyy. I need a way out."

"Don't talk like that, Debi. You love your husband. You want to be with him."

"No, I really don't. I'm tired of being the wife, the maid, the cook, the doctor, the husband even. He leaves his shit all over the house. I have to tell him over and over again to pick his shit up off the floor. So, not only am I picking up behind him, I'm picking up behind the baby, too. I have to do everything. Everything! I am sooo tired. When I get home, my feet and back are hurting, and the first thing he asks me when I walk through the door is what's for dinner. His ass should have dinner waiting for me!"

"I understand all that, Debi. Maybe it's because he's not working right now. Once he finds a job, things will go back to the way they were."

"No, they won't. My marriage was a big mistake. I should've never married Eric. I realized that when I was pregnant. I need a man to help me, somebody that can do things for me. I hear you talk about these men that take you on trips and buy you nice things, and my husband can't even keep a fucking job. I married a loser, Skyy. Now, I have a son with him, and things are that much worse. Daycare, the mortgage, the car payment, it's all on me. He does nothing but give me a good fuck, and these days, I don't even want that anymore. I just want him to leave, but he won't."

Debi continued to cry uncontrollably. Skyy rubbed her shoulders, feeling sorry for her friend.

"I just don't know what to do. I tell him all the time that I want a divorce, but he keeps telling me he wants to go to counseling or he'll change or something ridiculous. I need a way out."

"Maybe you do need to try counseling, Debi. I mean, that might help. I don't know. Maybe I'm the wrong person to ask about marriage."

Debi wiped her face, smearing her make-up. The meltdown made Skyy a bit uneasy because she wasn't equipped to handle it; she was a hairstylist not a psychologist.

Debi took a deep breath. "I'm sorry for dumping this on you. I just can't tell anybody in my family. They wouldn't understand. They think I live this fairytale life with this great husband, when actually my world is upside down. They think Eric is holding it down at home, but he's not. What makes me so angry is that he thinks going to a fast-food restaurant or retail store to get a job is an insult. I mean, he brings in unemployment, but that's about enough to buy groceries. He needs to find something. To make it worse, he knows how to do plumbing. Has his plumbing license and everything. You think he's out there trying to get some plumbing work? Hell no. He doesn't want to do nothing, and I'm tired. I'm done."

"Can I help? I mean, do you need any money or anything? I can give you ..."

"Skyy, I appreciate it, but I can't take your money. What I need you can't give me. I have to figure this out by myself."

Skyy went back to her chair. She felt as if the meltdown was just about over, and she was clueless as to what she could do for Debi at that point. The initial intent of calling Debi to her office was to offer some financial assistance and to discuss her tardiness.

"Well, if there's something I can do to help, let me know."

"Since you have a way with married men, how about taking one off my hands?" Debi said jokingly.

"Hell no! You can keep his ass."

After they both finished laughing, Debi got up, pulled her too-tight Baby Phat shirt over her puffy abdomen, and opened the door.

Before exiting, she looked over to Skyy. "Thanks for listening. I really needed to get that off my chest," Debi said, then headed back to the front of the shop, leaving Skyy there with the negative energy still taking up space in her office.

Skyy felt sort of sad, when she really had no reason to be. She powered up her computer and grabbed a couple of envelopes from her desk. As she waited for the computer to boot up, she tore open the utility bills so she could schedule online payments for them. After looking at the balance due on each, Skyy decided to pay the water bill, electric bill, and cable bill. The lease payment wasn't due until the first of the month, so she would wait to make that payment. After making those payments, she looked at her supply list and realized it had been about a month since she'd had a shipment from her distributer. So, she wrote herself a note to call them first thing in the morning. A knock at the door broke her concentration.

"Yeah?" she said.

Coco poked his head in. "Hey, is Debi okay? She's not mad at me, is she?" he asked.

"She's not okay, but it's not you. It's Eric."

Coco entered the office, shutting the door behind him. "Spill the tea, honey."

"Coco, you better not say a word to anybody."

"I'm not. I promise."

"Coco, I'm serious. Not a word to Niya or Tiffany."

"Okay. I said I promise."

"Did Debi leave yet?"

"Yes, you know she had to get to the daycare by six. Now stop stalling and tell it. What happened?"

Skyy leaned in closer to Coco so she could speak softly and still be heard. She wanted to be careful in case Niya and Tiffany were standing outside of her office door eavesdropping.

"Debi wants a divorce from Eric. She said she hates him."

Coco gasped, grabbing his chest like Fred Sanford. "What? Are you serious?"

"Yep, as a heart attack. She told me she hates him and that her marriage was a mistake. She wants him to leave, but he won't."

"How sad is that. Why won't she just leave?"

"She wants *him* to leave. I guess since she's paying all the bills and . . ." Skyy stopped mid-sentence, realizing she was probably telling too much of Debi's business.

"Wait a minute. Are you saying that Eric ain't paying no bills? Oh hell naw! That nigga gotta go!"

"Coco, that part slipped out. Please don't say anything. If you do, I will never forgive you. Debi was a wreck when she came in here, and I think she really just needed someone to talk to. I think she told me too much, but it was too late. I know she wouldn't want Tiff and them to know about this. So, if it gets out, I will know it was you."

"Skyy, I already told you, I'm not gonna say a word. Girl Scout's honor." Coco put his fingers up in the air, forming the Girl Scout symbol.

Just then, Skyy's cell phone vibrated on the desk and the word 'Toyota' appeared on the display screen.

"Umph, that's Kyle. Let me see what's up with him." She waved Coco out of the room. "Hello?" Skyy answered, while Coco made a funny gesture before closing the door behind him.

"Hey, baby. I haven't talked to you in a few days. Where have you been?" Kyle asked.

"I was out of town. Went to Vegas with a few friends. What's going on?" Skyy responded.

"I need to see you, baby. I'm horny as hell."

"Damn. Straight and to the point, huh?"

"Come on, Skyy. You know how we do."

She knew exactly how things went with Kyle. He was the man that needed intimacy. Of course, Skyy shared intimacy with all of her men, but Kyle was the one who needed it the most. Kyle was a bit too uptight for Skyy, but his sex was off the chain.

Skyy met Kyle while shopping for cars. After spending about thirty minutes walking around the Toyota dealership, she finally fell in love with a jet-black, convertible Toyota Avalon. Ready to take the car for a test drive, Skyy followed the salesman into the showroom to get the keys and make a copy of her driver's license. Kyle happened to be walking from his office to the lounge for some coffee when he saw her. Skyy noticed him immediately.

At six-feet, two-inches tall, he was hard to miss. His sandy brown goatee complemented his bronze complexion. He wore his hair cut close, just enough for a nice round-up with attractive sideburns. His eyes were light brown, his lips were full, and his teeth looked like pearls when he smiled. The dimple in his right cheek made Skyy melt. The wedding ring on his left hand made her heart skip a beat. And the flat-front, black HUGO trousers he wore told an even bigger story. Not that his pants were too tight; it was more like his manhood was too big. Skyy was equally impressed with his Kenneth Cole slip-on shoes, which she remembered seeing in a Nordstrom's catalog. So, she knew he had taste. And by the way he looked at her, Skyy knew he cheated.

She pretended not to notice him when he walked toward her, even though she knew he was headed her way.

"Hi. You being taken care of?" he asked, knowing the answer to the question.

"You mean the car, right?" Skyy asked seductively.

"It can mean something else only if you want it to."

Skyy looked at his left hand before looking up into his eyes again. "How long have you been married?"

"Five years."

"Are you happy?"

"No."

Just then, the salesman approached them with car keys in one hand and temporary license plates in the other.

"Hey, Kyle, I haven't made the sale, at least not yet," the salesman joked.

Skyy and Kyle held their stare; the energy between them was intense and Skyy loved it.

"Kyle, huh? Why can't Kyle take me for a spin?" Skyy asked the salesman.

"Because Kyle is the manager. He doesn't sell. He closes all the deals for us."

"Don't worry. When you get back, I'll be here." He flashed his gorgeous smile and headed to the back of the showroom to the glass offices.

Skyy took the test drive, not really caring if the car drove smoothly or not. All she wanted to do was get back to the dealership to see Kyle. One would think the only reason she purchased the car was because it gave her an excuse to be face to face with Kyle again. In actuality, she would've gotten close to Kyle with or without buying the car. She just had that way about her. Besides, Kyle made sure Skyy got the best deal possible on the sale, making the car salesman a bit upset because it affected his commission.

Skyy and Kyle's relationship took off like a rocket. Kyle talked a lot about being unhappy with his wife and how he yearned for affection. He explained to Skyy that he was one of those men who needed a visual connection to a woman, and he felt like he made that connection with Skyy. He made it very clear that he needed to stay in his marriage because of his kids, and Skyy made it clear that she had no intention of being anything other than what he wanted her to be. So, they hit it off immediately.

"I was hoping I could see you today. Meet at our spot." Their spot happened to be the Embassy Suite Hotel on Emerywood Parkway, about ten miles west of the city. Since Kyle lived in Chester, Virginia, which was about thirty miles south of the city, the chances of running into his wife were slim. Besides, he always knew where his wife was whenever he planned a rendezvous with Skyy.

"What's in it for me?" Skyy teased.

"I got eight reasons why you should come, and I mean *come*."

"Umph, I don't know. Just eight?"

"Come on, Skyy. I'm sitting here getting hard just thinking about you. It's been two weeks, and I'm about to explode. Plus, I have a surprise for you."

"Oh, I love surprises. Give me a hint."

"Can you say Atlantis?"

"Atlantis as in Nassau, Bahamas?"

"That's right. Sunday through Wednesday trip. It's in four weeks. That gives you plenty of time to get your appointments straight. Meet me at seven. I'll text you the room number."

"Okay, I'll see you in a bit."

Chapter 3

Four weeks passed quickly, and Skyy was back on a plane, this time heading south. Kyle had purchased tickets for a chartered plane, and everyone on board was heading directly to Nassau, Bahamas. Before arriving in Nassau, the plane would leave Richmond and make one stop in Norfolk to pick up some additional passengers. Kyle specifically requested that their assigned seats be apart from each other because he wanted to keep things discreet until they arrived at their destination. Even at the airport in Richmond, they appeared to be strangers, texting each other as several rows of seats separated them.

As much as Kyle enjoyed having sex with Skyy, he didn't want his wife to find out about his affair nor did he want his marriage to end. He merely wished his wife would take the time to try and regain the perfect size 6 body she once had. Currently, she was a sloppy size 14, which was unsightly to Kyle because she tried to wear the same type of clothes she wore as a size 6. Since she didn't work, she just sat around the house with their two young kids, watching soap operas and eating up everything in sight. While Kyle was a member of American Family Fitness and worked out four to five times a week, he couldn't get his wife to work out with him to save his life. So, he did what he was supposed to do as a husband by supporting her and taking care of his kids, but looked outside of the marriage for intimacy.

His wife was suspicious of his cheating, but he made sure he was always careful when he stepped out on her. In spite of it all, he still loved his wife and didn't want to humiliate her by parading his mistress around town for others to see. He tried very hard to be discreet. What made it even better was the fact that Skyy was all for it. She would take Kyle under his terms because she made sure he understood they were her terms, too.

When they landed in Nassau, Skyy marveled at the beautiful palm trees that seemed to outline the small airport. Skyy considered Richmond International Airport mediocre in comparison to some of the airports she'd been in before. However, the airport in Nassau made RIC look like the airport in Las Vegas.

Before unbuckling her seatbelt, Skyy waited for the stewardess to make the official announcement that they had landed safely. Once the announcement was made, everyone on the plane seemed to stand up in unison, opening the overhead compartments to gather their carry-on items. Luckily for Skyy, she was seated in the sixth row, so she would be able to get off the plane quickly. Kyle was seated in aisle ten, so he would have to wait a bit longer.

Skyy grabbed her Gucci duffle bag from the overhead compartment, threw her matching Gucci tote handbag on her shoulder, and looked in and around her seat to make sure she'd collected all of her things. She adjusted her halter mini sundress, making sure her twins weren't trying to make an unnecessary appearance, especially since she wasn't wearing a bra. She followed the flow of traffic off the airplane, down the stairwell, and onto the pavement toward the airport. The ground was wet, but the sky was bright blue, which meant they'd just missed an afternoon shower. The sun was hot, and Skyy could literally feel the Palmer's Cocoa Butter Lotion melting on the back of her arms. While walking to the terminal, she searched her tote for a scuncii so she could pull her hair up in a ponytail. Feeling the sweat accumulating on her neck and in the crease of her back, she couldn't wait to get to the hotel to take a shower.

Kyle was a few steps behind Skyy, watching her every move. Everything about her turned him on. From her calf muscles, up to her round, thick butt, and even from the back, she looked good to him. As she pulled her hair up into a ponytail, the back of her sundress rose up a bit, almost exposing her behind. Some of the native men stared at her, probably wondering if she was alone. It excited Kyle. He waited until they were inside the airport before he walked up behind her, put his arms around her waist, and whispered in her ear.

"I can't wait to get you to the room. I'm gonna tear that ass up."

Skyy smiled. "Is that so?"

"Hell yeah, it's so."

Skyy rubbed her butt on Kyle's manhood and could tell he was already excited. "Umph, feels like you're already ready."

Skyy had to admit, Kyle turned her on in every way a man could. He was easy on the eyes, had a body built for the NBA, and his package was definitely enough to please any woman. She couldn't imagine why his wife didn't take the time to accommodate him by doing one thing—keep herself up. Skyy felt sorry for Kyle. He wanted to be faithful, but it was his wife's fault. She was the one who let herself go. One thing Skyy learned after dating married men was that fifty percent of the marriage was the sex, the intimacy. The other fifty percent included the kids, the finances, and everything else. Married men confided in her that when the honeymoon was over, it was truly over. No sex, no communication, the whole marriage thing felt more like a business arrangement than a permanent relationship. That's just the way it was. And Skyy didn't mind being the one to give up the fifty percent that most married men missed having in their marriage.

Since Skyy was the sort of female who hungered for intimacy and had a stupendous sex drive, this gave her the opportunity to have her needs met while fulfilling theirs. It didn't hurt that she got nice trips and lavish gifts out of the deal. She felt like her job was done when she sent her men home to their wives smiling and satisfied. Did she consider herself a whore? No. Her friends debated that argument with her on several occasions. Skyy made them understand that she was only doing what she wanted to do. Besides, why was it so wrong for her to get something out of the deal? Hell, there were plenty of women sleeping with *un*married men and couldn't even get a Happy Meal from McDonald's. She only wanted to have fun; there was no emotional connection to any of these men. Skyy realized they could call her one day to say it was over, and she would be fine with that.

After Kyle found their luggage, they made their way to the taxi stand outside. Numerous locals solicited their taxi services, all trying to get their taxi full to capacity for a trip to the various resorts. Some had minivans, Lincoln Town Cars, and even limousines, all converted into taxis. A burly, dark-skinned native approached Kyle.

"Where you going?" he asked with a Bahamian accent.

"Atlantis," Kyle replied.

"Okay. Come, come. I'll take you to Atlantis."

He opened the door to his converted limo, and Kyle and Skyy got in. The burgundy velvet interior was terribly worn, and the air was stuffy. The air from the air conditioner was warm, and Skyy hoped the ride would not be too long.

"Cable Beach, Paradise Island, Atlantis!" the taxi driver yelled, trying to get additional passengers so he could fill his limo to capacity in an effort to maximize his trip.

Kyle sat close to Skyy, and with his arm wrapped around her shoulder, he eased his hand into her dress to cup her left breast. He massaged her nipple until it got hard. Since Skyy didn't protest, Kyle kept this up until a middle-aged couple and their teenage son entered the taxi. The husband had a ruddy complexion, with thinning, sandy brown hair. He was clad in plaid golfing shorts and a polo shirt, and he wore a sun visor. He probably was not that bad looking in his younger days. The wife, a blonde Barbie lookalike, could stand to take a break from the tanning salon because her t-strap summer dress exposed skin that looked more like leather. Their son, who looked to be about thirteen, had his ears plugged with iPod earbuds and concentrated on his PSP handheld game.

The trunk slammed shut and the taxi bounced when the taxi driver sat in the driver's seat.

"Cable Beach and Atlantis, hey?" he said, awaiting confirmation.

"Yes," Kyle and the husband answered in unison.

What sounded like a Bahamian church service blared from the car's front speakers. The heavy Bahamian dialect of the preacher made it hard to understand exactly what his sermon was about. However, the driver seemed to understand every word, chiming in with a random "That's right" and "Amen".

"So, where are you two from?" the wife asked.

"Richmond, Virginia," Skyy answered.

"Oh really. We're originally from Fredericksburg, Virginia, but we live in Dayton, Ohio, now. So how long have you two been married?"

Some women have a way of prying into other people's business even when they don't know them. Since Kyle's left hand was sitting on Skyy's shoulder, his wedding band was in full view.

"Oh, we're not married. We're just friends," Skyy responded.

"Oh," the wife said, realizing she should've kept her mouth shut.

The husband and Kyle seemed to communicate with their eyes, and then it was as if the whole situation clicked right away for the husband, because he formed a small smirk on his face. It took the wife a minute or two to truly "get it", and that's when her smile turned to a frown. All sorts of thoughts went through her head, angry that this married man had the audacity to bring another woman to such a beautiful place. Not that it was any of her business, but she looked at her husband like she was expecting him to make a comment.

"What?" he asked, not sure of what she wanted him to do or say.

In a huff, she sucked her teeth and fumbled through the papers in her bright green beachbag.

The rest of the ride, Kyle and Skyy whispered and giggled like teenagers. The wife sneered while the husband wished it was him. They passed several modest homes that were nestled beyond palm trees. For every modest home, there appeared to be a concrete shell of an unfinished home. It was clear that either the recession in the United States had some sort of affect on the economy in the Bahamas or hurricanes had caused major delays in construction. Before long, they were in resort areas, because timeshare communities with restaurants and shops started to appear. Sun-tanned Americans walked amongst the brightly-colored buildings, spending their money for handmade strawbags and overpriced t-shirts. Every hotel chain imaginable started to pop up, and before long, the burly taxi driver yelled out, "Cable Beach!" He then pulled into the driveway of the Radisson Cable Beach and Golf Resort.

The teenager, still hypnotized by the music coming from his iPod, got out first. The wife rolled her eyes at Skyy, but the husband nodded at Kyle in agreement. Men had their own language; it didn't matter the color, nationality, or religion. From one married man to another, the husband probably wanted to ask Kyle how *he* could manage to get his secretary to the Bahamas while leaving his wife at home. He waited for the taxi driver to finish unloading the luggage, while his wife went inside the hotel to get them checked in. After paying the taxi driver, he disappeared among the other travelers who were entering the hotel.

Again, the driver made the taxi bounce when he got into the car. "Off to Atlantis," he said to them.

While scurrying through the busy traffic, the taxi driver hummed an unfamiliar tune. A couple of times he honked his horn, waving at other taxi drivers in passing. He seemed to be concentrating on getting Skyy and Kyle to their hotel as quickly as possible so he could head back to the airport to make some more money.

Kyle leaned over and pulled up Skyy's dress slowly. He kept his eyes on the driver, making sure he wasn't watching them.

"What are you doing?" Skyy asked.

"You know what I'm doing."

Kyle slid the dress up just far enough so that a portion of Skyy's bright orange thong showed. He rubbed his finger up and down the front of her thong until Skyy moaned softly, an indication that Kyle had reached her spot, and he continued working it until Skyy squirmed a bit in her seat. She opened her legs wider, giving Kyle access to her playground. With her eyes closed and head tilted back, Skyy no longer cared if the taxi driver saw them. Skyy's breathing quickened, and Kyle's hand worked her so fast that sweat was forming on his forehead. Kyle was about to cause her to erupt at any moment.

"Come on, baby. Come for me," he whispered in her ear. "Right here. Do it in the car."

The taxi driver was still humming his tune, oblivious to the encounter happening behind him. Skyy's moans got lost in the music blaring from the radio. Before Kyle could get his finger deep inside her, Skyy got stiff and her juices began to flow. Kyle sat back on his seat, about ready to have his own eruption, realizing he would have to wait until they got to the hotel before he could reach his peak. He was satisfied, though. The thought of bringing Skyy to an orgasm with another person only a few inches away from them excited him. For a brief moment, Kyle thought about his wife and how, early in their relationship, they enjoyed an exciting sex life. That was one of the reasons he decided to make her his wife. She used to have a sex drive that mirrored Skyy's. That was before the kids came.

Kyle licked his finger before pushing his tongue into Skyy's mouth. They kissed long and hard, so much that the driver cleared his throat. It was obvious to them that he was not interested in being a spectator in their love game. So, Kyle adjusted Skyy's dress, sat back in his seat, and enjoyed the rest of the ride. The ocean water was in full view, and they could see the Atlantis hotel. All that separated them from the hotel was a long bridge, which appeared to put a substantial distance between the hotel and the rest of Nassau. A voice came over the radio, summoning the driver.

"On my way to Atlantis. I'll be der in about twenty minutes, no?" the taxi driver answered.

The voice on the radio gave instructions for the driver to stop at the Holiday Inn Resort on his way back to the airport. The taxi driver grumbled before confirming the pick-up.

Skyy watched as the Atlantis hotel got closer. The pictures on the internet didn't do the majestic place justice. Unlike most of the resorts and hotels in Nassau, Atlantis seemed to occupy a space all its own. All of the towers were grand in stature, and the Royal Towers reminded her of five stacks of uneven playing cards with an arch in the middle, except this archway was actually a strip of presidential suites that most celebrities rented when they stayed at the Atlantis. Along with the Royal Towers were other sets of Atlantis hotel towers: the Coral Towers, Beach Tower, the Cove Atlantis, and the Reef Atlantis.

"Are you going to the Royal Towers?" the taxi driver asked.

"Yes, the one with the casino," Kyle responded.

"Okay, no problem."

As the car eased closer, Skyy's eyes grew bigger watching the majestic view. Palm trees outlined the property, and just as the Atlantic Ocean encompassed the legendary island of Atlantis, turquoise blue water enveloped the Atlantis Hotel and Casino.

"Wow, this place is beautiful," said Skyy.

"I knew you would like it," Kyle replied with a smile.

The taxi pulled into the front entrance of the Royal Towers, and a bellman quickly approached. The taxi driver quickly opened the trunk and removed their luggage, handing it over to the bellman.

Kyle exited the taxi first, followed by Skyy. He was the ultimate gentleman, holding her hand, assisting her from the vehicle. After paying the driver, Kyle followed the bellman to the front desk. As if the outside of the Atlantis wasn't amazing enough, the inside was just as astounding. The murals on the walls were snapshots of Egyptian times. Oversized columns with intricate designs adorned the open lobby area, which was filled with elegant marble floors and Louis XIII style furniture. Even the light fixtures made of detailed brass were elegant.

"I'll be right back, baby," Kyle told Skyy.

He walked up to the reservation desk while Skyy continued to admire the breathtaking view. She watched the passersby, all appearing to be relaxed and worry-free. This was obviously where people with money stayed while in Nassau, at least that was Skyy's thought. She wondered how much Kyle was spending for the four-day, three-night trip. Even though Kyle made pretty good money at the dealership, Skyy knew he was the sole breadwinner of his household, so his discretionary income was pretty limited. Sure, he didn't mind taking her to nice restaurants in Richmond and surrounding areas, sending her flowers, and even buying her low-end jewelry from Kay Jewelers (although she preferred jewelry from Fink's), but this was her first time leaving the state with Kyle. Traveling was something she normally did with the music mogul. Skyy realized Kyle was trying to step up his game a little, probably trying to compete with her other men.

"You ready?" Kyle asked.

Skyy nodded and they proceeded to the elevators. They took the elevator to the eighth floor and then followed the arrows to room 835. Upon entering the room, Skyy realized Kyle's money was definitely not as long as the music mogul's. Even though they were staying in the Royal Towers, their room was the most basic the hotel had to offer. The austere room was adorned with Caribbean-themed prints and contemporary furniture. A king-sized bed took up space on one side of the room and directly across from it was an armoire with a flat-screen TV. A maple wood table and two chairs were to the right of the armoire. Sunlight filled the entire room by way of the oversized patio door, which provided an awe-inspiring view of the beach.

"Yeah, this is what I'm talking about. What do you think, Skyy?"

"This place is beautiful. I could retire here."

She opened the patio door and stepped onto the patio, letting in the warm ocean breeze. The sounds of eclectic Caribbean music and ocean waves filled the air. Skyy leaned carefully on the banister, taking in the view. So immersed in the moment, she didn't hear the bellman at the door with their luggage. Kyle handled the luggage while Skyy continued to admire the view. After closing the door behind the bellman, Kyle walked up behind Skyy and kissed her on the neck. She leaned back into him, closing her eyes.

"Well, what do you want to do first?" Kyle asked.

"I want to take a shower. I feel so sweaty."

"I like it sweaty."

Skyy turned around and faced Kyle, pulling his face to hers. "Don't you need to make a call first?" she asked.

One thing about Skyy, she always made sure her men did a good job covering themselves. She knew Kyle needed to check in with his wife to let her know he'd arrived safely.

"No, I can't call yet."

"Why not?"

"Because, technically, I'm still supposed to be flying. I told her I was going to a meeting in California at headquarters."

"Mmmm-hmmmm." Skyy unbuttoned his white linen shirt, exposing his full chest and six-pack abs. "Then let's take a shower together," she said.

Skyy took him by the hand and led him to the bathroom. She started the water in the shower, then they both undressed each other. There were very few words exchanged between them; most of their communicating would be done through sex.

They entered the fiberglass stand-up shower, allowing the water to saturate their bodies. After grabbing a washcloth and soap, Skyy slowly lathered it on Kyle's chest. He reciprocated by rubbing soap on Skyy's breasts, making her nipples hard. Touching was the ultimate foreplay for them, and it seemed like the more lather they generated, the more aroused they both became. Skyy washed Kyle's manhood, but it felt more like masturbation to Kyle. He reached down to Skyy's valley, putting his finger in its familiar place. She put her foot up on the soap dish and pulled him close to her. Kyle grabbed the condom, which he conveniently placed on the soap dish when they got in, and gave it to Skyy. She got down on her knees and took Kyle in her mouth to make sure his manhood reached its maximum length. She sucked him hard and felt his muscle get bigger and bigger. Kyle moaned in ecstasy, trying hard to stop an eruption from happening in Skyy's mouth. She rolled the condom on his swollen muscle before standing up and putting her foot back on the soap dish. Because Kyle was so big, Skyy opened her vaginal lips, giving him full access. The soap and water were the perfect lubricant, and Kyle entered her easily. Gaining their rhythm, they both moaned to the sound of two wet bodies smacking against each other. Climaxing came quickly for Kyle, a sign that he probably hadn't had sex since the last time he was with Skyy.

*   *   *

The sound of the patio door opening woke Skyy. The sun would be setting within the hour, so the water had a picturesque view. She turned to watch Kyle, whose back was to her. She could tell by his body language that he was mustering up the energy he needed to call and lie to his wife. He dialed the number on his cell phone and waited for an answer.

"Hey, KJ. It's Daddy. What you doing, lil'man?" There was a brief pause. "I know, I know. Daddy misses you, too. Put Mommy on the phone. I know KJ, but I need to speak to Mommy."

Kyle went back and forth with his five-year-old son before his wife finally got on the phone. Skyy tried hard to hear Kyle's side of the conversation.

"Hey. I just landed. We got a little delayed, but I finally made it in." There was another brief pause. "Yeah, I have my luggage. I'm waiting on a taxi."

Kyle listened for a minute or so while Skyy imagined what his wife might be saying to him. Was she talking about the kids? Was she telling him that she missed him and loved him? Maybe she told him that she knew he was lying. Whatever it was, Kyle listened in silence.

Skyy eased out of bed and made her way to the bathroom. She decided to freshen up while Kyle finished his conversation with his wife. Not that she felt guilty, but she knew whenever one of her men was on the phone with their wives, it was her job to be quiet. She played the mistress role perfectly, which is probably why all of her men cared for her so much.

She returned to the room at the sound of the patio door closing. Kyle was sitting on the side of the bed. She walked over to him and put her hands on his shoulders.

"You okay?" she asked.

"Yeah, I'm alright." Kyle's mood had become somber.

"What's the matter, Kyle?"

"I . . . we . . . this . . . this whole thing is wrong. What if something happens to me while I'm down here? How will I explain it to my wife?"

Kyle was the type of cheater who enjoyed the thrill at first, then felt guilty afterwards.

"Kyle, if you want to go home, we can leave now. I don't want to be here if you're going to be moping around the whole time."

"It's not that. I want to be here. I just hate . . ."

"Kyle, don't unload that on me. We go through this every time. You invited me here. I didn't ask you for this. You called me, remember?"

"I know, I know."

"Well, I'm not forcing you to do anything you don't want to do. You're here because you want to be here."

Kyle wrapped his arms around Skyy's waist. He appreciated her reassurance. It was true; he asked her to go on the trip and not the other way around. Come to think of it, Skyy never really asked him for anything. It was always Kyle who volunteered his gifts, dinners, etc. It was probably because he felt guilty. Plus, Skyy fulfilled a need for him that his wife didn't. So, he felt it only right that he showed his appreciation.

"You are so special to me, you know that?" Kyle said.

"Hey, don't go getting all sentimental on me. We're supposed to be having a good time. Come on. Let's get dressed and go out to get some dinner."

"I prefer dessert first," Kyle responded.

Skyy smiled, realizing that Kyle's funk was dissipating and he was ready for round two.

Chapter 4

Skyy parked her car and headed to the salon. It had been a couple of weeks since her trip to the Bahamas, so it was back to business. She noticed the blinds were open, which meant Coco had already arrived at work. She unlocked the door with her key.

"Good morning, Ms. Coco."

"Hey, Ms. Thang. Oh, uh-uh, uh-uh! Where the hell did you get that handbag?" Coco said, noticing one of the newest additions to Skyy's designer handbag collection.

Skyy threw the Louis Vuitton Artsy tote bag on the front counter so she could flip through the appointment calendar. Coco looked her up and down approvingly, checking out Skyy's Seven jean capris and lime green tube top.

"Okay, I'm liking this ensemble, too, Ms. Fly. And you didn't tell me about this bag. It's fierce."

"Coco, I bought this from the Louis Vuitton store at Stony Point last week. I told you about it."

"No, you didn't." Coco left his customer in his chair and walked over to admire her handbag, grabbing it and putting it on his shoulder.

"Coco, come on back here and finish my hair. I told you I have to be to work at eight," said Coco's customer.

"Girl, you almost done. Calm down."

"Coco, what did I tell you about customer service?" Skyy said.

"Oh, Skyy, you trying to use your lil' authority? Okay, okay, I see you. Neisha, stop acting like you so concerned about that job. You trying to find a reason to call in anyway."

"I know, right?" the customer replied.

They all laughed. It was still early, so Coco and Skyy were the only two stylists in the salon. Coco went back to his customer's hair and put the final touches on her sew-in weave.

"You know we have a meeting this morning, right?" Skyy asked.

"Yep. I received your text message reminder last night. Is Debi gonna be on time?"

"I hope so."

A moment later, Debi entered the salon sashaying in a halter top and tight Rocawear jeans.

Coco looked at his wrist at an imaginary watch. "Debi? You here? And on time? I don't believe it."

"Good morning, everybody. Shut up, Coco," Debi said.

"Girllll, it's gonna snow, thunderstorm, or something today since Debi's at work before eight."

"Coco, I didn't know you were the designated timekeeper."

"I need to be the designated shoekeeper and take those cheesy shoes off your feet. Ewwwww!" Coco said, making reference to Debi's Payless specials.

"What's wrong with my shoes? I thought they were cute. They were only fourteen dollars." Debi turned her foot, giving Coco several different views of her brown leather slip-ons.

"First of all, nobody wears mules anymore."

"Mules? These are not mules, Coco. You make me sick," Debi laughed it off, but started to feel a bit self-conscious about her shoes. She was hoping Coco would give her a thumbs-up on her shoes. However, she now wished she had left the shoes in the store.

In addition to his other roles in the salon, Coco was also the fashion police. He didn't stop with Skyy. Everyone in the salon was open game when it came to fashion, and Coco did not have a problem giving good or bad feedback.

"Debi, don't listen to Coco. Your shoes are fine," Skyy said, trying to offer her friend reassurance.

"Mmmm-hmmm, that's what her mouth says, but I bet you won't catch her buying any shoes out of the P. Alright, Neisha, you're done," Coco said, while removing his customer's cape and turning her seat around until she was facing the large mirror on the wall.

Then Coco handed her a mirror so she could inspect his work. He moved the chair around slowly, giving her a chance to look at her hair from the front and get a view of the back. She handed Coco some cash, which he didn't take the time to count, and then stood up, taking one last look in the mirror before leaving.

"Put me down for two weeks, Coco. Six-thirty," the customer said.

Coco grabbed his appointment calendar from his station and flipped through several pages. "That's July 22nd. I got you down."

"Thanks. Y'all have a good day."

"Bye," they all chimed in.

As she exited the shop, Tiffany and Niya entered.

"Good morning," they said in unison.

"Morning, Tiff. Morning, Niya. I think you were right, Coco," Skyy said.

"What?"

"A hurricane or something is about to hit. Niya is here before eight."

They all laughed at Niya, the young, high school graduate who was leaving for college in the fall. Since she spent most of her nights hanging out with her friends, she found it difficult to make it to the salon early. That day, she really didn't need to be there for the meeting, but since she rode to work with Tiffany, she didn't have a choice.

"Alright, come on, y'all. Let's go ahead and get this meeting going. Niya, lock the door, please."

They all followed Skyy to the waiting area and took seats on the sofas. Skyy grabbed a notebook from her bag and sat on the sofa beside Debi.

"Okay, we have a little over a month before the hair show in Atlanta. I booked our rooms at the Embassy Suites for Saturday, Sunday, and Monday nights. Debi and Tiff are sharing a room, and me and Coco will share a room. I registered Coco for the fantasy hair competition on Sunday night. So, Coco, you have to be there on Saturday."

"I'm gonna be there. Who said I wasn't?"

"Because last year you went missing in action, and I started panicking."

"But I showed up, Skyy."

"Yeah, showed up *late*."

"Oh Lord, I am never gonna live that down. Let it go. Pahleeze, let it go."

"Coco, you can win this thing, but you have got to be on time and make it to registration, everything you didn't do last year that caused you to mess up the whole thing. Now, I already know you could win if you would just be where you're supposed to be."

"Okay, okay, okay, I'll be there. I promise. Girl Scout's honor." Coco held up one hand in the Girl Scout's symbol and put the other on his chest.

"I don't know why I need to go," Tiffany said.

"Tiff, I already told you there's going to be a spa seminar on Sunday morning that I want you to attend. They're going to be discussing new nail products and techniques. Plus, you need to help us get Coco set up for the hair show."

Tiffany sulked. She really didn't feel like being involved with the hair show. She would rather spend her time chasing behind her son's father. The thought of not being able to track him down upset her. She felt her absence would give him too much free time to run the streets.

"Can't you be away from your baby daddy for three days? Damn, girl, he got you gone. Y'all young girls need to learn the P's and Q's of dating," Coco said, smacking his teeth.

Tiffany rolled her eyes at Coco and crossed her arms. Niya, who really didn't need to be a part of the meeting, got up and went to the door when she saw a man walk up to the door.

"Who is that, Niya?" Skyy asked.

Before Niya could answer, Debi jumped up. "Oh, that's for me." Debi adjusted her too tight Rocawear jeans and walked over to open the door.

Skyy and Coco looked at each other in bewilderment because clearly, the tall, dark, and handsome man at the door was not Eric, Debi's husband.

"Excuse me. We're having a meeting," Coco yelled.

"Give me two minutes, Skyy. I'll be right back," Debi said, then stepped outside to talk to the mystery man.

No one said anything for about a minute or two. Everyone was too busy trying to read Debi's body language. The man was not dressed in a suit nor did he have a briefcase, so he didn't appear to be a lawyer. Plus, Debi's body language was too relaxed. They couldn't hear the conversation, but it was obvious from the way Debi playfully hit the man's arm that she was flirting with him.

"Uh-uh, what the f . . ."

"Coco!" Skyy interjected.

"What? You know you want to know just as bad as I do who that guy is."

They all stood at the window watching the interaction between Debi and the mystery man. After about another minute, he walked away, got into a silver Lexus LS with North Carolina tags, and drove off. Everyone but Skyy shuffled back to their seats and acted as if they hadn't been spying on Debi, who came in still smiling from the encounter.

"Hold up! Hold up! Hold up! Lucyyyy, you got some 'splaining to do," Coco said, imitating Ricky from the *I Love Lucy* sitcom.

"I know what y'all are thinking, but he's just an old friend. As a matter of fact, he's Eric's brother."

They all exploded in laughter.

"Yeah, right," Coco said.

"He is."

"How come we never heard you mention Eric's brother before?" Tiffany asked.

"Well, because first, he lives in North Carolina, and second, he and Eric stopped speaking years ago."

"Mm-hmm. I think the heffa is lying," Coco said.

"I'm serious. It's not what you think. We're just friends."

"Hmmm. So, if he and Eric don't even speak, what is he doing here talking to Eric's wife, huh?" Coco asked in a matter-of-fact tone.

"I thought we were having a meeting, not twenty-one questions starring Debi."

"We *are* having a meeting," Skyy said, directing her comment to Coco so he would turn his attention from Debi and back to the business at hand.

"Skyy, don't act like you don't want to know what Debi is up to. And, as a matter of fact, this heffa has make-up on this morning. Hmmm, new shoes, make-up, not a hair out of place, and all before eight a.m. Something smells fishy, and I'm not talking about you heffas either."

"Coco ..."

"Coco my ass. Bitch, you better tell us what's going on, or the next time Eric comes into this shop, I'm singing like a canary," Coco said playfully.

Everyone stared at Debi, obviously as eager as Coco to find out who the handsome brother was that had Debi smiling.

"Y'all don't give a sista a break. For real, it's nothing. He's just a friend. That's it." Debi could tell no one believed her. "Okay. His name is Landon, and he really is Eric's brother. I actually met Landon before I met Eric. We were friends. We're still friends, but nothing is going on. He called me a couple of weeks ago, right around the time I was about to have a nervous breakdown over Eric. He's just being a really great confidante right now."

They all looked at her sort of suspiciously.

It's as if Coco was recounting the story in his head, then he blurted out, "Hold up! Hold up! You met him before you met Eric? And they haven't been speaking to each other for years? Were you dating Eric's brother first?"

Debi looked at Coco, her expression giving her away.

"Ooooooh, you skank heffa! You dated two brothers?" Tiffany said.

"Who said anything about dating? I said we're just friends. Case closed."

"Well, I would be careful if I were you. Any time there is a male confidante involved, girl, you know you're playing with fire," Skyy said.

"Don't you have some nerve talking about me playing with fire. You play with fire every day." Debi voiced her comment with so much conviction that Skyy was actually offended.

"Mmph, so what I do gives you the right to cheat on your husband?"

"Who said I was cheating?" Debi shot back.

"You will, trust me. The recipe is already there."

Debi and Skyy threw invisible knives at each other, both offended by the other person's statements. Sure, Skyy was aware that everyone in the salon knew the source of all of her relationships, and it was their right to their opinion. She never felt ashamed about what she did or who she did it with. What Skyy didn't appreciate was her so-called friend making an off-the-wall comment about it when the conversation was clearly about Debi and not her.

"Look, can we just get back to the meeting? I have a customer coming in at eight forty-five," Tiffany said.

"Forget the meeting. I'm loving this *Bold and the Beautiful* episode going on right now," Coco said.

"Tiff is right. Let's get back to business. Coco, is Shakira still going?" Skyy asked. "Is she still going to be your model?"

"Yep. She has a cousin that lives in Atlanta, so she's going to stay with her cousin for the weekend. She came over my house Saturday night, and I tried a couple of things on her. I know my theme and everything. Trust me, we will be ready."

"Okay, Coco, I'm really counting on you for this. We need to put Richmond V-A on the map." Skyy then continued with the remaining business pertaining to the hair show, discussing the various seminars and party plans associated with the event.

The tension between Debi and Skyy could be felt, and it was clear both women had attitudes with each other. However, like in most hair salon environments, it would soon blow over, and they would be the best of friends by the next day.

Chapter 5

Skyy sat at her desk going through various invoices and bills, trying to reconcile her business checking account. As she read through each piece of paper, she typed the information into an Excel spreadsheet on her personal notebook computer, attempting to keep her business accounting as accurate as possible. Since she was a business owner, it was important for her to keep her records up to date so she could file her tax information on a quarterly basis instead of yearly like most people did that worked in the corporate sector. It was close to seven p.m., and Skyy was the only one in the salon. When the telephone rang, Skyy answered the cordless phone that was on her desk, but before doing so, she checked the caller ID and noticed it said 'Private Caller'.

"Blue Skyy's," she answered.

"Yes, I'm trying to reach Skyy Armfield," the anonymous male caller said on the other end.

"May I ask who is calling?"

"Yes, my name is Lawrence Richardson. I need to speak to Skyy Armfield. Is she there?"

"I'm sorry, Skyy is not here."

"Oh, so Skyy does work there? This is her shop, correct?"

At that point, Skyy realized the person was obviously trying to track her down for whatever reason. Of course, the first reason that came to mind was that someone's wife was having their husband followed and she had been caught in the crossfire.

"Yes, she does, but she's not here."

"Shoot. I'm trying to surprise my wife, and I wanted to talk to Skyy about getting my wife's hair and nails done on Saturday after we do massages. It's our anniversary."

"Oh. Is your wife an existing customer of Skyy's?"

"Yes."

Skyy sighed with relief. Her guilty conscious had gotten the best of her. She scheduled the hair appointment for the man's wife and checked Tiffany's appointment book for a nail appointment. After getting everything scheduled, Skyy went back to her paperwork, but before she could get started, her cell phone rang. She sucked her teeth, agitated by the interruptions. She desperately wanted to get the paperwork done so she could meet Kyle at their secret place for a night of dinner and sex. She looked at her cell phone and it displayed "J". A smile instantly appeared on her face at the thought of talking to her music mogul boyfriend. She hadn't talked to him in a few weeks because he'd been on the west coast on business, and the time difference made it hard for them to connect and talk.

"Hey you," she said.

"What's up? How you been?" J said with a strong, southern accent.

"Busy working. How about you?"

"About the same. Just got in a couple of hours ago. Tired as hell from jetlag, but I wanted to hear your voice. You know I miss you, gurl," J said.

"Ummm-hmmm, that's what your mouth says."

"I'm serious, gurl. You know the deal. So, you still coming down here for the hair show, right?"

"Yep, August 15th."

"You need me to get somebody to pick you and your crew up from the airport? I can get a car over there, you know."

"I know, J. We'll be alright."

"No, I insist."

"Okay, if you insist. You always insist."

"That's how I do. You know that. Oh, and I already have a hotel booked for you. Top of the line, of course. Nothing's too good for my gurl."

"J, remember, this is a business event for me and my employees. I can't play disappearing acts while I'm in Atlanta."

"Hey, I'm clearing my calendar to make time for you, so I think you need to reciprocate and make some time."

Skyy smiled. "J, we will see each other, I promise. But, I have to handle my business first."

"How many times do I have to tell you to quit that business and move down here close to me? I'll take care of you."

"I know you can take care of me, J. You do a good enough job now. But, I like having my own business, doing my own thing. Besides, what would your wife think if you moved some woman to Atlanta?"

"She don't care what I do. As long as I keep the paper rolling, she's fine, you know what I'm saying."

Skyy knew exactly what J was saying. As one of the hottest music producers in the industry, J was a multi-millionaire who started his own record label before he turned twenty-one. He was what people considered a natural talent. Back in 1989, when J was only fifteen years old, he was writing top hits for artists like Bobby Brown and Anita Baker. After writing and producing a number one hit for girl group C.H.A.N.G.E. when he was sixteen, J received his big paycheck. That's when people in the music industry began to take him seriously. Despite his age at the time, more and more artists wanted him to work on their albums. He used his money and invested in a record label, discovering some unsurpassed hip-hop artists in the industry today. The only thing he regretted was the fact that he married his first girlfriend and never signed a prenup.

As his career heightened, his wife seemed to sit stagnant, never taking an interest in anything but having babies and spending J's money. The more money he made, the more reliant she became of him. She expected J to do everything for her financially. During the early years of their marriage, the intent was for her to go to college, get her business degree, and work as J's business manager. However, she dropped out of college, had three kids, and became one of Atlanta's most prestigious housewives. In fact, she'd been approached by the Bravo network to be one of *the* Atlanta Housewives. However, J would not approve of it. Not that it was necessary. Everyone in Atlanta, as well as the music industry, knew his wife because she used her husband's celebrity status to create her own. Their relationship was volatile, strictly a marriage of convenience. Even though J had enough money to divorce his wife, give her half, and still be well off, he didn't want to give her the satisfaction of it all. He preferred to be in control of how much money she deserved to spend on a regular basis instead of a judge giving him orders on how much to pay her.

As selfish as it sounded, J was comfortable with the arrangement because he'd been cheating on his wife for over ten years.

At first, he targeted women in the industry, but it became too messy because of his wife's notoriety. Lately, he targeted women who were not in the industry in an attempt to keep his mistresses under wraps and out of the limelight. Skyy happened to be a perfect choice for J. After meeting her at the International Fashion and Hair Show in Atlanta last year, he fell hard for Skyy.

Even though J was not as easy on the eyes as Kyle was, he made up for his looks with his extremely large bank account. His sex wasn't half bad either. For a short guy, he was heavily endowed and could do things with his tongue that Skyy had never felt before. What Skyy appreciated about him the most was the fact that he never had a problem spending his money on her. Sure, the money he spent on her didn't put a dent in his bank account, but Skyy took whatever he gave her, and she did it with a smile. J not only gave her expensive gifts, but he also gave her large sums of cash. Nothing was too good for her, and J was always trying to convince her to move to Atlanta to be closer to him. Skyy felt like it was only a matter of time before J found another mistress to play around with. However, for now, J wanted to make Skyy a permanent fixture in his life ... as the woman on the side, of course.

"J, don't start that. You know I'm not leaving Richmond. I'm staying right here with my salon and my friends."

"But you can have a salon down here. I asked you to think about it the last time we talked. Have you even considered it?"

"No. There's nothing to think about. I'm staying here. You knew this would be long distance when we met."

"Yeah, but I was hoping I would've convinced you to move by now."

"J, you're getting too heavy. I thought we were gonna keep things cool, you know?"

"You know how I feel about you, Skyy. I haven't felt like this about a woman in a long time, and I just can't stand to think about you up there, being with another nigga and shit."

"J, you're the one that's married."

"Yes, and you know my situation with her."

39

"Are we gonna have this conversation again? I would rather you fly up here and see me. You know can't nobody handle this like you," Skyy said, boosting J's ego.

Skyy knew J thrived off of being complimented about how good he was in bed, so she tried to tell him the things he wanted to hear.

"I see you. You trying to change the subject, but it's cool. Don't you realize I can have any woman I want, and I choose to be with you?"

"Yes, I do. I also know at any minute, you can decide you don't want me anymore and throw me to the side like garbage, which is why I would prefer to keep my life here in Richmond."

J grew silent because he knew he was fighting an uphill battle. "Okay, baby. I won't sweat you about it," he finally said. "It's cool. You still my gurl, though."

"I hope so."

Skyy could tell J felt defeated once again. They'd been having the same conversation for several months now, but Skyy continued to stand her ground. There was no way she would pack up and leave her life in Richmond to move to Atlanta to be someone's mistress.

"So, the hair show is not until next month. I gotta wait until then to see you?"

"You can see me anytime. You know that. You're the one with the busy schedule. Besides, you have plenty of women down there keeping you satisfied. So, don't try to make it seem like it's all about me. I know better."

"Stop trippin'. You know how I feel. See, there you go again."

"Okay, okay, when do you want to come up here?"

"I have a meeting in New York next week. I can stop by on my way up."

"Okay, I'll be here."

"I got you something while I was in L.A., too. It's in the mail. You should get it in a couple of days."

"Okay. So we good, right? You not mad at me?"

"Naw, gurl, we cool. I told you that. I'll holla at you later."

"Okay," Skyy said, ending the call with J.

As much as he made her happy, she felt like he was getting a bit too clingy, even from a distance. The only good thing was the fact that he was not willing to leave his wife. Therefore, she knew as long as he was still married, she still had him where she wanted him.

*   *   *

It was a sunny Sunday afternoon, a day when the salon was closed. However, Coco and Skyy were in the salon preparing for the hair battle in Atlanta. Coco decided to choose a Chinese theme, and each style he would design would be asymmetrical with sharp edges. While in the salon, Coco practiced his routine on three dummy heads, trying to master the cut he would administer on his client in the hair show. One of the rules of the show was that the routines had to be timed. Each stylist only had a few minutes to create hair masterpieces. So, Coco decided to have his client wear hairpieces that he would cut right in front of the audience.

While Coco practiced, Skyy did some heavy-duty cleaning of the salon. Whenever she had a weekend that she was free, she used Sundays as the time when she would wipe down the workstations, scrub the floors, and clean the shampoo bowls as well as the bathroom. Music blared from the radio speakers while Coco and Skyy concentrated on their individual tasks. The more it appeared that Skyy was making progress, Coco continued to spur hair around as he cut.

"Coco, am I working for nothing?"

"Skyy, nobody told you to come in here trying to clean when you knew I had to practice."

"Why didn't you practice at home?"

"Because I didn't want to get hair all over my white carpet."

"So you just make more work for me?" Skyy said, rewiping the counters.

Coco turned to Skyy, giving her much attitude.

"Whatever, Coco."

"I think I'm about done here anyway. I need to go home and get some sleep. You know I didn't get in until four this morning."

"Where did you go last night?"

"Chile, we went to D.C. to this new club, and I tell you, the kids were in full force. Talk about some pretty boys. Ump humph umph. And what did you get into last night?"

"Nothing much. I talked to Davin for about two hours."

"The mortgage broker, right?"

"Yeah. He was really depressed. His wife had to go out of town on business, as usual. So, he was home alone and just needed someone to talk to. She treats him like trash."

"Umm-hmm, and you were right there to pick him up off the curb, too, huh?"

"Really, Davin and I have only slept together once. The majority of the time he wants conversation. All he really wants is some attention."

"Why do you waste your time with that? Sounds depressing."

"Because he's a nice person. I like to boost him up, make him smile, and just give the man some emotional support. Our friendship isn't built on anything physical; it's more emotional."

"I still don't understand why you waste your time, especially when you have your hands full with the other two. Besides, what are you getting out of the deal?"

"Who said I was getting something out of the deal?"

"Because if you weren't getting anything out of it, you wouldn't be in it."

"That's cold, Coco. I'll have you know that Davin stimulates my mind just as much as I stimulate his. We have very nice conversations. We have a lot in common. We like the same music; he wants to open a barbershop. So, we talk about that."

"I thought he had his own business?"

"He does. He has his own mortgage company. He's a mortgage broker, but he hates his job. He wants to pursue his dream, but his wife won't let him venture out and do the barbershop thing. I think he appreciates the fact that I actually listen to him and understand his need to want to pursue his dream."

"Can I ask you a personal question?"

"Of course, Coco. Not that you need to ask permission."

"Have you ever been in a monogamous relationship? As long as I've known you, you have never been in an exclusive relationship."

Skyy chose her words carefully because she knew Coco had a way of bringing out the good and the bad in her.

"Are you being genuine, Coco, or are you trying to be funny?" she asked. "I don't have a desire to be with one person. Not now, not ever. I've told you that before."

"Yes, you have, but you have never told me why. And you still didn't answer my question."

Skyy frowned a bit, and Coco could tell she was getting a bit uneasy.

"Well, let's just say I have learned a lot from all of my relationships, past and present. Therefore, I prefer to live my life accordingly."

"Not answering my question again."

"Coco, what do you want me to say? I had a difficult childhood and have a problem with commitment. Is that what you're looking for?"

"Skyy, it was a simple question. Have you ever been in a monogamous relationship?" Coco asked again, this time slowly and firmly.

"No."

"Was that so hard? I'm not trying to be your therapist, honey."

"So why did you feel the need to know the answer to that question?"

"Because sometimes I wonder how you can be so, so . . . I don't know, unfeeling about certain things."

"Coco, come on, don't start with me today. I am who I am, okay? I don't judge you because of your lifestyle, do I?"

"No, you don't, and for real, you don't know what I had to endure growing up as a gay black man. I know sometimes I walk around and it seems like I have it all together, but trust me, honey, I have my bad days. Life hasn't always been easy for me. I think the reason why I gravitate to you is because you have always treated me with so much warmth and respect in spite of who I am. I also see how you live your life so freely, and it makes me wonder sometimes if there was something you had to overcome to get to this point in your life. You know what I mean?"

Skyy looked at Coco and noticed he had tears in his eyes. Coco was using the moment to dig down deep inside himself to try to connect with Skyy somehow. It was as if Skyy was a page in the *Richmond Times Dispatch* newspaper, and Coco was reading her. However, in usual Skyy fashion, she refused to open up.

"I just don't have commitment in me. That's all there is to it."

Skyy's past was as big a secret to Coco as his gayness had been to his father when he was in high school. However, it was Coco's father who beat Coco in a rage when he found out about his lifestyle. He thought by beating Coco that he could make him tough, make him a real man. That beating, which caused Coco to have a fractured rib and broken nose, resulted in Coco attending numerous therapy sessions in his adult life. Every time he thought about his past, he thought about the pain and suffering he endured at the hands of his own father. Coco also knew, however, that there was something Skyy kept secret about her past that he wanted her to share. Just when Coco thought he'd gotten her to that place, a place where Skyy would be willing to open up, Skyy immediately shut down. Coco was only familiar with Skyy's life from ten years ago to the present. Anything or anybody from her past was a mystery.

Chapter 6

"Ladies and gentlemen, the captain has turned on the seatbelt sign. Please return to your seats, and make sure all seats are upright and tray tables are up. All electronic devices should be turned to the off position as we prepare for landing." The stewardess gave final instructions for the passengers on the Airtran flight that Skyy, Coco, Debi, and Tiffany were aboard.

The International Hair and Fashion Show in Atlanta was finally upon the group, and they were all (except Tiffany, of course) excited about the weekend's events. Skyy and Coco were seated in the exit rows, and Debi and Tiffany were seated a few rows behind them. After flying for about an hour and a half, Flight 230 arrived at the Hartsfield-Jackson Atlanta International Airport just around noon, giving the group plenty of time to get checked in and settled before the festivities of the hair show began. Bronner Brothers, the producers of some of the top hair products for African-Americans, was the host of the national hair show. The hair show, which ran from August 15th through August 18th, was an international event that celebrities and everyday people from all over the country came together to celebrate African-American hair care.

The airplane touched down with force, hitting the pavement and causing the passengers to shake uncontrollably. Everyone seemed to sit as far back in their seats as possible, bracing for the landing, and Skyy closed her eyes for a few seconds. Landing was the thing she hated the most about flying. Her head moved from side to side, sort of like a bobblehead, until the airplane came to a complete stop.

"Ladies and gentlemen, on behalf of Airtran Airways, we would like to welcome you to Atlanta, Georgia. Please remain seated until the aircraft comes to a complete stop. We realize you have several choices in flying, and you chose to fly Airtran. Thank you for flying Airtran Airways. We hope you enjoy your stay."

The intercom clicked off, and Skyy opened her eyes just as the airplane came to a complete stop. The sound of the engine started to slow down and get lower. Almost simultaneously, seatbelt buckles began to unclasp, and passengers stood up to grab their carry-on luggage from the overhead bins. Skyy followed suit, grabbing her matching Gucci travel tote and duffle bag.

"ATL, we are here!" Coco shrieked. He said it so loud, some of the passengers turned to look at him. He hissed at them before sucking his teeth and rolling his eyes.

"Coco, we haven't been here for two minutes and you're acting up. Behave," Skyy told him.

"Honey, I ain't misbehavin'," Coco said in a southern belle-type accent.

They continued to collect their things, making sure they weren't leaving anything behind. Skyy fumbled through her Gucci handbag until she located her BlackBerry. Then she powered it on, checking to see if there were any messages. The message indicator flashed, letting her know she had several text and voicemail messages. She was sure the messages were all from J, who was probably eagerly awaiting her arrival. The passengers who were seated in the front half of the airplane had made their way off of the aircraft, so Coco and Skyy followed the flow of traffic.

"Thank you," the stewardess said.

Skyy and Coco nodded. They made their way to the terminal, which was full of life, spilling over with people trying to make their way to other destinations.

"Wait right here, Coco. I have to go to the bathroom."

Skyy put her purse on her shoulder and placed her other bags on one of the seats in the waiting area before making her way to the ladies' room while checking her text messages. Coco nodded in agreement while checking his voicemail messages. Skyy bumped her way through the crowd, only to be greeted with a long line at the restroom. While standing in line impatiently, she deleted each text from J telling her to call him as soon as her flight landed. Since there were about ten people ahead of her, she decided to give him a quick call.

"Hey, I just landed. What's wrong?" Skyy asked, wondering why J had sent her so many messages.

"Hey, I'm glad you made it safely. I wanted to catch you before you left the airport in a taxi. I have a car there to pick you up and take you to the hotel. The driver has a card with your last name on it near baggage claim, so be on the lookout, a'ight?"

"J, you didn't have to do that."

"Gurl, don't tell me what I didn't have to do. You're in my town now. I'mma be the ultimate host. I got you all set up at The Mansion on Peachtree. Five-star hotel, of course."

"J, I have reservations at the Embassy Suites with my staff."

"No woman of mine is gonna stay in the Embassy Suites. You're staying in one of the Presidential Suites. I got it all taken care of."

"I told you I'm here on business, J. So, I can't be holed up in a hotel with you all weekend."

"Come on now. I'm trying to do something really nice for you. Don't blow it."

Skyy tried to keep her cool because she knew this was J's way. Somehow, he always managed to make it appear that he was doing her a favor by spending time with her.

"I didn't ask you to make reservations for me. I have a reservation at the Embassy Suites, which will work out for me just fine," Skyy snapped back.

"Okay, okay, shawty," J said.

"Hey, I told you about calling me shorty," Skyy interrupted.

J released a heavy sigh, apparently agitated by Skyy's treatment. "Look, do we need to start this thang over? I mean, you in a bad mood about something? If you're not trying to spend any time with me, that's cool."

Still a bit groggy from the flight, Skyy rubbed her eyes. She wanted to see J; she just had to get her bearings. However, she wanted him to understand that he could not command all of her attention while she was in Atlanta.

"I do want to spend some time with you, J. I'm sorry. I'm standing in this long line, trying to go to the bathroom, and my head is throbbing. I really just want to get checked in and get a nap. I was up all night packing. You know how I wait until the last minute."

Skyy paused, hoping J's mood would lighten a little bit. The last thing she wanted was for him to be pissed off at her while she was in Atlanta. J was a major asset for Skyy and her friends while they were in town. If there was a party or a club that they needed to get into, J was sure to have one of his people get them in, VIP treatment and all. Plus, it didn't hurt that J would lace Skyy with some nice gifts, cash, and out-of-this-world sex.

"Come on, J. You know how much I want to see you. I've been looking forward to it since I saw you last month. I went and got something nice for you from Victoria's Secret."

"Yeah?" J said.

"Yep. I need to see you in the worst way."

"A'ight, that's what's up. Keep it hot for me."

"All for you, baby." Skyy softened her tone in an effort to get back in J's good graces.

"Well, catch that car. He'll take your crew to the Embassy. You go over to The Mansion. The suite is already reserved, and the driver has the room key. I'll meet you there in a couple of hours."

Skyy bit her lip, almost wanting to get J straight about being so bossy. Sometimes he talked to her like she was one of his "people", and it rubbed her the wrong way. But, this wasn't the time for it. It was his way, and Skyy just chalked it up to a man with power. Sometimes he had a hard time disconnecting from his business persona.

"I'll see you later," Skyy said before ending the call.

She was finally next in line for a bathroom stall, and she was feeling the wrath of the cranberry-apple juice she drank on the flight. After relieving herself, she washed her hands, checked her hair in the mirror, and applied some MAC lipgloss to her lips. She adjusted her halter top around her neck, popped a piece of Orbit spearmint gum into her mouth, then made her way back to Coco and the rest of the gang. She could hear Coco talking before she could actually see him.

"Well, listen. This is neither the time nor the place for this discussion. You want to take it there, then take it there. But right now, I'm on my way to the hotel, and I don't have time for this." Coco abruptly slammed his flip phone shut.

Tiffany and Debi were sitting, waiting for Skyy.

"Coco, who was that?" Skyy asked.

"Honey, nobody important. That's for damn sure. Let's go."

"Hey, before we go, would you all mind if I stayed at a different hotel?" Skyy asked.

"Hell yeah, we mind. So you think you're gonna just have us staying at the Motel 6 while you're at the Four Seasons? Oh hell nawwww!"

"Coco, the Embassy Suites is not the Motel 6."

"Mmm-hmm, so where you staying, Miss Thang?"

"Some hotel called The Mansion."

Coco gasped really loud, placing his hand over his mouth in dramatic fashion.

"What?" Skyy asked.

"The Mansion? You talking about The Mansion on Peachtree?" Coco asked.

"Yeah."

"Oh no, you're not staying there without me. Uh uh, uh uh! No way, honey. That place is all that from what I hear. I have a friend who had a client that stayed there."

"It's just a room, Coco. No different than what we already have. Besides, this way, you can have the room to yourself in case you have company."

"Don't try to dissuade me, Skyy. I want to stay at The Mansion with you," Coco whined.

"Oh, Coco, stop acting like a baby. What difference does it make where you stay, as long as you have your butt at the hair competition tomorrow," Debi said.

"Shut up, Debi. You're such a lil' hater," Coco said.

"Come on, y'all. Let's get our luggage. I hear there's a car waiting for me . . . I mean, for us," Skyy said.

"You were right. It's waiting for *you*. We just squirrels. It's your world, Skyy," Coco said, as Skyy stuck out her tongue.

The group made their way through numerous terminals and down a couple of escalators before making it to the baggage claim area. They searched the display screens until they found the one that read 'Flight 230 arriving from RIC'. Passengers from the flight were surrounding the conveyor belt, waiting for it to start moving. The airport was crowded, and Skyy wondered how many of the travelers were actually in town for the hair show. Some were blatant, wearing matching t-shirts blazoned with salon names like T & M's Hair Salon and Nu Look Hair Design. Skyy wished she'd thought of getting her small team matching t-shirts, but decided against it after noticing Coco's overstated, one-piece, denim, short jumpsuit and cowboy boots. He would've never wanted to arrive in Atlanta wearing just a t-shirt and jeans.

Skyy looked around to see how close they were to ground transportation since she knew the car that J had sent for her would be there. She noticed a short, brown-skinned brother with long dreadlocks holding a sign that read 'S. Armfield Party'. He didn't have the conventional look of a driver, which meant he was more like one of J's yes-men instead of an actual chauffeur. Just then, the conveyor belt started to rotate and luggage slowly appeared.

"Hey, Coco, I'm going over to let the driver know we're here."

Coco nodded, still carrying on a heavy conversation on his cell phone. Tiffany, who had been quiet the majority of the flight, kept dialing number after number on her cell phone, attempting to reach her baby's father, but to no avail. She was disgusted because she knew he was probably over his other baby mother's house. Debi was away from the group by the airline's Lost and Found office, obviously carrying on a private conversation. The past several weeks, Skyy noticed how Debi was spending more time on her appearance and taking more of her telephone calls in private. Skyy suspected Debi was still using her brother-in-law as a confidante, but she refused to touch on the subject again. Skyy walked toward the driver, who was standing clad in baggy jeans and an oversized polo-style shirt.

"Hi, I'm Ms. Armfield."

The driver looked Skyy up and down approvingly. "Wassup. I'm Tron. Where's the rest of your group?" he asked.

"Oh, they're getting their luggage. I saw you over here with the sign, so I wanted to catch you before you moved or something. This airport is so big; I didn't want to lose you."

"No problem. The car is right outside. Let me come help you with your bags."

Skyy took the lead and could feel Tron studying her butt from behind. He was such a tiny, little guy that Skyy wasn't sure he would be much help with their luggage. In addition to the luggage with their clothes, they had a huge trunk that contained Coco's hair equipment and props he needed for the hair competition. Skyy noticed her bright red matching luggage was propped against the wall near Tiffany, who'd already gotten her one piece of luggage. Coco was struggling to get his trunk off the rotating belt, so Skyy went over to assist him. Tron fell right in behind her, providing the muscle they needed to successfully remove the trunk.

"Thanks, Tron. This is Coco, one of my stylists."

"Wassup?" Tron said cooly.

"How you doin'?" Coco said, mimicking Wendy Williams, while Tron scoffed.

"Coco, do you have everything?" Skyy asked.

Coco put the trunk on a pushcart, then piled his rolling luggage on top of it. "Yes, honey. Let's go give Atlanta a whirl." Coco placed his oversized Chanel sunglasses on his face, wrapped his long scarf around his neck once, and proceeded to push the cart.

Tron frowned a bit, obviously a bit homophobic.

"Come on, Debi and Tiff," Skyy said, grabbing her luggage.

They followed behind Tron as he walked toward the automatic doors. Outside, the Georgia air was stuffy and the sun was hot. Tron walked over to a black on black, ¾-ton, 2009 Chevy Suburban, with tinted windows and shiny alloy wheels. He opened the trunk and began to load the cargo area with the lugguage they lined up beside him. Coco unloaded the cart and then pushed it to the bellcap so he could place the cart back inside.

"It's hot as hell out here," Coco commented, but no one really acknowledged him.

Tiffany's cell phone blared 'I just wanna be, I just wanna be successful', an indication that she had an incoming call. She answered abruptly.

"I've been calling you all morning since before I left Richmond. Didn't I tell you I was leaving today? You didn't even come over and see me before I left." Tiffany paused to listen to the lie she was being told by her son's father.

"Uh-uh, you sound so, so desperate. Ewwww," said Coco.

"Coco, mind your business," Skyy said.

Tron closed the trunk and opened the driver's side door of the truck. Skyy got in the front seat, while Tiffany, Debi, and Coco piled into the back. When Tron started the engine, the loud bass from the

51

music caused them all to jump. Tron turned down the volume just enough to hear Skyy speak.

"Did J tell you to drop them off at the Embassy Suites first?" Skyy asked.

"J? Oh, that's what you call him? Ha, that's cute. Yeah, he got you booked at The Mansion, right?"

"Yes. I've never been there. Is it nice?"

"Hell yeah, it's nice." Tron bobbed his head to an unfamiliar rap song that was playing on the radio. The song had a mixture of hip-hop, reggae, and pop beats all rolled into one sound. The rapper sounded like a cross between Ludacris and Kid Cudi.

"Yeah, that lil' nigga can flow," Tron said out loud, but he was really talking to himself. He continued to bob his head to the music of the mystery rapper, while heading toward the place where the Atlanta skyline was more defined.

* * *

After getting her troupe checked in at the Embassy Suites, Skyy was taken to The Mansion Hotel on Peachtree in downtown Atlanta. Pulling up in front of the hotel, Skyy was sure she'd seen the tall building from the airport. The architecture on the outside of the hotel was chic and modern, giving the look of large jigsaw puzzle pieces. The lobby didn't disappoint either, with contemporary leather furniture, white and black symmetrical marble floors, and a black marble fireplace. Skyy took in the view while waiting for Tron to bring in her bags. She was very impressed by the hotel J picked for her, and she couldn't wait to thank him.

When Tron came in with the luggage, the concierge stiffened up. "Can I get a bellhop to get those for you, sir?"

"No, that's okay. She's already checked in. I got these."

With Skyy on his tail, Tron headed to the elevators. They stood there, both feeling a bit awkward while waiting for the elevator.

"So, how long have you worked for J?" Skyy asked.

"About three years. He's my cousin, and I'm trying to get my music thang up and runnin', you know what I'm saying?"

Skyy nodded in agreement, but really didn't know what he was saying. As they rode the elevator in uncomfortable silence, Skyy couldn't wait to get to the room. She continued to follow behind Tron before reaching the Presidential Suite. Skyy didn't feel like she was entering a hotel room. It felt more like a posh, upscale New York condominium. The ceilings were eleven-feet high, and there was clearly more than 2,300 square feet of living space. The custom drapes were open, displaying a panoramic view of the Atlanta skyline.

"I'm gonna leave your key right here on the table. Ju .... I mean, J should be up soon."

"Thanks, Tron. Wait. Let me give you a tip." Skyy dug to the bottom of her purse, searching for her wallet.

"No, uh-uh, I can't take a tip from you. We straight. Have fun."

Tron left, leaving Skyy standing in the middle of the colossal hotel room. She headed to the separate bedroom, which had beautiful ice blue draperies that hung at the head of the bed. The headboard of the oversized queen bed was quilted, and it matched the draperies. The furniture was contemporary but refined, with fresh flowers delicately placed throughout the suite. The view from the bedroom window was just as incredible as the view in the living room. Atlanta's ostentatious skyscrapers seemed to touch the end of the earth.

Skyy took in the view a little longer, then decided to take a bath before J arrived. She headed to the bathroom, which didn't disappoint either. The marble ceramic tile seemed to envelope the entire room. Natural sunlight shone in through the glass block windows that were right above the heightened Jacuzzi-style garden bathtub. The bathroom was bright and inviting, and Skyy couldn't wait to enjoy it.

She turned on the faucet, filled the tub with bath beads, compliments of the hotel, and let the steam fill the room. She noticed the plush robe hanging on the back of the door and couldn't wait to wrap herself in it. While Skyy waited for the tub to fill, she headed back to the bedroom to get some clothes from her suitcase. She didn't feel like unpacking yet, just wanted to take a hot bath, slip into some Victoria's Secret loungewear, and catch a quick nap before J got there. Skyy knew she had to be ready when he came. She needed to have all of her energy. Unlike Kyle, who was the gentle, adoring lover, J brought a totally different flavor to the table. He approached sex as a sport, and their lovemaking was wild and uncultivated. J was the kind of lover that left a woman walking like a cowboy for a day or two. He expected Skyy to bend into every position imaginable, and he felt the most comfortable with Skyy's legs propped up high on his shoulders. He believed in going as deep as he could, touching the very tip of Skyy's utopia.

Skyy laid out a pair of pink shorts, a white tank top, and pink and white polka dot thongs. Of course, she had no intention of wearing a bra. She undressed in the bedroom, leaving her clothes in a pile on the floor, and headed back to the bathroom. The tub was almost filled, and Skyy knew by the time she got in, it would be filled just enough. She stepped in slowly, letting her body adjust to the hot water. Thanks to the bath beads, the water felt like silk on her body. She turned on the Jacuzzi and leaned back, letting the eight powerful jets thrust water onto different areas of her body. The Jacuzzi bath took her to another level of relaxation, and she hoped J wouldn't be there anytime soon. The dream was broken when Skyy heard the door to the hotel room open. At that moment, she wished she had a five-hour energy drink to help her get through the next couple of hours.

"Skyy?" J's voice echoed throughout the hotel room.

"I'm in the bathroom," she yelled.

A few seconds later, J entered the bathroom clad in a pair of Hudson jeans and an Ed Hardy t-shirt. He appeared a bit shorter than usual, probably because the garden bathtub sat up high off the floor.

"You got started without me? Wassup with that?" he asked.

"I was actually trying to catch a nap before you came. I didn't realize you were going to be here so soon. How you doin'?"

"Good now that you're here."

J made his way to the tub, leaned over, and kissed Skyy hard on the mouth. He removed his Tag Heuer watch and placed it on the floor before reaching into the tub to explore Skyy's body. He caressed her breasts forcefully, encouraging her nipples to swell, before finding her valley. Skyy moaned in ecstasy to the rhythm of the swishing water that was a product of every thrust he made going in and out of her valley with his finger. He used his other hand to yank her head back with her hair so he could suck on her neck. Skyy grabbed J's hand to keep him from causing her to have a premature eruption.

"Come on. Get in with me," she said softly.

"Uh uh, get out," J said, breathing heavily.

While continuing to kiss her, he pulled Skyy from the tub, not caring that her body was soak and wet as he pressed her close to him. Skyy wrapped her arms around him, feeling cold and hot at the same time. With their bodies intertwined, they walked toward the bedroom. Skyy lay back on the bed, and J dropped to his knees, forcing Skyy's legs as far apart as he could. He went straight to her clit, hungrily licking and sucking it, making it swell. Skyy's moans got louder and louder because J always hit the right spot when he ate her out. He put his two fingers in her pussy as he sucked her, and Skyy's back started to arch.

"Come on. I need you to fuck me," she purred.

"You want this dick, don't you? Tell me again."

"Yes, baby, I want it now. Fuck me."

J unbuckled his jeans and pulled them down just enough to set his muscle free. He lifted Skyy's legs up on his shoulders, bending them back as far as they would go before easing his way in. He thrust deeper and deeper inside her until there was nowhere left for him to go.

"Come on, baby. Fuck me," Skyy begged.

This caused J to go into third gear. He pushed back and forth, back and forth, with so much force that the backboard bumped against the wall. His thrusts were wild and uninhibited, and Skyy hurt so good. This went on for minutes, with J panting and breathing heavily before he forced Skyy to turn over on her stomach. J wanted to hit it from the back, one of his favorite positions, because not only did he like to watch the way Skyy's ass wiggled like jello the harder he forced himself inside of her, but he also liked the option of anal sex.

"You like this shit, huh? You like this shit?" J panted.

"Yes, yes, yes!" Skyy groaned, trying to breathe through every push of her chocolate walls. She bit down on her lip, as J groped her breasts and pulled her hair simultaneously. "Oh, oh, oh!" she squealed.

J's speed quickened, almost like a locomotive, and then he stiffened. When his body got limp, he flopped on top of Skyy. Since J was a little guy, his body didn't smother her, not like Kyle. He kissed her on her back, then rolled over on the bed.

"Damn, gurl, that shit is good. What you do, put some hot sauce on it this time or something?"

Skyy rolled over, exposing her erect nipples. "You so crazy. I need a towel, blanket, or something. It's freezing in here," she said.

J got up and headed to the bathroom, grabbing the fluffy robe from behind the door. He threw the robe to Skyy from the bathroom before gargling with the hotel-provided mouthwash.

"What time you and your crew heading out tonight?" J asked.

Skyy wrapped herself in the robe, feeling more relaxed than ever. "I don't know. The comedy show is later on, but that's about it. The hair battle and fashion show are tomorrow night. I want to take a nap before we go out, though."

"You gonna have enough time to have dinner before the comedy show?"

Skyy looked at him. "What? Look, I don't want no trouble, J. I mean, it's one thing to be holed up in this hotel room, but out around town, *your* town, I don't know."

"She's in Florida visiting her parents. She left yesterday."

"What about her friends?"

"What about her friends? Look, I pretty much do what I want, Skyy. You know that. We talked about this. I sent her away for the weekend so we could be together. Let's just enjoy each other while we can. Can we do that?"

"If I walk out of this hotel and somebody shoots at me, I'm blaming you."

"Believe me, you don't have to worry about anything like that. Oh, before I forget, I got you something."

J grabbed a mint green jewelry box from the dresser and handed it to Skyy. By the color of the box and the silver letters engraved in it, she knew J had been to the David Yurman store. A smile instantly appeared on her face.

"You got me some Yurman?" Skyy said, grabbing the box and not expecting an answer.

She opened the box, revealing a diamond encrusted 10-millimeter bangle. The bracelet would match perfectly with her collection.

"Oh, J, you know what I like, don't you!" she shrieked.

"Yeah, and so do you." J smiled with a devilish grin.

Chapter 7

"What's up A-T-L!" the overexuberant MC yelled to the crowd of thousands in attendance at the hair show.

Today was the big day, when Coco would compete for the $2,000 grand prize, a trophy, and of course, bragging rights for a year. The fantasy hair competition was established to allow stylists an opportunity to showcase their creativity. The hairstyle, theme, and make-up had to complement each other, proving technical and artistic capability. Having chosen a Chinese theme, Coco's model was wearing an ankle-length, bright red cheongsam with bright red pumps. Coco had styled her hair in an asymmetrical blunt cut, with one side long, one side short, and slanted bangs. Coco also put a few spikes in her hair for a dramatic effect, along with a spicy red rinse. Her face had been made up with fire-like colors: yellow, red, and orange eyeshadow, blush, and bright red lipstick. Her eyes were melodramatic, as she was wearing very long eyelash extensions and heavy mascara, perfect for the fantasy competition.

"Ladies and gentlemen, before we finish the fantasy competition for the evening, I want to thank all who came out to the comedy show and after-party last night. The turn-out was phenomenal, so much that we had to turn some people away. Our surprise guest, the baddest, boldest, and bossiest housewife from *The Housewives of Atlanta*, was in the house, and she agreed to be a judge in our competition today. Come on out!"

The MC pointed to the stage entrance, and the tall, honey-blonde haired housewife appeared. The crowd roared as she took the stage. Skyy, Debi, and Tiffany were front and center, while Coco was backstage with his model. He would be upset that he wasn't standing with them to see his favorite housewife live and in person. She came on stage, looking flawless in a short, wrap mini-dress and stiletto heels. She spoke to the crowd, telling them how excited she was about being a part of the event. The atmosphere in the arena was electrifying with flashing lights and loud music blaring. There were a total of a hundred models in this particular competition, and Coco's model was number sixty-four. The Atlanta Housewife took her place at the judges' table, along with the four other judges, and the competition began. Each contestant came out one by one, modeling their attire and hair for the judges and the crowd. Cameras were flashing and the crowd was boisterous. Skyy and her crew remained composed, saving their applause for Coco. The models seemed to come and go very quickly, and before they realized it, Coco's model was on stage.

"Chinese tradition has come to America, y'all! Straight out of Richmond, Virginia's Blue Skyy's Hair and Nail Salon, we have a creation by Coco. The model is wearing a customary Chinese dress, which complements the emphasis of the 2010 version of the Chinese bob. Fabulous! Let's give her a hand!"

Coco's model walked the stage, showing off Coco's creation. Skyy, Debi, and Tiffany screamed and applauded like their life depended on it. Others in the crowd did the same, obviously impressed with Coco's design. Skyy tried to read the judges' faces to determine if they were just as impressed. Skyy caught a glimpse of Coco from the area backstage where all of the competing stylists were. She gave him two thumbs-up to let him know his model was absolutely fabulous.

The remaining models graced the stage, some mediocre, some high-tech. From futuristic, to throwback to the sixties, they all seemed to have their own style and flair, which was needed for this competition. When the competition was over, the models took their place on stage, all of them wearing their respective numbers. This allowed the judges one last peek at the models before they voted. The MC reappeared, this time wearing a long, black Cher wig, a black skintight cat suit, and stilettos. The vision might not have been so odd if the MC wasn't male. The crowd roared in disbelief at the sight of him strutting on the catwalk, posing as if on a photo shoot for a magazine. As Madonna's song "Vogue" blared from the speakers, the MC started to vogue, using his hands to make imaginary squares around his face. Skyy, Debi, and Tiffany cheered him on, giving the MC his moment. Finally, after giving the crowd much attitude, the MC grabbed the microphone.

"Wasssssup, A-T-L! What, y'all thought I wasn't gonna get in on the action tonight?"

The crowd yelled. He continued to pose like the camera was on him at every angle, leaning back on four-inch stilettos like a professional.

"Okay, okay, let's get down to business. I'm going to call out ten numbers. These are the models that are the top ten vote-getters of the competition. If your number is called, please join your model on stage," he spoke directly to the stylists. "Alright, ladies, as I call your number, head to the stage as quickly as possible."

A man dressed in a black suit walked up to the stage and handed the MC an envelope. The MC roared like a cat at his presence. The crowd erupted with laughter.

"Okay, here we go. Number thirty-two, number twenty-six, eight-nine, ninety-seven, eleven, fifty, sixty-four, sixty-nine, nineteen, and thirty-three."

Debi, Skyy, and Tiffany jumped up and down in pure hysteria. Coco headed to the stage dresssed in black liquid leggings, thigh-high leather boots, and a black stylist smock emblazoned with the words "Blue Skyy's Hair and Nail Salon" on the back. Of course, Coco accessorized by wearing a long black scarf around his neck and oversized Jackie Onassis Chanel sunglasses. He jumped up and down in excitement. All of the finalists stood anxiously awaiting the final results.

"Okay, here we go. Coming in third place is ... Harvette Dupree from A Cut Above, Compton, California!"

Harvette and her model, number eleven, hugged each other before Harvette made her way to the MC to get her trophy. The MC moved the third place trophy from below the podium and handed it to Harvette along with a check.

"In second place, we have ... Coya Tomlin from Touch of Class, Frederick, Maryland!"

Coya screamed and jumped up and down like someone who'd just won the Publisher's Clearinghouse Sweepstakes. She ran and hugged the MC before getting her check and second-place trophy. Then the stage lights appeared to get still and a loud drumroll started to play.

"And now, for first place and the $2,000 grand prize . . . Coco Sheridan from Blue Skyy's Hair and Nail Salon, Richmond, Virginia!"

Coco exploded, jumping around on stage like a hot potato. Skyy, Debi, and Tiffany screamed at the top of their lungs as the remainder of the crowd cheered Coco along. Coco paraded to the front of the stage, looking more like a Miss America pageant winner, to collect his prizes. He fanned his face with one hand, while covering his mouth in disbelief with the other. The judges were all standing and applauding. At that moment, Coco noticed his favorite Atlanta Housewife, and his eyes got big as lemons.

"Coco, congratulations! The judges all agreed that your design was unique and original, artistic and ingenious. The presentation was superb and fabulous!"

Coco leaned into the microphone and yelled out, "Thank you," numerous times before the MC took control again.

"Can I get the staff of Blue Skyy's Hair and Nail Salon to join Coco on stage, please?!" The ladies obliged, moving quickly through the crowd to the side of the stage near the steps. "Celebration" blasted through the speakers, and confetti began to fall from the ceiling. Flashes from numerous cameras lit up the dark room. Many of the pictures were of Coco and his model.

"One more time for our special guest host, our winner, and all of the contestants!" the MC tried to shout over the commotion.

The audience began to dissipate a bit, while the crowd on stage grew. Skyy and her crew all gave Coco congratulatory hugs.

"You did it, Coco! I knew you could do it!" Skyy shouted.

They all danced around, continuing to hug and cheer for Coco.

"I can't believe it! I won! I won! Yes, honey, I did it!" Coco screamed.

Even though the show was over, there was still a bit of chaos in the convention hall with all the noise and people. Coco's model disappeared to the area backstage where she could change her clothes.

"Come on. Let's go outside to the lobby," Skyy said, leading the rest of the group away from the excitement.

Coco noticed the Atlanta Houswife snapping photos and signing autographs. "Now you know I cannot leave Atlanta without taking a picture with the diva," he said.

"Coco, I know you're not going over there acting like a fan, trying to take a picture with her?" Debi said.

"What? Are you crazy? I'm the superstar tonight, honey. She should want to take a picture with me." Coco snapped his fingers three times in a semi Z motion and sashayed toward the Atlanta Housewife for his photo op.

"That damn Coco is mess. Come on, y'all. Let's go out in the lobby and wait for him. I can't bear to watch him make a fool of himself," Debi said.

"Shoot, by the time Coco is finished with her, he'll have her thinking he truly is the superstar," Skyy said, while she and Tiffany roared with laughter. Debi was too busy responding to a text message she'd just received to share in the laugh.

"Hello?" Skyy said to Debi, trying to get her attention.

"What?" Debi replied, with her eyes still fixed on her phone.

"Who the hell are you texting so much that you can't even pay attention to us?"

"Whatever, Skyy. I'll be right back," Debi said hurriedly, before leaving them standing there.

"Debi! Debi!" Skyy yelled, but Debi ignored her.

"What is going on with her?" Skyy asked Tiffany, not really expecting an answer.

Tiffany just hunched her shoulders, unconcerned, wishing she could leave herself.

Skyy looked around, trying to find Coco. In true Coco form, the paparazzi was snapping picture after picture of the Atlanta Housewife and Coco, who were giving the cameras everything they desired. When they were done, they kissed each other on both cheeks. Skyy just shook her head in amazement and then continued to the lobby area with Tiffany on her heels.

When Skyy opened the door, she was taken aback. Debi and her brother-in-law were exchanging a kiss, but it wasn't an 'I'm happy to see you' kiss. It was more like an 'I can't wait to get you back to my room' kiss. Debi's brother-in-law had his arms around her shoulders, and whatever he was whispering in her ear made Debi giggle. Skyy was wondering, first of all, what he was doing there, and second of all, why they were sharing such a passionate kiss. Skyy and

Tiffany eased back into the convention hall where the hair show had taken place, trying to avoid being seen by Debi.

"Did you see that?" Skyy asked Tiffany.

Tiffany's mouth was still open in astonishment at what she'd just witnessed. "I can't believe, Debi. I bet that's who she was with last night," Tiffany said.

"What are you talking about?"

"Hmph. After the comedy show and the party at the club, we went to our hotel, but she told me that she had to go to the front desk to check on something. Then, when I got to our room, she called me on my cell and said she was going to have a drink at the bar and that she would be up later. She told me not to wait up for her. So, I took a shower, went to sleep, and didn't wake up until I heard her coming in this morning."

"What?! Debi? Are you serious, Tiffany?"

"Yep. Debi is creepin'."

Skyy cracked the door open just enough to get another look at Debi and her brother-in-law, who were still hugged up in the corner. Coco walked up behind them, giving them a scare.

"Who are y'all spying on?" Coco asked.

Skyy opened the door a little wider so Coco could get a view. Coco gasped when he saw Debi's brother-in-law smack her on the butt.

"What is she doing?" he said.

A few people passed them, telling Coco congratulations, but he was too busy trying to get the scoop on Debi to even acknowledge them. Skyy tried to shush Coco so Debi wouldn't hear or notice them. The three of them almost looked childish, spying on their friend. They were beginning to bring attention to themselves, especially since Coco had just been seen taking pictures, and on top of that, winning the grand prize. All eyes were already on him.

"Look, my public is starting to take notice. So, either we're going to go over there and read that hooker her rights, or we're going to leave her alone and make our way to the after-party," Coco said sarcastically.

"After-party? I don't feel like going to the after-party. I just want to go back to the hotel," Tiffany said.

"Ewwww, you are so, so, boring. Why are you being a party pooper?" Coco said.

"Look, the only reason I came down here was to go through this hair show and take that class. Y'all know I would rather be at home with my baby and my man," Tiffany snapped.

"Chile, please." Coco rolled his eyes and then redirected his conversation to Skyy. "Are you going to the party or do you have plans with Mr. Music Mogul?" he asked Skyy.

"I'm going to the party first. I'm not hooking up with him until later tonight," Skyy replied.

"Damn, I was hoping he would show his face. You know I'm dying to know who it is, even though I have a good idea of who it might be," Coco said. "Shoot, you and Debi getting room service like nobody's business. Ms. Coco needs to find her a maintenance man tonight, okayyy?!" Coco added, rolling his neck and bucking his eyes radically.

"TMI, Coco, TMI," Skyy said.

"I know, right?" Tiffany agreed.

"Y'all are just haters. Thanks so much for the motivation." Coco took his sunglasses from the top of his head and placed them on his face. He opened the door to the lobby, while Skyy and Tiffany followed behind him. They noticed that Debi was gone, and so was her playmate.

"Did that skank leave us?" Coco asked.

They walked over to the escalator to get a better view of the second level. They searched through the multitude of people that seemed to spill out of the convention hall into the lobby to socialize. They continued scanning the throng of people, trying to spot Debi, but she was nowhere to be found. Skyy took her BlackBerry from her purse and dialed Debi's number. It rung several times before Debi's voicemail picked up. Just as Skyy was about to leave a voicemail, she received a text from Debi. *'I'm not going 2 tha party. I have plans. Will cll u ltr'*. Skyy showed the text to Coco, then to Tiffany. Tiffany shook her head.

"Umph, umph, umph. She has lost her mind. I'm gonna tell her about herself."

"Coco, mind your business. That's Debi's business."

"Well, she just put her business all out on Peachtree Street, so now it's all of our business. Wait 'til I see her. Just wait."

"Come on. Let's head to the party."

"Skyy, would you be upset if I went back to the hotel? I don't feel like hanging out tonight."

Skyy wanted to do like Coco and tell Tiffany about herself, but instead, she didn't give her a hard time.

"Tiff, are you sure you don't want to go to the party? They're having it at the Tongue and Groove Club. It's closed to the public, so everyone there will be in the hair business. This could be a great networking opportunity."

"Skyy, I do nails. That's all I do. What the hell do I need to network for?"

Skyy took a deep breath and tried to choose her words carefully. Frankly, she was getting sick and tired of Tiffany bringing down the mood. The trip had been very enjoyable for everyone except Tiffany. But, Tiffany brought this on herself. She didn't want to enjoy herself. She was so unhappy with her life that she walked around with a chip on her shoulder, down in the dumps, when really she had no reason to be. She was never satisfied with anything or anybody. Skyy realized that no matter what, there would be no pleasing Tiffany. Until Tiffany was happy with herself, she would never be happy with anyone else.

"Tiffany, if you want to go back to the room, that's on you. However, I refuse to let you put a damper on this fantastic evening. Coco just put our spot on the map by winning a national competition in one of the hair capitals of the world. Instead of you being happy for him, you'd rather be down on yourself. I wanted all of us to come to this event in an effort to learn some new things. You're the only nail technician in my salon. I thought you took your job a bit more seriously. You need to learn new techniques in order to stay competitive and gain a broader clientele. That was my goal for all of us this weekend."

"I'm not being down on myself. I just didn't want to be here, that's all."

"Yeah, well, you're here, so deal with it. Can we turn the channel from the soaps, please?" Coco said.

"Coco, mind . . ."

"I know, I know. Mind my business. I'm just saying, Skyy. Stop pacifying her like a newborn. Hell, if she don't want to hang out and have some fun, let her go sit in the room and think about her baby daddy all night. I bet you this, he ain't thinking about you right now, which is all the more reason you should be out enjoying yourself."

"Coco, that was mean. Why would you say that?" Tiffany said.

"Girl, wake up and smell the fuckin' Starbucks mocha latte. He is your baby daddy. He is not your husband. He is not your boyfriend. He is your baby daddy. Period. So, stop trying to make it something that it ain't, and move on. Okayyyyy?"

Tiffany sneered at Coco.

"Coco, you apologize to Tiffany," Skyy demanded.

"For what? Truth hurts, don't it? I just say what everybody else is thinking."

"Fuck you, Coco." Tiffany walked off in a huff, disappearing in the crowd.

"Coco, why did you do that? You hurt her feelings. That was not nice and you know it."

"Skyy, Tiffany has gotten on my last nerve this trip. She should've kept her ass in Virginia if she was gonna act like this."

"But, Coco, you know she's trying to make things work with her baby's father. Why would you say that to her?"

"You heifers are too damn sensitive for me."

"Like you aren't."

"I know, right?" he replied, and they both laughed.

The crowd was thinning, and Skyy and Coco exited the convention center, following the flow of traffic outside. Everyone was either going to the parking deck to get their cars or they were loading into one of the yellow taxicabs that were conveniently parked along the street.

Tiffany grabbed a taxi by herself and went back to the hotel. Coco's words had struck a nerve with her so much that she cried the entire way to the Embassy Suites Hotel. In spite of it all, the first thing she did when she got to the room was dial her baby father's cell phone number. She would spend the rest of her evening alone, since it was evident that Debi wouldn't be coming back any time soon.

Chapter 8

The chime on Skyy's alarm clock chirped softly at first and then crescendoed loudly until she hit the snooze button. The last few days spent in Atlanta had taken a toll on her, and she wished she didn't have any customers today. Unfortunately, she had five of her regulars scheduled, so there was no way she could get out of doing their hair. She turned over to focus her eyes on the time, realizing she forgot to set the clock for a six a.m. wake-up. The alarm clock was still set for seven o'clock a.m., which was the time she needed to be up when she left to go to Atlanta.

"Shit!" she yelled, recognizing the fact that she was going to be late.

Rolling over in her king-sized sleigh bed, she pushed the duvet cover away from her body, sat up, and slipped her feet into her furry slippers. She grabbed her cell phone to call Coco so he could tell her customers that she was running late but would be there a.s.a.p.

Skyy's pathway to the bathroom was illuminated by the sunlight. It was the early sunlight, the kind that had an orange tint to it. She tried to move as fast as she could, but her body was too tired. After finally making her way to the master bathroom, which was adjacent to her bedroom, she turned on the shower. Steam filled the bathroom quickly, causing condensation to cover the mirror above the sink. Skyy wiped the mirror so she could get a good view of herself while brushing her teeth. She wouldn't fully wake-up until she got in the shower and the water from the dual showerheads were beating down on her.

After showering and dressing quickly, she threw on a purple maxi sundress with black, flat Gucci thong sandals. There was not enough time to do much to her hair, so she applied some hair crème from Carol's Daughter, brushed her hair back into a ponytail, and headed out the door in record time.

* * *

"Look, that boy is just as zesty as he wants to be. My gaydar tells me that he is definitely one of the kids," Coco said.

"Coco, I don't believe that. He has like three kids with three different celebrity women. I refuse to believe he's gay," his customer replied.

They were going back and forth about some rapper and the rumors of him being on the downlow. There were only four people in the salon: Coco, his customer, and two of Skyy's customers. Neither Debi or Tiffany had made it in yet. The blinds shook against the door when Skyy entered.

"Good morning, everybody. Karen and Sheena, I am so sorry I'm late. I forgot to set my alarm clock. We didn't get in until late last night; our flight was delayed; and I'm just all out of sorts."

"It's okay, Skyy. My boss isn't in the office today, so I can be a bit late. I'll ease on in," Karen replied.

"And I'm off today," Sheena said.

"Good morning, sunshine. You look like hell," Coco added.

"Thanks, Coco. I appreciate your honesty. I need to call Debi to see if she can stop by Starbucks and do a coffee run. Come on, Ms. Karen," Skyy said. She motioned for her customer to come and sit in her chair so she could put a cape on her. Systematically, she put a neckstrip around her customer's neck before swinging the black nylon cape over her body to protect her clothing. "What are you getting today?" she asked.

"Just a shampoo and roller set."

"Okay, go to the bowl. I'll be there in a second." Skyy dialed Debi's number on her BlackBerry, but it went straight to voicemail. "Damn, her phone is off. Coco, do you know if Debi is coming in today?"

"No, Skyy, I don't have Debi's calendar tattooed on my chest."

"You so damn smart. Can you check her book for me, please?" Skyy hurried over to her customer.

"Okay, you act like I'm not servicing one of my customers right now. Don't get mad at me because you're late and behind schedule." Coco wiped his hands on his smock before going over to Debi's station, looking for her calendar. She only had two customers listed, and they were afternoon appointments. "She won't be in until 3:30," Coco said.

Skyy turned on the water in the sink and let it run a while until it was warm. She soaked her customer's hair quickly before squeezing a large amount of shampoo into her hands. Skyy worked the shampoo into her hair vigorously, being sure to scratch her scalp.

"Are you itching?" she asked.

The customer shook her head. Fortunately for her, Skyy was doing a great job with washing her hair, so she didn't have an opportunity to say her scalp was itching.

"Call Tiffany. I need my Starbucks fix. I mean, if it comes down to it, I can do 7-Eleven, but I prefer Starbucks." Skyy washed her customer's hair a third time, rinsed it, and then applied some leave-in conditioner, combing it through. "Let that sit for a few minutes," Skyy said before waving her other customer to her chair. "Come on, Sheena."

"I'm gonna need for you to get it together, Miss Thang. I'm only operating off of a few hours of sleep, too, so get it together, honey," Coco told Skyy.

It was obvious Skyy was still a bit sluggish and worn out.

"What are you getting, Sheena?" she asked her customer.

"I think I need my edges touched up," Sheena replied, fingering the short hair around the sides of her head.

It wouldn't take much for Skyy to do her hair because she wore a very short hairdo with a few spikes on top. Skyy applied some relaxer around the sides and to the back of Sheena's hair after wrapping her in a protective cape. She then raced to the shampoo bowl and rinsed the conditioner from her other customer's hair. She squeezed the water from her long hair before combing it out, then placed a plastic cap on her head to keep her hair from air drying.

"Go to my chair and switch places with Sheena." The customer did as she was told, while Skyy yawned loudly. "I'm sorry, y'all. I need to wake up." She worked the relaxer on Sheena's head with her fingers, testing the straightness.

Just then, the blinds on the door shook, signaling that someone was entering the salon. Everyone turned their attention to the door.

A tall, delicious carbon copy of Idris Elba walked in, sporting an oversized striped polo and jeans. All of the women stared at him and smiled, wondering whose man he might be.

"Can I help you?" Skyy asked while walking toward the man.

"Yes, my name is Shamar Wiggins. I'm looking for Skyy Armfield. Is she here?"

Skyy spoke before using caution as she normally would do. "I'm Skyy. How can I help you?"

"Oh, you're Skyy. Well, I'm a private investigator from . . ."

"Oh hell no. Uh-uh, this conversation ends right here. I don't talk to private investigators," Skyy exclaimed.

"But, you don't understand. I . . ."

"I understand fully, and I would appreciate it if you would leave my salon before I call the police. Like I said, I don't talk to private investigators. So, whoever paid you to investigate me, tell them I wasn't here or something. This conversation is over."

Skyy opened the door for the private investigator, wanting him to exit the salon. Coco walked over to Skyy and stood behind her as reinforcement, not that he would be a match for the six-foot, two-inch barrel of muscles that stood before them. Coco may have had the height, but he definitely couldn't match the muscles. The private investigator paused before placing his business card on the counter.

"When you feel like talking, please give me a call." He flashed a set of perfect white teeth and a set of matching dimples in his cheeks.

Skyy's heart fluttered slightly, but not enough to ease up on the man.

"That won't be necessary. Thanks, but no thanks." Skyy shut the door behind him, but not before checking him out one last time.

"Ooooh, that is one big piece of chocolate I wouldn't mind melting in my mouth," Coco said.

"Coco, you so crazy." Skyy walked back to her customer who was sitting at the shampoo bowl giving her the evil eye.

"Oh, I'm sorry, Sheena. Let me rinse that relaxer off your hair."

"So, Skyy, what do you think that was all about?" Coco asked.

"I have no idea. I thought he was coming in here for Sheena or something."

Coco grabbed the business card from the counter. "He's from Baltimore. Who have you been screwing in Baltimore?"

Skyy raised her eyebrows. "Baltimore?"

"That's what this says. And he has a Baltimore number listed." Coco walked over and showed the card to Skyy. He held it close to Skyy's face since she was washing her customer's hair.

"Let me ask again. Who in Baltimore have you been screwing?"

"Coco, mind your business." When Skyy grabbed the shampoo from the shelf, it slipped from her hands, spilling on the floor. Coco noticed that Skyy appeared to be nervous.

"You okay?" he asked.

"I'm fine." Skyy reached down to pick up the shampoo, only for it to fall from her hands again.

"Shit!" she yelled loudly, causing everyone to turn and look at her. Skyy rubbed her temples and then put her face in her hands. "I'll be right back. Coco, finish rinsing her for me, please," she said before running to the bathroom and slamming the door.

"What the hell is wrong with her?" Coco asked, not talking to anyone in particular.

He picked up the shampoo bottle, grabbed a towel from the shelf, and laid it on the floor to cover the spilled shampoo. He finished rinsing Skyy's customer's hair, applied the conditioner, and put a plastic cap on her head.

The blinds on the door shook again, catching everyone's attention. This time, it was Tiffany and Niya. As they all exchanged good morning greetings, Niya took her seat behind the counter at the front of the shop, and Tiffany put her purse in the drawer at her nail station.

"Well, well, well, is that a smile on your face? I haven't seen that smile since last week before we left for Atlanta. I guess it's safe to say you saw baby daddy last night," Coco teased.

"Coco, do you have to start with me this morning? I'm too sleepy to even care about what you're saying," Tiffany said.

Skyy came out of the bathroom, and she didn't look well.

"Skyy, are you okay? You don't look so good," Coco asked.

"Good morning, Tiffany and Niya," Skyy said.

"Hey, Skyy," they both said.

"No, I don't feel good. I don't know if it's something I ate yesterday or what, but my stomach just got upset all of a sudden." She walked over to her station to finish her customer's hair.

"You want me to get you a ginger ale from the soda machine? You look awful."

"I'll get something in a minute. I need to finish my customers first." Skyy became unusually quiet from that point on.

Coco wondered if her change in demeanor was a result of the visit from the private investigator. He tried to analyze the situation. It wasn't just the private investigator, but the fact that he was from Baltimore that got Skyy upset. Coco wasn't sure who Skyy had been involved with in Baltimore, but it was obvious he or she was trying to track her down. Better yet, it could have been something from Skyy's past catching up with her that she didn't want to confront. Coco had to figure out a way to get Skyy to open up. He needed to know what had her so jilted.

Chapter 9

Skyy locked the door behind her last customer before closing the blinds. It was about eight o'clock, the sun was setting, and Skyy was dog tired. It was a big mistake for her to schedule so many appointments for the next day after returning from a trip. Normally, she wouldn't do such a thing, but it was obvious she wasn't thinking this time.

Her BlackBerry vibrated on the counter. It was Kyle. She didn't feel like meeting him tonight. Quite frankly, she was still a bit sore from her weekend with J. Their sex was always wild and passionate, but when it was all over, Skyy sometimes needed a few days to recover. She touched the ignore icon on her phone so it would stop vibrating, and then she walked to her office to sort through the mail, trying to determine what was junk and what was important. The computer made its Windows chime as it turned on so Skyy could check her business account.

Without warning, the sky opened up, and it started pouring outside. Skyy could hear the rain hitting the large window in the front of the salon. She knew it had to be heavy, because the sound vibrated through the entire salon. Thunder pulsated like African drums, and she was sure there was lightning that followed. The power in the salon blinked a couple of times, prompting Skyy to turn off her computer. She learned her lesson the hard way while on her computer once before while it was storming. The storm had caused her power to go out, which resulted in her computer being blown, as well.

She walked back to the front of the salon to check her drawer for an umbrella, before realizing she'd left it in her car. Peeking outside through the blinds, she caught a glimpse of the rain and how hard it was pouring. It was pouring so hard that she could barely make out the images in front of the salon. There were a couple of people walking by who were getting soaked; their umbrellas served no purpose. Skyy decided it would be best to just wait out the storm. So, she walked to the office to get her throw cover out of her cabinet and made herself comfy on the brown leather sofa. Since she was already tired, it didn't take long for her to dose off.

*   *   *

The knocking on the door startled Skyy at first, and she paused for a few moments before moving to be sure she wasn't dreaming.

"Skyy, Skyy, let me in. It's Eric."

"Shit," Skyy mumbled to herself.

Eric was the last person she wanted to be face to face with. After Debi's behavior in Atlanta, Skyy did not want to play question and answer with her husband. She looked at the clock; it was almost ten o'clock. Skyy couldn't believe she'd been sleep that long. She also couldn't believe Eric was standing outside the salon door asking to come in. Skyy slipped her feet into her sandals, rubbed the sleep from her eyes, and peeked out the blinds. She could see Eric's silhouette leaning against the door. The smell of Grey Goose vodka consumed her the moment she unlocked the door to let him in. Eric stumbled in, tripping over the landing. Skyy had to catch him so he wouldn't fall face first on the ground.

"I, I need to talk to you." Eric's speech was slurred, and he could barely stand up.

"Eric, what are you doing here? How did you get here?"

Skyy guided him over to the sofa so he could sit down. Then she hurried back to the door so she could lock it. Eric began sobbing.

"Eric, hey, what's wrong?"

"She's cheating on me. I know she is. Debi's cheating on me, and now she wants a divorce." Eric slumped over, cradling his face in his hands.

"Eric, you really need to talk to Debi. What are you doing here?"

"Because she told me that she was at work. She told me she was here, but I don't think she even came to work today."

Eric was right. The two customers that Debi had on the book for the day must've cancelled or rescheduled, because Debi said she wasn't coming in.

"Eric, I think you need to drink some coffee, sober up a little, then go home and talk to Debi. This is something you and Debi need to talk about."

"Don't you get it? She, she don't want me no more. She told me last night that it's over. Said I have to get out."

"But, Eric, you and Debi can work through this like you always do."

"It's different. She's been with someone else. I know it."

"You don't know that, Eric."

"I know my wife, Skyy. When she got home last night, I knew. I just knew." Eric continued to sob, leaving Skyy helpless.

She sat down beside him, rubbing his back. "Eric, really, I think you need to talk to your wife."

Eric looked up at her slowly. Skyy couldn't figure out why Debi would cheat on such a nice-looking man.

"Tell me the truth, Skyy. I know you know the truth. Is Debi fucking around on me?"

Skyy felt uneasy, especially since she knew the truth. But, it was not her place to tell Debi's husband that she was cheating.

"I'm sorry, Eric. I don't know. You need to talk to Debi. How did you get here?"

"I walked from Shockoe Bottom."

"You walked? All that way?"

"Yeah. I'm too wasted to drive, and I, I just needed to clear my head. I'm trying as hard as I can, Skyy. I want to be the man I used to be, but I can't find a job. Believe me, I'm trying. But, Debi doesn't understand how it feels to be the man of the house and not be the breadwinner."

Skyy sighed heavily. Quite frankly, she couldn't care less about any of this. This was Debi and Eric's problem, not hers. All Skyy wanted to do was go home and get in her bed.

"I'm sorry, Eric. I wish there was something I could say to make you feel better."

"You know the last time we made love? Four months ago. I can't even touch her. That's how I know she's cheating. Debi never turned me down before. Never. But, for the past four months, I can't even touch her."

Skyy rubbed his knee, while Eric continued to sob. She started to feel sorry for Eric, especially since she knew Debi was screwing around on him with his own brother. All she could think of was how crushed he would be if he found out. She sure as hell wasn't going to let that cat out of the bag.

"Do you want me to call Debi? See if she will come and get you?"

"Are you listening to me? She told me she was at work. How is it going to look if I ask her to come and pick me up here? I'm supposed to be at my boy's house shooting pool. Let me just sit here for a minute and get myself together."

Angst covered Skyy's face. She desperately wanted to go home, and Eric sitting on the sofa letting his drunkenness wear off was not her idea of a good time.

"Eric, look, I really need to get home and get some rest. As you know, we didn't get in until late last night, and I had early customers. I'm beat. I can call a friend or call you a cab or something, but I really need to go."

Eric struggled to stand up. His linen pants and shirt were still a bit wet from walking in the rain. Skyy couldn't help but notice how his pants clung to him and how thick his manhood looked through the slightly damp pants. Feeling throbbing between her legs, she bit down hard on her bottom lip.

"Eric, you really have to go," she told him.

Skyy had to force Eric out of the salon because she did not want to cross that line. Debi was her friend, a cheating friend who didn't want this man; however, she was still her friend. Eric caught Skyy staring at his manhood. She stood up, now feeling a bit uneasy, like a kid being caught with her hand in the cookie jar.

"Come here," he said, reaching for Skyy and pulling her close to him.

"Eric, come on now. You're drunk."

Eric caressed Skyy's butt while grinding on her. Skyy took a mental measurement of his penis in her head.

"Come on, Skyy. I need this. I won't tell if you won't."

He planted soft kisses on her cheeks, her neck, and even sucked her ears. As tired as Skyy was, she had to admit he felt good to her. She tried to push him away, but she got weaker with each kiss.

"Eric, please, you have to stop. This is not right."

Her lips said one thing, but her body told a different story. Eric bit at her nipples through her dress, causing them to get erect. He was hungry for a woman, any woman, and he was way past due for sex. Since Debi wasn't dishing it out, the only sex he received was in the form of his right hand, pay-per-view, Vaseline, and Scott paper towels. He felt like he had nothing to lose at this point. His wife was cheating and had made a decision to leave, so fuck it.

"Come on, Skyy. Just one time, please."

Skyy didn't resist as he moved his hand up her dress and between her legs. As sore as she had been earlier, somehow, her brain had sent a different message to her vagina now. He felt for her clitoris through her thong and knew he had her spot when she let out a purr like a kitten.

"Eric, we can't, I can't . . . ."

"Shhhh, one time, just one time," he whispered.

Eric put his tongue in her mouth before laying her down gently on the sofa. He raised her dress up over her waist and explored her body, putting his tongue in every crevice available. By the time he was ready to make his entrance, Skyy was almost in climax mode. Even in a drunken stupor, Eric touched her in ways that most men took years to learn. He sucked her breasts, each one very slowly and sensual. Eric didn't even pull his pants all the way down before entering Skyy's valley. He couldn't hold out much longer. With half their bodies on the sofa and their legs hanging off, they found a way to make it work; they had a rhythm going, even though they were in an awkward position. His breathing was heavy, which made the stench of the vodka even more noticeable. It didn't take long for Eric to reach his peak, and when he did, he got so stiff that Skyy thought he had passed out. He took a deep breath before standing up.

Skyy felt overcome with guilt. She felt like one of those people on *Jerry Springer* who sat on stage and said, 'I don't know. It just happened'. She never knew how any adult could come out of their mouth and say 'it just happened', but now, she found herself on the other side of that theory. Guilt built upon Skyy minute by minute. She adjusted her dress and refused to make eye contact with Eric, who paced the floor while rubbing his forehead. It suddenly occurred to her that Eric was not as drunk as he appeared to be when he first got there. The alcohol was slowly wearing off. Then again, she wondered if he was really drunk at all, or if it had been an attempt on his part to get back at Debi.

"I think you need to go," Skyy said.

Eric turned to look at her, feeling ashamed. "I'm sorry, Skyy. I, I just don't know what I'm doing anymore. I'm a fucking loser all the way around." Eric continued to pace, shaking his head, disgusted with himself.

Skyy continued to sit there, holding herself, feeling equally ashamed. It didn't matter that she slept with countless married men; this time, it didn't feel right to her. It wasn't right. Debi was her employee, her friend. Debi confided in her, and what did Skyy do? She screwed Debi's husband. That was the lowest of the low. How could Skyy face Debi without feeling guilty?

Skyy stood up. "Eric, you really need to go."

Eric's eyes were sad. They were both guilt-ridden; the mood was awkward. Skyy wished she could rewind the clock and erase what had just happened.

"Come on. I'll walk you to your car. You think you can drop me off at my car?"

Skyy nodded. Sulking, Eric's shoulders were slouched, and he hung his head low. Skyy walked to her office to make sure she'd turned off all the lights. Then she grabbed her things from her station before following Eric out into the darkness.

They walked down Broad Street in silence, passing numerous abandoned buildings and several homeless people on the sidewalk. Skyy anticipated leaving the salon while the sun was still up, so she had parked her car almost a block away. The air was stuffy, the aftermath of a thunderstorm when it hit Richmond in the middle of summer. For a Tuesday night, Broad Street was unusually busy with traffic. Skyy breathed a sigh of relief when she finally reached her car. She used her car remote and unlocked the door, placing her tote bag in the trunk before getting in the driver's seat. Eric got into the passenger seat. Before she turned the key in the ignition, Eric touched her hand and leaned close to Skyy so he could see her face in the darkness.

"I'm sorry. I'm so sorry. I've never cheated on Debi before, and I, I think I just had too much to drink tonight. I was upset and, shit, I fucked up."

Skyy sat back in her seat without starting the car. She realized she and Eric needed to put closure to this right then and there.

"Eric, as far as I'm concerned, tonight never happened. Whatever happens between you and Debi, please don't let it involve me. Deal?"

"Deal."

Skyy stared into his eyes. "I'm serious, Eric. You really need to bury this thing that happened tonight. I mean, if you want to try and get Debi back, telling her about us will not help your case. You know what I'm saying?"

Skyy tried very hard to convince Eric that keeping their quickie affair a secret would be in his best interest. In actuality, Skyy didn't want to hurt Debi, not in this way. Of course, she knew about Debi's affair, and maybe that's what made it a little easier to allow Eric to use her the way he did, but the fact still remained that Debi was someone she considered a friend.

"Skyy, I shouldn't have brought you into this. I need to work on my relationship with Debi, try to win her back before it's too late."

Skyy started the car and let the music set the mood for the drive to Shockoe Bottom. She eased down Broad Street, turned on Fifth Street, and merged onto Main Street, taking it all the way down to the bar in Shockoe Bottom where Eric left his car. Once near the Farmer's Market, Skyy slowed down, waiting for Eric to instruct her on where to turn. She noticed the personalized license plate 'D&E 2007' on his blue Ford Expedition, which was parked on Main Street to the left of them. So, she pulled up behind it. Eric looked over at Skyy apologetically before exiting the car.

Skyy pulled off, not even waiting for Eric to get into his truck. She circled the block so she could get back on Main Street going the opposite way, turned on Franklin Street, then jumped on the interstate. Her BlackBerry had been vibrating for over an hour, and she tried to take a quick peek at her messages while keeping her eyes on the road. She noticed there were three missed calls from Kyle, two missed calls from Davin, four text messages from J, and two voicemail messages. She hit the envelope on her touchscreen to play her messages; both voicemails were from Davin. She hadn't talked to him in a while, and he wanted to know if she wanted to go hang out Saturday night. His wife was in Chicago on business for two weeks, and he was feeling a bit lonely. She saved his message and decided she would call him the next day. Her day had gone a lot differently than she'd originally planned. She just knew she would already be at home in her comfortable PJ's, asleep on her 400-thread-count sheets. So much for that.

Chapter 10

The weekend before Labor Day meant a lot of things to a lot of people—back-to-school shopping for the kids; the last official weekend of summer; an extra day off from work; an overabundance of cookouts. For those in the hair industry, it was one of the busiest weekends of the year, the second busiest to Easter weekend. The salon was crowded. Every chair in the waiting area was filled, all of the dryers were being used, and the shampoo chairs were full. The blinds shook, and in walked the neighborhood hustle man with two plastic bags full of stuff to sell.

"Yo, whassup, Niya. Got those Gucci and Louie bags. What you need?" he said, sitting his plastic bags on the floor in front of the counter. He pulled a couple of his counterfeit designer bags out of one of the plastic bags and held them up for everyone in the salon to see. "Yo, yo, I got those Gucci bags!" He yelled this time, trying to get the customers' attention.

"Gator, I'm looking for some DVDs. What you got new?" Skyy asked.

"Don't you want a nice designer handbag? I'm letting them go for only sixty dollars, Labor Day special."

"Gator, how many times do I need to tell you that Skyy doesn't do fake, honey," Coco yelled from the shampoo area.

"Hey, let me see," Debi said, walking towards Gator's inventory.

A couple of customers from the waiting area followed Debi, who proceeded to pull additional handbags from the plastic bags.

"Hey, this one looks just like your black one, Skyy," Debi said, holding up a cheesy version of Skyy's Pelham Gucci handbag.

Skyy just smiled, thinking to herself how that bag looked as fake as a three-dollar bill.

"Oh, I'm getting this one. How much?" she asked.

"Every style, sixty dollars. I'll even throw in a free keychain."

Debi reached into her smock and pulled out three twenty-dollar bills. She'd made a lot of money doing hair that day. So, she figured she could treat herself, especially since her brother-in-law had been giving her money to help with her bills. Eric didn't know Debi was communicating with his brother, let alone having an affair with him. However, Debi was following Jill Scott's advice by living her life like it's golden.

"Come on, ladies. I need to get rid of all these bags today, end-of-season sale. These are great for the fall." Gator grabbed several bags, hung them from each of his arms for display, and paraded around the salon. He walked over to the women who were sitting under the dryer so they could get a better look.

"What you think, Skyy?" Debi said, showing off her new bag.

"It's cute," Skyy lied. She did a quick look-over and noticed the leather was fake and stiff. The hardware was too shiny, and the bag had a funny smell.

Debi put her new bag on her shoulder, proud of her newest investment. Coco looked at Skyy, and they made faces at each other, making a mockery of Debi's fake handbag. Neither of them would be caught dead sporting a knockoff handbag.

The blinds on the door shook again. This time, Eric and Debi's one-year-old son entered. Skyy's smile disappeared, and she immediately found a customer that needed her assistance near the shampoo bowls.

"Hey, Eric," Niya said loudly so Debi could hear her.

"Hey, everybody," Eric said, while placing his son down on the floor so he could try to take a few footsteps with assistance from his daddy.

Debi rolled her eyes at the sight of Eric, but became overly excited at her young son.

"Hi, Mommy's little pumpkin. What are you doin' here?" The baby burst into laughter at the sight of his mother.

"Hey, Debi, we came by to see if you wanted to do lunch with us," Eric said.

"Does it look like I have time to take a lunch break, Eric? Don't you see all these customers?" Debi replied. When the baby grabbed Debi's legs, she picked him up and hugged him tight.

"You still have to eat. How about I go and grab you something from Lee's Chicken?"

"That's okay. We ordered food from the Jamaican restaurant down the street." She continued to play with her son, giving him quick kisses on his chubby cheeks while trying her best to ignore her husband.

Eric glanced over at Skyy, who turned away quickly when she noticed him looking at her.

"Hey, what's up, Skyy!" he yelled over the noise in the salon.

Skyy waved, avoiding eye contact. Coco noticed Skyy's uneasiness while lifting the hood of one of the hairdryers to check his customer's hair. He ran his fingers through it lightly to detect wetness before replacing the hood over her head.

"About ten more minutes," Coco said, before heading back to his station.

"Heyyy, Eric," Coco sang, waving his hand high in the air.

Eric nodded his head as if to say 'what's up' and then turned his attention back to Debi.

"We really need to talk. What time do you think you'll be home tonight?"

"Don't know. We're getting a lot of walk-ins, so it's hard to say."

Eric leaned in close to kiss Debi on the cheek, but she pulled away.

"Debi, I love you. What can I do to make this work?"

"Don't do this here. This is not the time. Take the baby home. I'll see you later."

"Debi, I'm trying. I'm really trying ..."

"Eric, go home. Please, just go home."

Skyy, Coco, and Tiffany tried to hone in on Debi and Eric's conversation without being obvious. They all appeared to be CIA agents in the middle of a sting operation the way they looked at each other and then back at Debi and Eric. It had been almost a month since their Atlanta trip, and they all had given Debi the third degree about her behavior on the trip. All except Skyy, of course. Of all people, she had no right to talk to Debi about cheating, especially since she'd gone as far as she did with Debi's husband.

Eric looked over at Skyy again before grabbing the baby from Debi. Coco noticed again. The baby started crying, kicking, and screaming because he wanted to stay with Debi. Eric struggled to console the baby, but he wiggled and fought to get back to Debi.

"Go ahead, Eric. Just leave so he can stop crying," Debi said.

"I love you, Debi." Eric hurried out of the salon with the boisterous baby, unable to wave goodbye to anyone in the shop.

Skyy seemed to breathe a sigh of relief. Coco eased over to her.

"Mnmmm-hmmmmm," he said to Skyy.

"What?"

"What was that about?"

"What are you talking about, Coco?"

"I saw that."

"I saw them, too."

"No, no, Miss Thang, I'm talking about you. Why did Eric keep scanning the room for you?"

"Coco, why do you always have to start drama? Eric ain't checking for me, so why would you even say that?"

"Skyy, I could've sworn I saw Eric wink at you or something."

"Coco, for real, you're going to piss me off talking stupid."

"Mmm-hmmm, call it what you want." Coco swung his head and snapped his neck before strutting back to his station. He reminded Skyy of a peacock because he had decided to grow a mohawk, and the portion of his hair on top was spiked and dyed bright orange.

Skyy was hoping guilt wasn't oozing from her pores after being in the same room as Eric. It was the first time she'd seen him since the "incident", and she felt uneasy just being in his presence.

The salon phone seemed to be ringing off the hook, and Niya was busy transferring calls and taking appointments. Gator had made his rounds in the salon, pleased that he was able to sell a few of his handbags. He put his remaining inventory back into his plastic bags.

"Yo, Skyy, when I get those DVDs in, I'll come back by. A'ight, shorty?"

"Okay, Gator. Thank you."

"Y'all need anything else, just let me know. Thanks, ladies."

A few people waved and said goodbye to Gator as he left the salon. Skyy, Debi, and Coco were all at their stations, styling hair and trying to get the customers in and out as quickly as possible.

* * *

Several hours passed, and the sun was starting to set. The salon was still jumping, but it was not as busy as earlier in the day. Skyy was flat ironing one of her customer's hair, Debi had a couple under the dryer, and Coco still had three in the waiting area. Tiffany was finishing up a manicure, when her baby's father came storming through the door. Clad in a wife beater, sagging denim shorts, a pair of Timberland boots, and shoulder-length cornrows, he headed directly to Tiffany's station.

"Yo, I need to talk to you."

Whatever he needed to talk to Tiffany about must've been important, because you could see the steam coming from his ears. Moreover, he ignored everyone else in the salon and focused all of his attention on Tiffany. She looked up at him with a bit of apprehension.

"What's wrong with you?" she asked.

"I'd rather talk about this outside. It won't take but a minute."

Tiffany got up in a huff, leaving her client at her station. "I'll be right back," she said before following him outside.

Skyy, Debi, Coco, and Niya looked at each other in bewilderment.

"He's so trifling. I don't know why she deals with him," Niya said.

"I wonder what's up with that," Coco stated.

They all went along with their business, keeping a close eye on Tiffany and her baby's father outside. It was obvious to everyone watching that they were arguing, with him doing most of the talking. Tiffany's body language was that of someone on the defensive, so they all began speculating on what she could've possibly done to piss him off. At one point, her baby's father pointed his finger in Tiffany's face and got so close that he could almost kiss her. Yet, this encounter was anything but affectionate. Skyy realized Tiffany had been outside for at least five minutes, and her customer was getting a bit irritated.

"Do you want me to go out there and get her?" Coco asked.

"No, I'm going to get her," she responded.

Skyy put her Chi flat iron carefully on the counter and wiped her greasy hands on her smock before heading to the door to get Tiffany. However, before she could get to the door, the baby's daddy smacked Tiffany across the face so hard, she almost lost her balance.

"Oh hell naw! Coco, dial 9-1-1! He just hit her!" Skyy yelled before rushing to open the door. "Are you crazy? Why are you out here hitting on her? She's a female!" Skyy screamed.

"Look, this don't have nothin' to do wit' you. You need to carry yo' ass back in the shop and let me talk to Tiff. This between me and her."

Tiffany held her hand to her face and cried softly.

"Tiffany . . . Tiffany," Skyy called her name repeatedly, but Tiffany refused to look at her.

By now, Coco had made his way to the door and pushed past Skyy. "Excuse me, but is there a problem?" Coco said.

"Look, like I just told Skyy, this shit right here is between me and Tiff. Both of y'all can go back in the shop and mind yo' fuckin' business."

Coco sized up Tiffany's baby's daddy. He was shorter than Coco by a few inches, but he made up for it with his weight. It was obvious he'd been in jail pumping iron based on his pecks. On top of that, Coco noticed a couple of jailhouse tattoos on his neck. Still, Coco was not fazed or intimidated by any of that. In fact, Coco seemed to put his femininity in his pocket and put on his manhood, because he did not back down from baby daddy at all.

"Look, I just saw you put your hands on her, and I don't care what got your panties in a bunch, but I'm not gonna stand by and let you hit on her. So, either you carry your lil' swole ass on somewhere and cool off, or you're gonna have to deal with me. Believe me when I say, I've had bigger niggas on top of me, honey. So, I ain't afraid to pump some weight, you know what I'm saying?" Coco said.

"You better take your faggot ass back in the shop before I slap the shit outta you next time," baby daddy shot back.

"I got your faggot ass, nigga. As a matter of fact, I want you to slap me. Please slap me so I can show you just how much of a faggot I really am. Don't let these tight skinny jeans and mohawk fool you,"

Coco scowled, getting in his face while Skyy walked over to console Tiffany.

"Come on, Tiffany. Let's go inside," she said.

Coco held his position, waiting for something to jump off, while Skyy led Tiffany back in the salon.

"Tiff, I ain't done yet. Yo, Tiff, I said I ain't done!" he yelled.

"Guess what? She is. Now I think you better leave before the police get here. I would hate for them to look you up and find out you on parole. That would be a shame," Coco taunted.

Baby daddy sucked his teeth, hit his fist in his hand, and then decided it would not be worth him going back to jail for fighting Coco.

"You lucky," he said before taking off down the street.

Several customers were in the window watching the finale. Coco went back inside to check on Tiffany. Skyy had taken her to the office in the back to make sure she was okay. The people in the salon applauded when Coco entered.

"Go, Coco," one customer said.

"Yeah, that's right, Coco," another said.

"Coco, I can't believe you stood up to that hoodlum. He's not to be played with," Niya said.

"Look, I'm no slouch, honey. Besides, he's a punk, hitting on women. Any man that hits a woman can't whip a man anyway," Coco said.

"We know he can't whip a man, but what about you?" Debi replied jokingly.

Some people snickered at Debi's comment.

"Shut the hell up, Debi. Maybe if yo' husband slapped yo' ass around a little bit, maybe you'd like his ass a little bit more and like his brother a little bit less."

Random 'oooohs' filled the salon.

"See, Coco, I was just joking, but you always have to take shit too far."

"Take shit too far? Oh what, you can say what you want to say to me, but I'm supposed to bite my tongue? Fuck that. I go out there to help that lil' young girl who has a big overgrown nigga slapping her around like a rag doll, and instead of you saying 'Good job, Coco', you ridicule me." From the tone of Coco's voice, he was upset and his feelings were hurt.

"I was just joking, Coco. Damn! Since when did you get so sensitive?" Debi said.

"Probably around the same time you started wearing clothes that fit," Coco snapped, then went to the office to check on Tiffany. Debi stood there appearing defeated and now with her feelings hurt. Coco knocked on the door before entering.

"Hey, you okay, Tiffany?" he asked.

Tiffany had a red bruise on the side of her face for which Skyy had given her an icepack.

"Yeah, I'm okay. I'm so embarrassed. I'm sorry for bringing all this drama to the shop today, Skyy," Tiffany cried.

"Look, you don't have to apologize for anything," Skyy said.

Tiffany turned to Coco. "Thank you, Coco. I'm so sorry."

"Tiffany, stop apologizing. This is not your fault. He has no right to put his hands on you. Can I ask you a question? Has he hit you before?" Coco asked.

Tiffany looked down at the icepack in her hands, moving it around uncomfortably. She didn't want to answer the question, only because this was not the first time she'd been hit.

"Okay, I got it. Tiffany, I'm going to say this and then let it go. If you don't get out of this relationship, it's going to get worse. Now, luckily, Coco was here to stop him from beating your head in this time, but what about next time? You need to think about yourself and your son. He doesn't need to see all that. Now, I said my piece. I have customers, and so do you. But, if you need my help, let me know. I'm here, okay?"

Skyy didn't want Tiffany to feel like she was judging her, only that she was there to support her. It wasn't the time to judge. Tiffany was still young and needed to learn a lot about life. At twenty-four, her idea of being in love was by taking punches from a man who claimed to love her so much. He was the first and only man she'd ever been with, and he pretty much controlled her. Skyy was just surprised Tiffany allowed him to hit her and was pretty sure it had been going on for a while.

"And I'm here, too, for reinforcement," Coco added, patting his pocket like he was touching an imaginary gun. They all laughed.

"Thank you, Skyy. You, too, Coco. Let me work this out. It's not that serious. I'm just ashamed he did that in front of everybody. But, I'm okay. Let me get back outside to my customer." Tiffany handed Skyy the icepack and returned to her station.

"We need to keep an eye on her. I don't like that at all," Skyy said.

"Yeah, I know. I almost had to jack up that huzzie Debi a few minutes ago."

"Why? What happened now?"

"She made a rude comment, but that's alright. I got her ass back. Honey chile, I can't wait to get home and soak in the bathtub. This day has worn me out."

"Yeah, me, too, Coco. Come on. Let's go finish these customers so we can get out of here."

Skyy followed behind Coco, feeling the burden of the day's events on her shoulders. First, there was Eric and the uneasy feeling she experienced upon seeing him. Then there was Tiffany's fiasco, and now to top off the evening, she was getting a text message from Kyle, telling her that his wife may have found out about their affair. She took a deep breath before deleting the message. What else could go wrong?

Chapter 11

Frankie Beverly and Maze's "Before I Let Go" blasted throughout the building, which resulted in the majority of the thirty-plus crowd taking to the dance floor. Skyy and Coco decided to attend the Labor Day Ocean Blue Bash that was being held at the expansive Showplace venue. One of Coco's customers had given him tickets, so they attended the party together. There was a tropical and Carribean theme for the party, and all of the partygoers were ordered to wear some shade of blue.

Coco was wearing a navy blue linen, button-front shirt with matching linen cropped pants. The outfit was not as loud as Coco would normally have it; however, he made up for it with his tan platform sandals that crisscrossed up his legs. He also wore a matching tan Gucci messenger bag, which was thrown across his body.

Skyy was wearing a pair of Persian blue wet-looking leggings with a matching aqua blue, off-the-shoulder charmeuse top. She wore black peep-toe platform wedges that were Gucci, of course, with a matching Gucci horsebit handbag. Her hair rested on her bare shoulders, and she wore minimal makeup.

They'd only been at the party for about thirty minutes, so the crowd was still a bit meager. The Showplace had been decorated with loads of balloons in various shades of blue. Because the venue was so large, white leather sofas were scattered throughout to provide some intimacy, and there were also tables with chairs that surrounded the dance floor. Skyy and Coco were seated on one of the leather sofas closest to the bar. Skyy was enjoying the old school music that the DJ played, while Coco found it a bit boring.

"Okay, for real, he needs to play some Gucci Mane or something. This music is so antique."

"Coco, this is the good stuff, music that makes you feel good. Not all that stuff that has to get bleeped every other word."

"I don't know about feeling good. Feeling tired, yes."

Skyy nudged Coco playfully. They scanned the crowd, watching people as they entered, analyzing their outfits, shoes, handbags, and of course, their hair. They'd already decided they needed to pass out twenty-two business cards so far. The DJ changed the music up a bit, this time putting on some go-go.

"Oh, this is my jam," Skyy shrieked as Rare Essence's "Overnight Scenario" played.

A throng of people rushed to the dance floor, but Coco was not impressed.

"Come on, Coco. I want to dance."

Skyy grabbed Coco by the hands and forced him to go to the dance floor with her. On the way, Coco noticed a towering, muscle-bound thug checking him out. He bobbed his head to the beat while watching Coco at the same time. Coco tried to appear uninterested, knowing he would probably see more of the guy as the night progressed. He and Skyy found a small amount of space on the floor to get their dance in as the DJ played a mixture of go-go, from Rare Essence to Chuck Brown. Skyy danced so hard that she broke a sweat. Thirsty, she shouted over the music for Coco to walk with her to the bar to get a drink. They both exited the dance floor, fanning themselves. At the bar, there was a huge line. So, they took a spot behind a fluffy girl wearing an aqua blue maxi dress that was two sizes too small.

"Twenty-three," they said in unison after noticing the girl could use a relaxer, trim, and color. Then they chuckled at their private joke.

"What are you drinking?" a man standing closest to the bar asked Skyy.

Initially, Skyy didn't hear him because she assumed he was talking to the lady beside him. Therefore, she ignored him and continued her conversation with Coco, who wiggled his way to the bar and ordered two vodka and cranberries. The man leaned in close to Skyy, which caught her off guard, so she jumped.

"I was gonna get that for you. What's your name?" he asked.

Skyy, who hadn't really paid the guy any attention, turned and took a quick look at him. The first thing that got her attention was his eyes. In a weird way, Skyy felt like she knew him or had seen his large almond-shaped eyes before. His goatee was full and thick, and he sported a bald head. He appeared to be about five-feet, eleven-inches tall, and he was very muscular.

"Why?" Skyy answered, trying to play hard to get.

He smiled at her while rubbing his goatee. Skyy noticed the sparkle from his wedding band. *Just my type,* she thought to herself.

"Well, if I buy you a drink, I at least want to know your name. I'm Kelvin by the way."

"Kelvin, huh? I don't think your wife would appreciate the fact that you're trying to buy me a drink, don't you think?"

Skyy tried to feel him out. Most of the married men she dated never really let her know right away that they were married, and they certainly were not walking around flashing their wedding band at her.

"I like meeting new people. She knows that about me. Now, are you gonna tell me your name or not?"

"Skyy with two y's."

"Skyy? Like the sun in the sky?"

"Yep, but with two y's."

"Somehow, that name fits you perfectly. So, where's your man, Skyy?"

Coco interrupted and handed Skyy her drink. "Mmmmm-hmmmmm, you know how to pick 'em, don't you?" Coco said softly to her.

"I'm going to see Sheena. She just texted me and said she was here. Text me when you're finished." Coco looked Kelvin up and down before disappearing into the crowd.

"What was that about?" he asked.

"Oh nothing. That's just Coco." Skyy took a sip from her watered down drink.

Kelvin picked up his beer. "Can we go somewhere and sit down and talk?"

Skyy hunched her shoulders, and Kelvin followed her to an empty sofa. Skyy sized him up in a sly manner, trying not to look so obvious. His blue ensemble consisted of a light blue True Religion button-down cowboy shirt with faded washed True Religion jeans. He finished his look with a pair of crisp white Nike Air Force Ones. Skyy looked on approvingly as he got comfortable on the sofa.

"So, Skyy, what do you do?"

"I do hair. I own a salon downtown. What about you?"

"I'm a police officer for Henrico County."

"A cheating cop. Isn't that sort of an oxymoron?"

"Who said I was cheating? And how is that an oxymoron?"

"I thought police officers were honest, law-abiding citizens."

"Police officers are humans, just like everybody else."

"Mmmm-hmmmmm."

Skyy sipped her drink seductively. The more she looked at Kelvin, the finer he became to her. Even though it was dark in the Showplace, Kelvin had gotten so close to her that she noticed a few freckles on his nose and cheeks. Something about a man with freckles always turned her on. She also noticed his almond-shaped eyes were light brown. To top it all off, he smelled good as hell.

"So, can I call you sometimes?"

"Sure, why not?"

"I don't have to worry about any boyfriends calling me back when I call you, do I?"

"You're the one that's married. I should be asking you that question."

"Me and my wife, we have a special arrangement. We're only together for the kids. She does her thing, and I do mine."

"I've heard that before."

"No, I'm serious. As soon as my son gets old enough, we're getting a divorce."

"Okay, whatever you say."

Skyy figured it couldn't hurt giving Kelvin her number. Besides, she and Kyle were going to have to cool things down since his wife might be tracking his every move. Kelvin would work well as a fill-in, as long as he stayed married, of course. Skyy put her number in Kelvin's phone, and he did the same with her BlackBerry.

"I'll call you tomorrow, okay? Maybe we can do dinner or something."

"Sure, give me a call," Skyy replied.

He flashed his pearly white teeth, then stared at Skyy for a few moments before getting up to leave. Skyy watched him walk away until he disappeared into the restroom. She sank back on the sofa and crossed her legs, relaxing a bit while she did a bit of people watching and enjoyed the music. A few minutes later, the muscle-bound dude from earlier came over to her.

"Yo, wassup?" he said, a major turnoff for Skyy. She hated for a guy to approach her with 'Yo'.

"Nothing much," Skyy replied dryly.

"Can you pass this on to your friend for me? I'm a promoter, and I need to do some flyers for an event. Let him know I might be interested in shooting him for the flyers."

Muscle man handed Skyy a business card that she didn't bother to read. She just slipped it in her purse.

"I'll give it to him."

"Thanks."

Skyy knew the drill. Muscle man was into boys, but he wanted to give his friends the impression that he was trying to get at Skyy. To outsiders, it probably appeared that way. His approach? Hand off the business card with his phone number. But, it was obvious to Skyy that he wanted Coco. She chuckled to herself at his effort. She was still holding her BlackBerry, so she sent Coco a text: 'muscle man lft his nbr for u'. She hit the send icon and waited for a reply. She grabbed her drink from the table beside the sofa and finished it off. From out of nowhere, Coco appeared.

"I knew that boy was a little tender honey. They sure can't fool me. Can we go now? This party is full of old people. I'm ready for some new school hip-hop."

"Coco, one minute you act like you're so grown, and the next minute you act like a young kid. Which one do you want to be?" she asked.

"Whatever, Skyy. You're just mad because you're enjoying this tired party. This old music is killing me."

"Well, why don't you go up there and ask the DJ to play some new stuff?"

"I did already. He said he would later. I need me another drink. You want another one?"

"Yeah." Skyy reached into her purse and grabbed a crisp twenty-dollar bill.

"Here, I'm buying this round."

Coco grabbed the twenty, and as he headed toward the bar, Skyy noticed an old head coming her way. He was sporting an apple jack hat and a bright, electric blue suit. It was obvious he was way out of Skyy's league.

"Hey, baby, how you doin'?" he said, sporting a gold crown on his front tooth. Another major turnoff for Skyy.

"Fine." Skyy tried to look past him.

"Can I sit down?" he asked, but sat down anyway. "You got a man, sweetheart?"

"Yeah, I do actually. He's gone to the bathroom," Skyy lied.

He got up quickly, so as not to disrespect Skyy's imaginary boyfriend. "My bad. I saw you over here by yourself and thought you were alone. Let me ask, are you happy?"

"Very," Skyy answered, flashing a fake smile.

The joker's ego was deflated. He buttoned his suit coat and strutted away much like Richard Roundtree, in a black-exploitation-movie-kind-of-way. Skyy shook her head in repulse, wondering why the man had the audacity to approach her. She so hated the party scene, which is why she normally stayed away from it. Coco, on the other hand, enjoyed mingling and meeting new people. Skyy would rather be at home in her pajamas, watching a DVD.

Her BlackBerry vibrated, and she noticed a new text message. When she opened it, the text was from Kelvin. 'U look lonely.' She responded, 'I'm fine.' 'I know ur fine. But u still look lonely . . . lol.' 'I'm not lonely.'

Skyy looked around to see if she could spot Kelvin watching her. She couldn't find him, though.

'Stop looking 4 me. I got my eye on u.'

That statement made Skyy a bit nervous. She didn't know if Kelvin was a stalker or what. She decided to text Coco, telling him she was ready to go. The night was still young; Coco could hook up with his other friends and hit Skittles Nightclub. Skyy would go home and get some much-needed rest.

Chapter 12

Skyy's BlackBerry vibrated loudly, almost falling off the nightstand beside her bed. Skyy rolled over to check the time, which illuminated from her alarm clock. She wondered who would be calling her at almost three o'clock in the morning. Since the person had called her back to back, she decided to see who it was. She looked at her phone and saw four missed calls from J. He was in L.A. and must've forgotten the time difference. Skyy put the BlackBerry back on the nightstand and was just about to snuggle under her covers to continue her sleep, when her phone vibrated again. This time, she decided to answer, thinking maybe there was something wrong.

"Hello?"

"Hey, gurl, what took you so long to answer the phone?" J asked.

"J, it's almost three o'clock. I was asleep. What's wrong?"

"Nothing's wrong. I just want to see you. How about flying out to meet me in Vegas tomorrow?"

"I cannot believe you woke me up to ask me to meet you in Vegas. Are you serious?"

"Of course, I am. And I'm sorry. I forgot about the time difference. I wasn't even thinking."

Skyy noticed J's voice was slurred. "J, have you been drinking? Are you drunk?"

"I'm decent. Been to a party tonight. Horny as hell. Meet me in Vegas. Come on, baby. I can have the ticket waiting for you at the airport."

Skyy thought about her schedule for the next day. She had a wedding party to do, so she couldn't possibly drop them to fly out and meet with J. She was a bit perturbed that J had the audacity to call her and expect that she drop what she was doing to fly across the country. His approach was a bit outrageous, as well.

"J, I have customers tomorrow."

"So! Tell them you can't do them. I'm asking you to fly out to Vegas, free of charge, and all you can think about are your customers? Shit, have that faggot Peaches do them for you."

"First of all, his name is Coco, and don't call him that. Second of all, he has his own clientele. I resent the fact that you think you can just pick up the phone and call me at any time and I'm supposed to just jump because you say jump."

"Look, shawty, I could've left the party with any of them tricks I wanted. But, naw, I come home and call you, asking you to spend some time with me. A nigga like me don't need to beg no bitch to be with him."

"Bitch? Did you just call me a bitch? Oh hell no!" Skyy yelled. By this time, she was wide awake and fuming. "Hello?" she said, waiting for a response. "J? Hello?"

All of a sudden, she could hear snoring coming through the phone. J must've been drunker than Skyy imagined, and he probably wouldn't remember their conversation in the morning. She disconnected the call and powered off her phone. She would hate for J to awake from a drunken stupor and try to call her back again.

Skyy turned on the lamp and searched the floor with her feet for her bedroom slippers. The event caused her to be fully awake, so she went to the kitchen to grab something to drink. She walked down a short hallway until she was at her living room, which was completely dark with the exception of the light that glowed from her Glade Plugin. She had to walk through the living room to get to the kitchen. Out of paranoia, she took a peek out of her living room window. Immediately, she noticed what appeared to be a Henrico County police car driving past her house very slowly. Skyy wasn't sure if it was a coincidence or if in fact that was the guy named Kelvin she'd met recently. The part that frightened her was she hadn't told him where she lived. They'd only gone on a couple of dates, which didn't lead to anything major.

She peeked out of the window again, and the police car was gone. Skyy decided she was just being paranoid. It was possible the police officer wasn't Kelvin, and that the officer was cruising through the area for something totally unrelated to her. Just to be safe, she decided to check her locks on the front door before proceeding to the kitchen.

The jars on the door shelf of the stainless steel refrigerator shook when Skyy opened it. She looked over her options and decided on some Ocean Spray apple cranberry juice. After taking a few sips straight from the bottle, she placed it back on the shelf, closed the refrigerator, and headed back to her bedroom. Skyy tossed and turned, trying to get her last two hours of sleep before she had to be at the salon. She suffered from mild insomnia, so J did more damage than he knew when he called and woke her up. Before she knew it, it was time for her to get up and go to work.

The sun was making its appearance for one of the first days of fall. Even though summer was officially over, the temperature still made it feel like summer. Skyy was ready for fall. The leaves changing, shorter days, and longer nights made having her affairs a little less troublesome. It was much easier to sneak around during the night than it was during daylight hours.

Since her house was in the far west end of town, it normally took Skyy about twenty-five minutes to get to the salon. Tack on an extra ten minutes for her to get her Starbucks fix, and she only had five minutes to spare by leaving the house at ten minutes to six. Traffic was light on 64-East, so the commute on the highway was trouble free. She took the downtown expressway to Cary Street, where she would exit to make her stop at the Starbucks in Carytown. Cary Street carried her to the boulevard and on to Broad Street, where she found a parking spot directly in front of the salon.

She was actually the first one in. So, she unlocked the door, turned off the alarm, and opened the blinds. A black Toyota Camry pulled up behind her car, and two of her customers exited. One was the bride-to-be and the other was her sister. The three others in the bridal party weren't expected to arrive until eight, eight-thirty, and nine. As Skyy sipped her coffee at leisure, feeling the caffeine kick in slowly, the blinds on the door shook and the two women entered.

"Good morning, ladies."

"Hey, good morning, Skyy."

"Good morning."

"Go ahead over to my chair. I'm going to turn the TV and radio on, bring this place to life."

Both women walked over to Skyy's station. The bride-to-be sat in Skyy's chair and her sister sat in Coco's chair.

Skyy yawned and stretched, still feeling a bit tired from her interruption of sleep. Thinking about J calling her at three in the morning made her realize her BlackBerry was still powered off. She grabbed her Louis Vuitton handbag and searched for her phone. When she powered it on, she noticed the small envelope was at the top corner, indicating there were voicemail messages. However, she decided to get started on her client's hair. She would wait until she got them both under the dryer before tending to her personal business. Skyy slipped on her smock and then covered her customer with an oversized cape.

"How you doing this morning, Michelle? You ready for your big day?" Skyy asked.

"Girl, I will be so glad when it's all over. This wedding has worn me out."

"Well, just think, tomorrow this time, you will be married, and the whole thing will be over and done with."

Michelle's sister sucked her teeth and rolled her eyes before crossing her arms. Her body language clearly told Skyy that she did not approve of the marriage.

"Don't start, Trice. I don't need your crap today. I don't want you causing any trouble on my wedding day."

Skyy carefully applied the relaxer to her customer's hair, while listening as the women began a discussion about the upcoming nuptials.

"Michelle, I mean, I'm here for you and everything, but you know how I feel about you marrying that slacker. Why won't you at least wait until you've known the man longer? Six months is just not long enough to know somebody before you marry them, I'm sorry."

"Didn't I just say I didn't want to get into it with you today? I'm marrying Tee, so deal with it."

"Yeah, you're marrying him and his baby momma drama. Skyy, let me ask you. Would you marry a man that you've only known for six months?"

"Honey, I'm the last person you want to ask about marriage. Trust me on that. I wouldn't advise you to marry a man after knowing him six years, let alone six months. That's just me."

"Well, anyone with any sense would know this man is rushing for a reason. He's after my sister's money."

Michelle jerked around and cut her sister a cold look. "Damn, can you let it go? I knew I should've let you go to your regular stylist. You're stressing me out, Trice."

Skyy listened as the sisters went back and forth until it was time for Michelle to get under the dryer. Skyy was glad that both of them were not regular customers, because they'd gotten on her nerves in the short amount of time they'd been at the salon already. This was only the third time she'd ever done Michelle's hair, and the first time she'd ever done her sister's hair. She hoped this would be the last, only because the drama was sickening.

By the time Skyy put the relaxer in Trice's hair and sat her under the dryer, Coco and Debi had arrived. Niya, who was splitting her time between Richmond and Petersburg while attending Virginia State University, didn't work during the week anymore and only worked every other weekend. This particular weekend was her weekend off, so the stylists had to chip in and split the administrative duties. Tiffany also helped out whenever she didn't have any customers.

Skyy looked at the clock and noticed it was about seven-thirty. Both customers still had some time left under the dryer, and her next customer wasn't due in for another thirty minutes. So, she sat in her chair and listened to her messages. *Hey, wassup, it's Kelvin. I was just thinking about you and wondered if we could do dinner or something tonight. I'm off duty all day. Give me a call.* Message two—*Hey, it's Kelvin again. I was hoping you would have your phone on. Wake up! Call me later.* Message three—*Okay, now, you really need to get up and go to work. Where are you? Give me a call.* The fourth message was a hang up, which Skyy assumed must've been Kelvin.

She was taken aback by the number of times Kelvin had called her, which had to be early since it wasn't even eight o'clock yet. As much as she liked Kelvin, she felt as if he was moving a bit too fast for her. They had interesting conversation, with Kelvin telling Skyy about his job as a police officer, giving her blow-by-blow details of various crime scenes he'd been in charge of. Their first date was spent in Fredericksburg, Virginia, which was only about a forty-five-minute drive from Richmond, where they saw a movie and had dinner at the Olive Garden. On their second date, Kelvin assured Skyy that going out to a spot in Richmond was not risky for him at all since his wife was visiting her parents that particular weekend. So, they decided to go to Lucille's Soul Food Restaurant for dinner and live jazz. Their other times getting to know each other had been spent talking on the phone. She often wondered when Kelvin's wife was home, because he always seemed to have time to call and talk to Skyy. She decided against calling Kelvin back, at least until she'd gotten all of her appointments done for the day. She needed to see what her day would shape up to be before making any plans.

Skyy walked over to check Michelle, whose hair was dry, and directed her to sit in her chair. Michelle noticed her friend coming in, and she ran over to hug her. Michelle decided she wanted all of the women in her wedding party to get their hair done in the same style, so she made appointments for all of them with Skyy. Skyy noticed that the girl entering the shop didn't have half as much hair as Michelle and Trice, which would prove to be difficult for the updo that Michelle wanted. Michelle brought her friend over to Skyy to introduce her and so Skyy could get a closer look at her friend's hair.

"So, Skyy, if you use some pieces, can you pin her hair up like ours, too?" Michelle asked.

Skyy examined the girl's hair, touching it on the sides and in the back to determine the length. It would be a challenge to give the girl an updo because her sides and back were shaved.

"Let me see the hair."

The girl pulled some human hair extensions from her bag and handed them to Skyy, who examined the hair.

"Hmmmm."

Skyy really didn't like working with weaves, and doing weaves on short hair was a bit of a nuisance. Coco was the master when it came to weaves in the salon.

"Would you mind if Coco did your hair?" Skyy asked.

She was agitated at the fact that Michelle didn't disclose that her friend only had a fistful of hair on her head. Not only that, but the color of the weave didn't match her natural hair color. This was definitely a job for Coco. Skyy didn't have the patience to deal with it. The girl shook her head, not really caring who did her hair as long as the bride was pleased.

"But, Skyy, is he going to do her hair just like mine?" Michelle asked.

"He can't do her hair exactly like yours because her hair is short, but he will work it out. Coco is one of the best in Richmond. You can bank on that."

Coco eased over to them after hearing his name mentioned. "What?" he asked.

"Can you squeeze her in? She's part of this wedding party, and they're all wearing their hair pinned up. Can you do her weave for me?"

Coco inspected the girl's hair, looking at it like an artist looks at his canvas before he paints.

"Of course, honey. No challenge is too great for Ms. Coco. You can go and sit in my chair." Coco squinted his eyes at Skyy, giving her a 'you owe me' look before tending to his new client.

Skyy smiled because she knew Coco was going to let her have it for throwing a customer in the middle of his appointments. He liked to keep his book on track, get his customers in and out, and working this weave in the mix would cause a bit of a delay for his customers.

Skyy pressed the silver bar at the bottom of the salon chair with her foot, and Michelle moved up as if in a spaceship about to take off. Skyy moved the chair around to make sure Michelle was perfectly positioned. They both looked up when Tiffany entered the salon; however, Michelle turned her head sharply.

"Hey, Tiff. How you doing?" Skyy said.

Coco and Debi chimed in with their good morning greetings, as well.

"Okay," Tiffany said dryly before putting her things in the drawer at her station.

Tiffany was wearing dark shades, which didn't seem odd right away until she sat down at her station without removing them. There was no way she would be able to do a manicure with dark sunshades on. Coco mouthed 'What's wrong with her?' to Skyy, and Skyy hunched her shoulders. Debi, who'd been engrossed in a heavy conversation on her cell phone since she arrived, put her hand over the receiver to ask Tiffany a question.

"Hey, Tiff, I have a customer on the way, and she wants to get a mani and a pedi with a French manicure. Can you do her?"

"Yeah, that's fine."

Debi went back to her conversation, which was obviously with her brother-in-law, because every other sentence was 'Landon, you so funny'. The group had come to the realization that Debi and her brother-in-law were hot and heavy, and Debi didn't care anymore that they knew. It would only be a matter of time before she'd be divorcing Eric anyway.

Tiffany fumbled around in her handbag before finally coming up with her cell phone. She dialed a number, placed the phone to her ear, and rubbed her forehead.

"Must be trouble in paradise," Coco said without looking up from his client's hair.

"Coco, mind your business," Skyy said.

"What? I am minding my business. But, we all know something must've popped off last night. Ms. Thang can't even show us her eyes. Probably swollen from crying all night."

"Coco! She can hear you," Skyy tried to whisper.

Like something out of the omen, Skyy's customer started to talk really loud, almost as if she wanted everyone in the salon to hear her.

"Yeah, Skyy, me and Tee are going to tie the knot today, girl. I'm so happy. I feel like I'm marrying my soul mate, you know what I'm saying?"

"You do? That's nice, Michelle. I wish you all the luck in the world."

"Luck? Honey, I've been lucky, trust that. I'm very, very lucky," Michelle said sarcastically.

Skyy gave her a strange look, wondering the reason for the sudden personality change. For the first hour of her visit, Michelle was very reserved and less assertive, but now, she'd transformed to something different. Skyy continued to concentrate on Michelle's hair, not noticing that her sister had come from under the dryer and was heading in their direction.

"I already know, Trice. I see her. But, I'm not fazed, not one bit," Michelle said.

Skyy looked up. "Honey, you're not dry yet," she said.

"Michelle, I cannot believe you. Why would you come in here knowing *she* works here?" Trice said, ignoring Skyy and motioning toward Tiffany.

Skyy's antennae immediately went up. At first, she wasn't sure if Trice was making reference to one of Coco's customers who'd just walked in, or if in fact, she was referencing Tiffany. It became evident it was Tiffany when Tiffany stood up, removed her sunshades, and proceeded toward Skyy's chair.

"I'm not thinking about her. Besides, I will be marrying my man in seven hours, so she can keep it moving," Michelle said.

By this time, Tiffany was standing in front of Skyy's chair, and her station felt a bit crowded.

"What did you say?" Tiffany asked Michelle.

"You heard me. I said, I will be MARRYING my man in seven hours. That's right, MARRYING him."

"You a motherfucking lie!" Tiffany yelled.

"Hey, hey, Tiff, we don't talk to the customers like that," Skyy said.

"She ain't no fucking customer, Skyy. This bitch came in here to taunt me. She's the bitch that's been fucking Trey."

Gasps seemed to echo throughout the salon. The only sounds that could be heard were the humming from the hairdryers and voices from the cartoon characters on the TV. Everyone was staring at them.

"Bitch? Hmph, the bitch is the one without the ring. And that's right, I have been fucking Trey, royally," Michelle said.

"Trey didn't give you that ring. You so damn gullible, you probably bought it yourself," Tiffany snapped back, leaning over and getting up in Michelle's face.

Skyy grabbed her, trying to move her away. "Wait, wait, this is not going down in here like this. Tiffany, relax. Michelle, you're marrying Trey? Tiffany's Trey?" Skyy asked.

By now, Coco and Debi were standing alongside Michelle's sister, forming a small semi-circle around Tiffany and Michelle.

"You mean *my* Trey?" Michelle said.

"You know what I mean. Is her baby's father and the man you are marrying today one and the same?" Skyy inquired.

"Unfortunate for her, but most fortunate for me, yes."

As dramatic as ever, Coco gasped and threw his hand over his mouth.

"How dare you come to my job telling these people all these lies about you and Trey!"

"Honey, I have no reason to lie to you or anybody else in here. Trey and I are getting married today. Oh what, you're the last to know? Trey was right. He said you wouldn't be able to handle it," Michelle said.

Skyy was trying to pull Tiffany away, but Tiffany's strength seemed to intensify with every word Michelle spat at her.

"You're a fuckin' liar! Trey ain't marrying you!"

"Come on, Tiffany, don't do this. You need to calm down." Skyy continued to struggle to hold Tiffany.

"Yeah, you need to get your girl. I would hate for something to happen to me up in here, and I have to sue," Michelle threatened.

"Oh, wait a minute, heffa. You're the one that brought all that drama up in this shop. Don't come in here talking about suing nobody. We're not having that," Coco said. "Look, whatever happens, y'all are not going to jump all over my sister," Michelle's sister said.

"Girl, ain't nobody thinking about your sister up in here. As a matter of fact, all y'all heffas can leave," Coco shot back.

"Wait a minute now. This drama is personal, but business is business. I don't want to be in the middle of this," Skyy voiced.

"Skyy, you need to put that bitch and her sister out! All this talk about a wedding is a lie!" Tiffany yelled.

"You got one more time to call me a bitch, and I'ma show you one. Don't hate because you weren't able to keep your man."

Tiffany pulled away from Skyy, dug down deep, and expelled a mouth full of spit that landed on Michelle's face. Michelle struggled to get to her feet because the salon chair was so high off the ground. She lunged at Tiffany, causing them to both fall to the ground. Michelle tried to pin Tiffany down while punching her, but not before Tiffany punched Michelle in the face and grabbed the updo that Skyy had just about finished. Coco, Debi, and Skyy tried pulling them a part while the other customers looked on in shock.

"Get off my sister!" Trice yelled, pulling at Debi.

The entire scene was chaotic with both women tussling. Finally, they were able to pull the ladies from on top of each other.

"Bitch, you lucky, real lucky!" Tiffany yelled.

Debi pushed Tiffany away from the scene and toward Skyy's office.

"That's alright. I'm calling Trey right now. He will come up here and fix her ass. This shit ain't over!" Michelle yelled. Her hair was disheveled, all of Skyy's hard work ruined, and there was a small cut on her lip. "Where's my phone?" Michelle screamed, while her sister tried to help her up from the floor.

"Come on, Michelle. This is ridiculous. You in here fighting like a damn teenager!"

"Look, at this point, I don't think it would be a good idea if you and your wedding party stayed. I mean, I can finish you and your sister up, but tell everybody else they need to find somewhere else to go. I can't have all this drama in my place of business," Skyy said.

"Tell that bitch to leave until we finish! We're paying customers!" Michelle yelled.

Skyy sighed heavily. Michelle had a point. They were customers, and they did have appointments. Still, Tiffany was an employee. Skyy was stuck between a rock and a hard place. She really didn't know how to solve the predicament.

"Oh my goodness, your lip is swollen, Michelle! And it's bleeding!"

"What?" Michelle turned to the mirror above Skyy's station and looked at her face in horror. "I can't get married like this! Oh no! This is not happening! Not on my wedding day!"

Skyy could feel a migraine coming on. Not only did she want those sisters out of her salon, but she feared they were going to take the drama to the next level by either calling Trey or even the police. And if they called the police, Tiffany could get into trouble because there were witnesses who actually saw her strike Michelle first and cause bodily injury.

"Okay, listen, let's do this. Let me get your hair straight and get your sister's hair straight so you two can be on your way. I really want this whole thing to be over with."

"My hair? Look at my face! I'm going to press charges against that bitch for what she did to my face! I can't get married looking like this!" Michelle yelled.

Skyy stood there helplessly, not really sure what options she had for fixing the situation at that point. All she wanted was for them to leave, whether they got their hair done or not.

Trice took her cape off and threw it on the chair. "Come on, Michelle. Let me call my girl. She can get us straight. We need to get out of here."

Skyy assumed Trice meant they would go to her regular beautician to get their hair finished, which was more than fine with her. Michelle removed her cape, also, and they gathered their things to leave.

"I really don't know what to say, but I wish you wouldn't have come in here starting stuff with Tiffany."

"All you care about is Tiffany? You better tell Tiffany to be on the lookout for that warrant in the mail, because I will see her ass in court!"

Michelle and Trice scoffed and left the salon in a hurry. Right on their heels was the bridesmaid who was supposed to get her weave done by Coco.

"Lord have mercy, I have seen it all up in here today. These young girls . . . I tell you the truth, honey. They will fight over a man like there is no tomorrow. Whewwww," Coco said, sounding as if he'd just been in a fight himself.

"Coco, go and check on Tiffany. Tell her they are gone. I'm so sorry, everybody. This is not how I run my business, and I hope you all realize that. For the inconvenience, everyone will get a ten percent discount today. Again, I am so sorry."

The few customers that were in the salon when the fight happened went about their business like the fight never happened. But, Skyy knew they were going to talk about it amongst themselves, especially when Tiffany returned from the back. They would be pointing and whispering about Tiffany and her sorry baby's daddy, who didn't have the decency to tell her that he was getting married. To top it all off, he'd only known Michelle for six months, while Tiffany had been putting up with his shit for two years. Some of that was during the time he was in prison, but she never got a ring. It was obvious to her that Michelle must have money, because there was no other reason Trey would put a ring on another woman's finger. At least that's what Tiffany thought.

Chapter 13

Skyy got off the highway and entered the parking lot of the Stony Point Shopping Mall. She maneuvered around the lot until she reached Fleming's Steakhouse, where she was meeting Kyle for dinner. They'd been on a hiatus for a while since Kyle's wife had become suspicious. Now, since his wife had pulled back a bit, he needed to see Skyy in the worse way. And Skyy could use a little therapy after all of the stressful events at the salon. Sex with Kyle was like therapy to her. His lovemaking was so gentle and kind, unlike the roughness she had with J. Skyy loved it both ways; however, that night, she needed soothing calmness.

She checked her oversized crystal Toywatch for the time. She still had a few minutes before Kyle was expected to arrive, so she decided to go inside and get seated, preferably at a corner table or booth. She parked her car, then checked her eye makeup and hair in the rearview mirror before exiting. Summer had officially made its exit, and the air was a bit chilly. Skyy pulled the collar of her leather jacket up around her neck and tightened her scarf. After locking her door with her key remote, the asphalt beneath her stiletto knee-high boots made a crumbling sound, similar to that of a snare drum. Skyy's black, leather mini skirt hugged her body tight, and she was sure Kyle would be pleased when he saw her. Skyy entered the dimly lit steakhouse and was welcomed by the maître d'.

"Hello, welcome to Fleming's. How many in your party tonight?" the maître d' asked.

"Two, please. I prefer a booth, if possible." Skyy knew sitting in a booth would be more discreet than sitting at a table.

"Do you want to wait for your guest before being seated?"

"No, I can be seated now. Thanks."

She watched as a hostess grabbed two oversized menus and followed behind her to a quaint, brown leather booth. Skyy eased in, sliding all the way to the wall, catching the white linen tablecloth part of the way with her. She quickly released the tablecloth from her bangles, being careful not to knock over the wine glasses.

"Your server will be with you shortly," the hostess stated before disappearing.

Skyy removed her leather jacket, revealing a sheer one-shoulder blouse. The flecks of glitter from her Victoria's Secret body lotion shimmered in the soft, recessed lights. The atmosphere was a bit noisier than Skyy expected, but the ambiance helped to set the mood. Skyy couldn't wait to eat dinner and head over to the Marriott to have Kyle as her dessert. She was long overdue for sex and needed it badly. She placed her BlackBerry on the table, anticipating an incoming call from Kyle. Within a matter of minutes, her phone vibrated.

"Hey," she said.

"Hey, you here yet?" Kyle asked.

"Yeah. I'm already seated at a booth near the back."

"Okay, I'm coming in now."

Skyy ended the call and looked through the crowd for Kyle. She knew he would come in searching for her, so she wanted to spot him first so she could try to get his attention. Numerous waiters and waitresses with oversized serving trays filled with bottles of wine and white china plates covered with select cuts of steak flurried throughout the restaurant. When Kyle appeared, Skyy waved her hand to get his attention, and he noticed her immediately. He smiled and headed toward her. Although Kyle's look was simply stated in Rock and Republic jeans, a blue Polo sweater, and a leather jacket, he still looked good to Skyy.

Before he reached the table, a waiter was standing before Skyy, asking her if she wanted a glass of wine. By the time the waiter rambled off his spill of about one hundred wines that Fleming's had to offer and handed Skyy a wine menu, Kyle was standing behind him. Kyle waited for Skyy to order a glass of Chandon sparkling wine before sliding into the booth beside her.

"Anything for you, sir?" the waiter asked Kyle.

"You can bring the bottle," Kyle instructed.

The waiter nodded in agreement and disappeared in the crowd.

Kyle put his arm around Skyy and rubbed her bare shoulder before kissing her on it. "Mmmm, you smell good enough to eat," he said.

"Well, I hope you're hungry," Skyy replied.

They giggled, amused by each other's flirting.

"You look good tonight. Where'd you get this nice jacket?" Skyy asked, admiring his soft, caramel-colored leather jacket.

"It was a gift. You know my birthday was two weeks ago," he said.

"No, I didn't. I'm sorry I missed your birthday. Happy belated birthday."

"Thanks."

"So, what's been going on with you? It seems like I haven't seen you in ages," Skyy asked.

"Well, it's been a while, that's for sure. We've missed you," Kyle replied, conveniently grabbing his manhood beneath the table so Skyy could see.

"You don't waste any time, do you?"

"We know what we're here for. No need in beating around the bush."

Skyy leaned over close to Kyle and whispered in his ear, "I want you to beat around in my bush. Can you handle it?"

"Skyy, we can skip this meal and order room service. Look at you. Are you horny or something, too?"

"Well, it's been a minute for me, so I could use a little help from you. Can you help me tonight?"

Skyy continued to tease Kyle with her words, while rubbing up and down his leg under the table. When she reached his manhood, she rested her hand there, softly caressing it. Kyle moaned, and they felt as if they were in their own world, surrounded by no one. They almost didn't notice the waiter returning to the table with the bottle of wine. He poured them both a glass before placing it back in a stainless steel ice bucket used to keep the wine chilled. Kyle and Skyy reached for their glasses, clicked them together, then toasted each other before both taking a sip. Scanning the menu with its assortment of steaks, seafood, and salads, Skyy decided on the petite filet mignon with lobster tail, but Kyle couldn't seem to make a decision.

"I hear the ribeye is good here," said a female, who had suddenly appeared and was standing at the booth.

Kyle and Skyy looked up instantly. Skyy noticed the color in Kyle's face seemed to disappear.

"Jody, what, what are you doing here?" Kyle stuttered.

"No, Kyle, the question is, what are *you* doing here? I thought you were going to play poker tonight with Steven and them."

It was obvious to Skyy that this woman had to be Kyle's wife. Kyle hadn't lied when he said she could stand to lose some weight. Peeking from beneath a bomber-type jacket, her Bebe rhinestone encrusted t-shirt hugged her body in an unattractive manner, showing every roll on her stomach. She was average looking, nothing to write home about as far as Skyy was concerned, and she probably hated the fact that the woman her husband was cheating with looked a whole lot better than she did.

"So, this is her? This is the bitch who has been fucking my husband so good that he won't fuck me."

Even though the restaurant was a little noisy, the people sitting at tables nearby could hear Jody, and a couple of women actually turned to look at them.

"Jody, you told me you were going to South Boston to see your mom. What are you doing here? What did you do, follow me?"

Kyle's wife leaned over on the table and got face to face with him. "What difference does it make? You lied to me! AGAIN! I asked you, Kyle, asked you if you were cheating. You swore on everything you loved that you were not having an affair. But, I knew it. All in my gut, I knew it. My husband has always had a healthy appetite for sex. So, I knew if he wasn't getting it from me, he was getting it from somewhere else."

Kyle's wife cut her eyes at Skyy and stared at her. Skyy looked down at her fork, wishing she could be anywhere else but there. It was not her place to address this woman because the situation was between Kyle and his wife.

"Sweetheart, please, let's step outside and talk about this."

"Step outside? Why? So I don't embarrass your little girlfriend? So now her feelings come before mine?" By now, Kyle's wife's voice had escalated to a point where the maître d' noticed and was looking across the room at them with concern. "Let me ask you one question. How long have you been fucking my husband?"

Skyy looked into her eyes, and it felt as if someone was shooting her through the chest with a dagger. "I think you need to talk to Kyle about that."

"It's obvious Kyle can't seem to tell me the truth, which is why I'm asking you. So, how long?"

Skyy could feel sweat beginning to build up on her back and under her arms. "Kyle, you need to talk to your wife."

"Look, don't talk to Kyle like you don't see me here, like I don't exist, because guess what? I do exist! I'm his wife. That wedding band on his finger? I put that there. I have his children. For five years, I've been washing his dirty drawers, cooking his dinner, cleaning his piss off the bathroom toilet seat, and all for what? So he can bring some trick to a fancy restaurant where he's never even taken me?" Kyle's wife pointed her finger in Skyy's face.

"Jody, come on. Let's go outside and talk," Kyle said. He stood up and tried pulling his wife away from the booth, but that only caused her voice to get that much louder.

"Get your hands off me, Kyle! What do we need to go outside and talk about, huh? I don't need answers from you because you can't be honest. I need to talk to her. She'll tell me the truth because she doesn't have as much to lose in all this like you."

"But, Jody, we're in a public place. I don't want to make a scene here. People are trying to have dinner. Please, let's go, and I will tell you everything you need to know."

Skyy remained silent, refusing to answer any questions thrown her way. It was not her responsibility to explain the nature of their relationship to Kyle's wife. That would be something Kyle needed to do. All Skyy wanted was to get the hell out of the restaurant. While Kyle tried to coax his wife out, Skyy stood up and grabbed her purse and jacket from the empty booth across from them. She waited for a window of opportunity (and enough space between the booth and Kyle's wife) to free herself from the messy situation.

"Skyy! Wait!" Kyle yelled.

Oh great, Skyy thought. *Now she knows my name.*

"Yeah, call Skyy. Tell her to come back so we can have one big party, Kyle."

Skyy hurried out the front door without looking back because she could still hear Kyle's wife screaming at him from a distance. She dashed to her car and got out of the parking lot so fast, she didn't even see Kyle and his wife exit the restaurant. Her heart was racing; she couldn't believe she'd been confronted by someone's wife. That had never happened to her before. Skyy was always so careful, and she thought Kyle had everything covered when he asked her out for dinner. His wife was supposed to be out of town at her mother's house. However, it made sense that she never really pulled back from Kyle, per se. She actually made him think she'd pulled back only to give him enough rope to hang himself.

Skyy jumped on the interstate, but not before calling Coco to tell him about her saga. Of course, Coco didn't answer, which meant he was probably inside a club partying or possibly having his own little rendezvous. Still a little shaken up, Skyy didn't really want to go home, so she decided to call Kelvin. He had called Skyy earlier in the day to ask her to go out, but it was after she'd made plans to go out with Kyle. She could use Kelvin's company tonight, though. And after the fiasco at the restaurant, she wouldn't even mind getting Kelvin to put in some real work. She'd already peeped out his package in his tight jeans. So, if he was willing, hell, why not? She dialed his number, and he answered on the second ring.

"Hello?"

"Kelvin? Hey, it's Skyy. Are you busy?"

"Not too busy for you. What's up?"

"Well, something came up, so my original plans fell through. I was wondering if you wanted to meet for drinks or something."

"Hell yeah. Where do you want to meet?"

Skyy thought for a moment about what was close by. She really wanted to find a hotel with a bar so she could have easy access to a room, should the need arise. She hadn't given it up to Kelvin yet, but she felt like tonight was probably going to be his lucky night.

"How quick can you get to Chesterfield?" she asked.

"Probably twenty minutes if I hit 288."

"Okay, how about meeting me at the Hyatt Place Hotel at the Arboretum? Meet me at the bar."

"Okay. Wait, what's going on? You don't sound like yourself."

"I really don't want to talk about it. I just need to get a drink. I'll see you there in a bit."

Skyy hung up without giving Kelvin an opportunity to say anything else. It was obvious her nerves were shot, and she couldn't wait to get to the hotel and get a real drink. She switched gears, taking Chippenham Parkway until she reached the Midlothian Turnpike exit. She headed up Midlothian for a few miles until the multicolored circles emblazoned on the side of the Hyatt Place Hotel appeared. She turned into the parking lot and found a space close to the entrance. Skyy decided she would get a hotel room so she could get Kelvin out of his clothes and into bed. Even though they'd only shared a few dates and lots of conversations, she didn't care. The mood she was in tonight, she would take anybody.

After checking in and getting her room key, she went to the smoke-filled bar where loud, contemporary pop music was blaring. She found an empty seat at the bar and ordered a vodka and cranberry juice. She took her time, sipping on it slow, so by the time Kelvin came, she would be ready for her second drink. It seemed as if an eternity had passed by the time Kelvin got there, and Skyy was four drinks ahead of him. The fact that she was already horny mixed with four alcoholic beverages kicked her into high gear, and she didn't waste any time when Kelvin came in. After he walked up behind her, Skyy turned on the barstool to face him and stood up. She put her tongue in his mouth. Kelvin was taken a bit off guard.

"Hey, you okay?" Kelvin asked. He liked the fact that Skyy was hot and bothered, and he knew his dream of being with her sexually was about to come true.

"Never better. Mmmmmm, you smell good," she replied.

Skyy handed him a glass of Hennessey, which she'd ordered for him a few minutes before he arrived. She almost stumbled when she tried to sit back on her barstool. It was apparent that Skyy was drunk. Kelvin wrapped his arms around her from the back, and it felt good that she wasn't rejecting him. On their previous dates, Skyy had been so reserved and standoffish that Kelvin started to feel like she really didn't like him. However, tonight, whether it was alcohol induced or not, Skyy was being the woman that Kelvin wanted her to be. Kelvin leaned over to kiss her neck.

"Hurry up and drink your drink. I have a surprise for you," she said, flashing the hotel room keycard.

Kelvin bucked the drink and slammed the glass on the bar. He asked the bartender for Skyy's total, peeled off a couple of twenties, and laid them on the bar. Then he took Skyy by the hand and followed the signs that read 'Lobby.' Skyy giggled while struggling over her feet, so Kelvin had to support her as they walked to the elevator.

"Skyy, do you know what you're doing?"

"Yes, so shut up and get us to the room," she said, trying to imitate a drill sergeant.

The elevator doors opened and Skyy stumbled in. When the doors closed, she rubbed her hands over Kelvin's manhood.

"Come on, let me feel that monster. You got a monster in there or what?" Skyy said.

"Keep rubbing and you'll see."

Kelvin took advantage of Skyy's intoxication by rubbing his hands all over her body, going down in her shirt, and even putting his hands up her skirt. They rode the empty elevator, fondling each other until they reached the fifth floor. When they found room 519, Kelvin used Skyy's key to open the door. The green light flickered and the door unlocked. Kelvin pressed on the knob and opened the door. Skyy pushed Kelvin into the room and down on the bed. Wasting no time, she climbed on top of him, pulling his shirt up and unbuckling his pants.

"Damn, Skyy, I don't know what's gotten into you, but I like it."

"Stop talking and fuck me, damnit."

Kelvin took his orders by flipping Skyy over on the bed and raising her leather skirt. She was also wearing opaque design tights and over-the-knee boots, so Kelvin pulled the tights and Skyy's thong down, leaving them to rest right above her boots. Kelvin spread her legs open with both hands, propping them apart so he could enter her with his tongue. He licked around her clitoris first before sticking his tongue in her valley. The thrust of Kelvin's tongue caused her back to arch.

"Yes, yes, suck that pussy, baby. Yes, do that shit."

The more Skyy talked, the more aroused Kelvin became. Skyy lifted her blouse and bra, exposing both breasts. She caressed them herself, using her tongue to suck on her nipples while Kelvin used his tongue on her.

Kelvin moved up to her breasts and played with them with his tongue. He licked his finger and used it to enter Skyy's valley, getting her cave ready for him to enter. Kelvin could hardly contain himself, so he eased his manhood into her valley slowly but firmly. Skyy wiggled to help his entrance, and in no time at all, they were rocking in a rhythm. Kelvin's breathing was heavy, and Skyy just closed her eyes, releasing the stress from the beauty salon and that night's events with each stroke. Kelvin drove harder and deeper; then his rhythm got faster and faster.

"Come on, baby, come on. Come for me. Come on. I'm coming," Skyy whispered in his ear.

Kelvin clenched up, sweat from his chest dripping into Skyy's face. She felt the warm sensation run down the inside of her leg. Kelvin rolled over and took a deep breath. Skyy, on the other hand, was too drunk to even keep her eyes open. All she wanted to do was sleep.

*   *   *

The sunlight peeking through the heavy drapes served as an alarm clock for Skyy. She opened her eyes slowly, trying to figure out where the hell she was. She lifted her head up and looked around when she realized she was not at home in her bed. She looked over at Kelvin, who was fast asleep. Her head throbbed a bit, clearly a hangover from the night before, and she was trying to remember how her night started out with Kyle and ended up with Kelvin. Then, as her brain decided to start working, she remembered the confrontation with Kyle's wife and meeting Kelvin for drinks. She was still partially dressed, even down to her boots, while Kelvin was only wearing his boxers. Skyy looked at her watch; it was seven a.m. The first thought that came to mind was the fact that Kelvin didn't go home to his wife. She tried shaking him a few times before he slowly stirred awake.

"Good morning, beautiful," he said to Skyy.

"Kelvin, it's morning. Don't you have to go home?"

"Go home? For what?" he asked, still half asleep.

"Your wife, that's what!"

"Oh, yeah. Ha! I guess I better be going."

Kelvin sat up and stretched. Skyy was sitting on the edge of the bed.

"What's the matter?" he asked.

"I have a terrible hangover. I don't know how many drinks I had last night, but damn, I'm feeling it now." Skyy rubbed her temples.

"You want to get some breakfast? Coffee or something?"

"Kelvin, go home," Skyy said.

"We don't have to rush, you know."

"Go home, Kelvin!"

Kelvin turned and looked at Skyy, but his look was empty and cold. Skyy really didn't care. All she wanted to do was go home, take a shower, and get in her own bed.

Chapter 14

"So, next thing I know, he's coming out of my bathroom wearing my hot pink thong. Chile, I didn't know whether to be excited or concerned," Coco said.

There was an eruption of laughter as Coco entertained the women in the salon. It was another busy Saturday, and this particular day, Niya was there.

"Coco, you're crazy as hell," Skyy said while flat ironing her customer's hair.

Debi was roller setting her customer's hair, and Coco was doing a sew-in. There were about ten people in the waiting area, Tiffany had a customer at her station, and the dryers were full. The Saturdays after payday were normally busy days for the salon, which is why Skyy had Niya come in on these particular Saturdays. Gator also kept track of the busy Saturdays, and that's when he normally made his rounds with his inventory. Just like the Saturday before last, Gator came in with a garbage bag full of items for sale. This week, he was selling Jordans, all sizes, for sixty dollars a pair.

"Yo, Debi, I got Jordans for babies, too, for thirty dollars," he yelled from the waiting area.

"Bring me a pair and let me see," Debi said.

Gator grabbed a small, black shoebox from the bag and took it over to her. "Damn, Debi, you looking good. What you been doing, working out or something?" he asked.

Debi blushed, but was elated that Gator noticed her fifteen pound weight loss. "Yeah, I go to the gym, and I'm doing Weight Watchers," she responded.

"Well, it's working for you."

"Thank you, Gator. Let me get these in a size 4."

Debi, who'd taken control of her life, thanks to the financial assistance of her brother-in-law and mister-ess, was indeed looking good. She was back to her pre-baby body weight, her body was tight, and she'd actually allowed Coco to take her shopping for more age-appropriate clothing. Even though she couldn't afford to shop at Saks or Nordstroms like Coco and Skyy, he took her to Marshalls where she could get some designer looks at a discount price.

"What about you, Skyy? You want some Jordans?" Gator asked.

"No, thanks, but when you get some Nike Shox, holler at me."

"Gator, don't believe the hype. Queen Bee ain't rocking no knock-offs," Coco said.

"Coco, mind your business."

"You know I'm telling the truth."

Skyy stuck out her tongue at Coco, and he rebutted by making a crazy face at her. The door of the salon opened, and in walked a delivery driver with a vase full of red, long-stemmed roses.

"Yes, can I help you?" Niya asked.

"I have a delivery for Skyy Armfield," he said.

"Skyy, you got flowers," Niya yelled.

Skyy looked up and wiped her hands on her smock before going to collect her flowers.

"Thank you." Skyy signed her name on the clipboard before the deliveryman exited. She reached for the card to read it. 'Thinking of you and thanking you. Kelvin.' Skyy tucked the card back into the tiny envelope, put the envelope in her pocket, and walked back to her station.

"Well?" Coco said.

"Well what?" Skyy responded.

"Don't be funny, Skyy. Who sent you the flowers?"

"Kelvin."

"Kelvin?"

"You know, the guy I met at the blue party."

"Oh yeah, Kelvin. Mmmm-hmmmm. I thought you two had only gone out a couple of times."

"Coco, mind . . ."

"I know. Coco, mind your business," he mimicked, as Skyy moved some things around on her station to make space for the flowers and then went back to her customer's hair.

Gator was still making his rounds, trying to sell more shoes, when Eric came in. Skyy looked up, and their eyes locked. She immediately looked away. She was shocked at how bad Eric looked. His facial hair was unkept, he'd lost a few pounds, and he had bags under his eyes.

"Hey, everybody. Debi, can I speak to you for a minute, please?" he said from the receptionist station.

"Not right now, Eric. I have customers."

Ignoring her words, Eric walked over to Debi's station. "How can you do this to me? You didn't even give me a chance. Divorce papers? I mean, I agreed to move out to give you space, but you promised it was temporary."

Debi put the flat iron on her station and turned to face Eric. "I am working. We cannot talk about this here."

"But you won't return my calls, and when I went by the house, you weren't there. How can you do this to me?" Tears welled up in Eric's eyes.

Skyy tried hard not to listen, but it was hard not to.

"I'll be right back," Debi told her customer. She grabbed Eric by the arm and led him to the hallway, stopping in front of the restroom and Skyy's office. "Eric, it's over. I'm moving on with my life. You're not a part of that anymore. Get yourself together, find a job, and move on."

"But, Debi, I love you. I don't want to move on."

"Well, you have to. I'm not in love with you anymore, Eric."

"We can go to counseling to try and save our marriage, Debi. You don't even want to try?" Tears were rolling down Eric's face, but Debi didn't feel any remorse for him. She was totally done.

"No, Eric. Now, please, just go."

"Tell me one thing. Does any of this have to do with Landon?"

Debi's eyes got as big as lemons.

"Don't lie to me, Debi. I mean, look at you. Losing weight, looking good. I know it's another man."

"Why does it have to be about another man, and especially Landon?"

"Debi, I'm not stupid. You might think I'm stupid, but I'm not."

"What do you want me to say? Yes, it's someone else. Is that what you want to hear? You don't need to hear that from me, Eric. Just accept the fact that this marriage is over, okay?"

"So, you won't tell me the truth?"

"Eric, I have customers. You need to leave so I can work."

He stared at Debi so coldly that it was as if he was looking through her. Seeing the hurt in his eyes, there was no way Debi could tell him about her and his brother.

"Well, since you won't tell me who you've been seeing, I won't tell you about me and Skyy." He frowned at Debi and turned to walk away.

"What did you say?"

He ignored her.

"Eric, what did you say?"

He turned around and looked at Debi. "You think you the only one fucking around? And here I was feeling guilty about fucking Skyy."

The noise in the salon was so loud that no one heard what Eric said but Debi. She took a few steps until she was up in his face.

"Eric, I know you're hurt, but saying that about my friend is not right. I'm trying my best to make this as easy as possible on you, but you want to make it painful."

"Make it painful? You made this painful months ago. You stopped talking to me. You stopped making love to me. All you did was resent me. I was, I mean, I am your husband, Debi. I can't believe you're willing to throw it all away because I can't seem to bounce back to the life we used to have."

"It's not just that, Eric. It's more to it than that."

"What more is it? If I was still working, would you want a divorce?"

Debi looked down at the floor. She didn't know how to answer that question. She knew the root of all their problems stemmed from the fact that Eric was not working. It sort of snowballed downhill from there. Maybe they would be happier if he was working, contributing to the household. She didn't know. What she did know was that there was no going back for her. She was moving forward, and her future didn't include Eric.

"Eric, I can't say it any other way than this. It is over. But, don't try to be hurtful by saying things about my friends. That's so unnecessary."

"Oh, you thought I was joking? I was telling the truth. I mean, what do I have to lose now, right? You wouldn't fuck me, so she handled it for me. Hmph, it wasn't bad either. It's all good. Like you said, move on. I got it." Eric sucked his teeth, looked Debi up and down, scowled, and frowned up his face. It was obvious he was upset, beyond upset, but was he telling the truth?

"Eric!" she called, but he left her standing alone.

Debi stood there for a moment, trying to absorb what Eric had just dropped on her like a ton of bricks. She wanted to think rationally about the whole thing. Was Eric saying that to cause her pain, or did he actually sleep with Skyy? Would Skyy sink that low by screwing Eric? Debi didn't want to believe that Eric was telling the truth. But, like he said, he had nothing to lose by telling her, did he? Debi returned to her work station so she could finish her customer's hair.

"I'm sorry about that, Mrs. Morgan. He just don't want to let me go. I'm so over it, it's not even funny."

Coco stopped what he was doing and faced Debi. "So, Ms. Thang, you confessed your sins yet?"

Debi rolled her eyes.

"Mmm-hmmm, just what I thought. You still playing with fire."

"Look, who I'm doing is no longer my soon-to-be ex-husband's concern, okay? We're separated, so he can do him and I'm gonna do me."

"Okay, so you wouldn't be mad if you found out he was getting his then?" Coco asked, glancing at Skyy.

Skyy frowned because she wasn't sure what Coco was leading up to. However, she was sure Coco didn't know about her and Eric, so why was he looking at her?

"I mean, I would hope he was getting his. He's a man."

"Okay, so what if it was somebody you knew?"

Debi immediately looked at Skyy as Eric's last words replayed in her head. She looked at Coco, then back at Skyy, and began thinking it was possible they were keeping a secret and maybe the joke was really on her.

"Coco, if you need to tell me something, spit it out."

"All I'm saying is, you doing somebody he knows. What if he was doing somebody you know? That's all. Would it be a double standard? Inquiring minds want to know."

"Coco, you know what? You really need to stop spreading my business through the shop. If I wanted people to know what and who I was doing, I would've announced it when I came in."

Debi was a bit perturbed at this point because Coco had a big mouth; she didn't appreciate him blurting out her business in front of the customers. She turned her back to Coco while fumbling around at her station. It seemed as if she was going to cry.

"Debi, I know you're not over there getting upset. We are just having a conversation. That's all. I was only playing devil's advocate."

Debi ignored Coco. Skyy, on the other hand, was vigorously tending to her customer's hair, hoping like hell the conversation would change. In the back of her mind, Debi wanted to confront Skyy, even though she really didn't want to know the truth if Skyy and Eric had actually slept together. It was one of those things where she didn't want to know, but at the same time, she did want to know. She battled with whether or not to confront Skyy about it. The anxiety would stress her out if she didn't, though.

"I tell you what. All y'all heffas got too much going on up in here. I'm the only one on the straight and narrow. Y'all need to try and mirror what I do. Live life a little less stressful, okayyy?" Coco said, snapping his fingers.

"Coco, you are not an angel, so don't even try it," Coco's customer stated.

"I prefer the term fairy, darling," he drawled.

"Wait, wait, y'all. Hold up!" Debi yelled, demanding attention from everyone. She turned to face them with tears rolling down her cheeks. "Turn the music off, Niya."

Niya grabbed the remote from the table in the waiting area that was strewn with magazines. Besides the TV and the humming of the hairdryers, nothing else could be heard.

"I'm throwing this out to anyone who might be able to answer this question for me. What would you do if you found out that one of your good friends fucked your husband?" Debi slowly moved her eyes to Skyy and held them there, transfixed on her. Debi crossed her arms and tapped her foot angrily, waiting for someone to respond. However, no one said a word, not even Coco, who stood with a look of horror on his face.

"No advice from anybody?" Debi held her stare on Skyy as she spoke.

Skyy shook her head, upset that Debi would be doing this with a salon full of customers. On top of that, she wished Debi would've pulled her to the side instead of opening Pandora's box right there in front of everyone.

"Ummmm, Ms. Debi, I'm not sure where all of this is going, but we have work to do. So, whatever it is that you need to announce, I need you to make it snappy," Coco said.

"You're right, Coco." Debi's voice dripped with sarcasm. She shook her head matter-of-factly and thought about her words before speaking. "Skyy, what would you do if you found out your friend fucked your husband? Oops, I forgot! You're in the husband fucking business. You might be the wrong person to ask."

Debi was condescending, evil almost, and Skyy felt like she was slowly melting away. She actually wished she was Bewitch and could twitch her nose to take her to another place. She'd rather be any other place in the world than standing facing Debi. The crowd appeared to be confused by Debi's behavior. There were a few quiet mumbles heard in the background as Debi demanded everyone's attention.

"Debi, this is uncalled for. If you need to talk to me, talk to me like a mature adult, not like a teenager having a temper tantrum in her parents' living room."

"Mature adult? Are you chastising me? How dare you chastise me! Let's set the record straight. I want everybody in here to hear this at the same time. My friend, my boss, the person I confided in, fucked my husband. That's right, ladies and gentleman. Skyy fucked Eric!"

Gasps along with numerous other negative sentiments filled the air.

"Debi, what are you doing?" Coco exclaimed. He ran to Debi and grabbed her shoulders.

"What am I doing? You need to be asking that backstabbing skank whore questions, not me."

Skyy looked around at everyone talking about her, turning their noses up at her. There was really nothing she wanted to say in front of the crowd, so she ran to her office. The pictures and mirrors on the wall shook from the intense door slam.

"Okay, everybody, I think the show is over. Carry on," Coco said.

He pointed the remote at the radio to power it back on so he could fill some space in the uncomfortable quietness of the salon. He then grabbed Debi by the arm and led her out of the front door. The customers started whispering amongst themselves, while Tiffany and Niya started their own private conversation. Coco felt like shaking some sense into Debi for making such a scene.

"Debi, you're out of order. Why would you do this? Why not ask Skyy first before accusing her? How do you know Eric isn't lying?"

"Coco, we're talking about Skyy here. You know she will fuck anything with a pulse. I never, ever thought she would betray me, though. Never." Debi's voice quivered.

"Debi, for real, girl, couldn't you have done this at another time?"

"When Skyy fucked Eric, they weren't thinking about an opportune time, now were they?"

"I'm just saying, right here, in front of everybody? Your customers? This was not the right time. I mean, I don't condone what Skyy did, if indeed she did it, but putting her out there like that in front of everybody wasn't cool, Debi."

"Oh, so now I'm the bad guy? She fucked my husband, Coco, and you're taking her side? You were the one asking what-ifs. I'm sure you knew."

"I didn't know about Skyy and Eric. Honestly, I didn't. I was simply playing devil's advocate. However, last time I checked, you were fucking your husband's brother. What if Skyy would've called a rally together to announce that?"

"That's different."

"How so? The way you feel right now, I bet my life that if Eric was to find out, he would feel the exact same way. You're being a hypocrite."

"Coco, I thought you were my friend, but you're on Skyy's side. That's okay. You stay here with that slut. After today, I'm leaving. I'll find another shop to work in. I can't work for someone I can't even trust."

Debi attempted to walk away, but Coco grabbed her.

"Wait a minute, Debi. Don't you at least want to hear her side?"

"I don't need details."

"But what if she says it's not true? You need to talk to Skyy first. Actually, you should've talked to Skyy first before pulling this. I cannot believe you! That's okay. I'm going to get to the bottom of this."

"Coco, this doesn't concern you. Just stay out of it." Debi burst into uncontrollable sobs. "I am so upset, so numb right now. I can't believe Skyy and Eric would do this to me."

Coco looked at Debi, wondering where all this lost love for Eric was suddenly coming from. She made it very clear that she didn't love Eric anymore, so why did she care so much that he cheated on her? Was she hurt because he fucked another woman or more hurt that the woman could possibly be Skyy? Those were the answers that Coco wanted.

"Look, come on now. Get it together, girl. I know you're angry. You have a right to be, but only if it's true. Go back inside, finish your customers, then you and Skyy need to have a talk. You got that?"

Debi wiped her face with the back of her hands before nodding in agreement.

"I'll go in and talk to Skyy, find out what's going on." Coco stared into Debi's eyes, looking through her pain. The past two months, he'd really gotten to know Debi, and even though he and Skyy were a lot tighter, he considered Debi a friend, too.

She managed a partial smile before they went back inside. Everyone seemed to stop talking when they entered.

"What? Y'all ain't never seen a pretty bitch like me before? What part of 'carry on' don't y'all understand?" Coco snapped.

Debi walked back to her station with a look of defeat. She sniffled while slowly placing rollers into her customer's hair.

"You gonna be alright, Debi?" her customer asked.

Debi stopped combing her customer's hair and put both hands up to her face. Her shoulders moved up and down with every sob. Her customer, a sixty-something regular whose wrinkles showed enough pain from her years of countless relationships and failed marriages, felt sorry for her.

"Debi, let's go outside and get some air."

"I'm fine, Mrs. Morgan. Let me finish your hair so you can go."

Mrs. Morgan turned to look into Debi's eyes. Debi was a long shot away from being fine. The pain and hurt she was feeling was written all over her face. Mrs. Morgan, wrapped in a black cape with a head full of blue hair rollers, looked more like a superhero than a human when she took hold of Debi's arm and escorted her back outside. The wind got under her cape, and it appeared she would take flight right there on the sidewalk. Debi took the opportunity to let the tears flow freely, releasing some of the pain she felt. The moisture from Mrs. Morgan's unrolled hair dripped on Debi's shoulders when Mrs. Morgan wrapped her arms around her to hug her.

"It's okay. Just let it all out." Mrs. Morgan rubbed Debi's back in a way that seemed to force the pain from deep down inside of Debi, out into the October air.

"Let me tell you something, Debi. No matter what the situation is with you and your husband, don't you ever allow yourself to be put down or humiliated. This stunt you pulled today? So unladylike. Listen, we are all human. Your husband—human. Your friend Skyy—human. Are they wrong for what they did? Of course, they are. But, you never, ever let their mistake become your misfortune. Now, weren't you just telling me that you were through with your husband?"

"Yes, but . . ."

"But nothing. If you're done, truly done, then why did you feel the need to make a scene? Whatever he did, or they did, it shouldn't matter to you enough where you're jeopardizing your job, business, etc. Honey, I have been through a lot of infidelities in my life by way of my men and so-called friends. Been there done that. However, one thing I've learned is you never, ever allow yourself to be the victim. You get what I'm saying to you?"

"But I feel so betrayed."

"And that's normal. I get that. But, one day, you will wake up. When the fog is gone, you will feel stronger. This whole thing will be a blur, a distant memory. Life is too short. Don't allow other people's actions make you lose control. Keep your dignity. Their actions speak for themselves, and at the end of the day, they will have to answer for them. Don't carry that burden."

Debi's tears were drying. She hugged Mrs. Morgan once more, consuming her scent of peppermint and cocoa butter lotion. "Thank you, Mrs. Morgan."

"Now, come on in here and finish my hair before I get pneumonia."

They walked back inside, arm and arm. Debi felt a little better. Although still angry with Skyy, she heard and understood Mrs. Morgan's words of wisdom. When they walked in, Skyy and Coco were missing, and their customers were sitting in their respective chairs. Skyy's customer appeared to be highly agitated. Debi looked over at Tiffany, who mouthed 'Are you okay?' over the noise. Debi nodded and asked where Coco was. Tiffany pointed in the direction of Skyy's office.

When Coco entered the office, Skyy was sitting behind her desk, arms crossed, staring into space.

"Skyy?"

Skyy sat there in silence.

"Skyy? You okay?"

"What do you think?"

"Don't get snappy with me. I came in here to check on you."

"I'm sorry, Coco. I'm so fucking angry. Why would Debi do this to me?"

Coco cleared his throat and raised an eyebrow.

"Oh, so you came in here to defend her to me, Coco? Come on now. Debi was wrong. If she wanted to discuss this, we should've done it in private."

Coco walked over and sat on the corner of Skyy's desk. He turned to face her. "Skyy, please tell me you didn't sleep with Eric."

Skyy stared at Coco, her eyes telling him what her mouth couldn't.

"Damn, girl. Why Eric? Didn't you think Debi would find out?"

She stood up and paced the floor of her cramped office. "Coco, I swear I never meant for this to happen. It was raining, and I was in the shop by myself. Next thing I know, Eric was at the door drunk, asking to come in. He was crying, and I tried, I tried to push him off of me, but he wouldn't stop."

"So are you saying he raped you?"

"No, I'm not saying he raped me, but, he, he just wouldn't stop, and I mean, it just happened. I told him it was wrong. He was just so drunk and depressed, Coco. I didn't want this to happen, honestly. I felt horrible afterwards. Eric did, too."

"So that makes it alright because you felt horrible?" Coco's head shook with over-exaggeration.

"I'm not saying it was right. I'm saying that I'm sorry it happened. I never wanted to hurt Debi."

"Too late for that now. Skyy, I have known you for a while, and I hope I can be open and honest here. I think you need to reassess your life, honey. Sleeping with Debi's husband, you crossed a dangerous line."

"Don't you think I know that? It just happened, Coco. You have to believe me. I didn't approach him or anything like that. He threw himself on me, and he begged, and . . . ." Skyy just shook her head, trying to make sense of the entire situation.

"Well, even if that was the case, it still doesn't change the fact that you slept with him. You need to talk to Debi. Explain the situation to her. Maybe if you tell her how it all went down, she might find it in her heart to forgive you. I don't know. But, you really need to go back out there and handle your business, because the chick in your chair is a bit salty at this point."

"I know. You want to go and finish it for me? I can sneak out the back," Skyy said jokingly.

"Girl, please. I got my hands full already. Plus, I need to hurry up and get out of here because I have plans tonight. Look, everybody out there knows the deal. Debi and I talked, and she's cool for now. So, you don't have to worry about any more unexpected announcements. Sure, they're gonna stare at you, but you have a job to do. Go on out there and handle your business. Then later on, you and Debi need to have a talk."

Skyy smiled at Coco. He made her feel a little better, even though she still dreaded going back to her station. Facing Debi was the last thing she wanted to do, but she couldn't stay holed up in that office forever. She may as well get it over with.

Skyy and Coco stood up in unison. She gave Coco a hug, a nonverbal way of thanking him for being her friend. At that moment, he was probably the only person in the entire salon that wanted to be her friend. Every woman in the salon despised her now. Sure, the staff all knew she dated married men, and that was cool. However, knowing that Skyy had slept with one of their men brought a new element to Skyy that they didn't like. She broke an unspoken rule among women friends, and no one in the salon—customers and staff—would look at Skyy the same way again.

Chapter 15

Skyy was relieved to have made it through the rest of her workday at the salon without any more conflict. She couldn't wait to finally leave the salon and go home to her safe haven. She and Debi hadn't had the opportunity to talk yet since Debi left immediately after finishing her last customer, without speaking a word to Skyy. However, Skyy planned to call Debi that night to put everything out on the table.

She turned down her tree-lined street and drove past several modern bungalows before reaching her all-brick rancher. The houses in her neighborhood were pretty new. They all shared a similar shape, but some of them were brick and some had vinyl siding in different colors. Since Skyy lived in the suburbs, there were no street lights, so the streets were dark. The moon was bright, and it provided some illumination to the nightsky. The leaves were all various shades of fall hues, and some had begun to fall. The leaves on the streets reminded Skyy of confetti, and she wondered when the county would come around to clean the streets.

She slowed her car to pull in front of her mailbox first, but there was a dark-colored sedan parked in front of it. As she got closer, she noticed it was a Chevy Malibu, which happened to be the same kind of car that Kelvin had. She could see a silhouette in the front seat of the car, but couldn't tell if it was Kelvin or not. The closer she got to the car, the more she realized it was Kelvin, and she was pissed. First of all, she hadn't told Kelvin where she lived, so she needed him to explain to her how he knew. Secondly, she didn't give him permission to come to her house. He took it upon himself to show up at her door unannounced, and Skyy didn't appreciate it. She pulled up next to his car and rolled down her passenger side window. Kelvin rolled down his driver's side window.

"What's up, baby? I've been waiting for you."

"Kelvin, what are you doing here?"

"I'm here to see you. I brought dinner and some wine. Thought I'd surprise you."

"How did you know where I live?"

"Skyy, I'm a police officer. That wasn't hard for me to find out. So, you want to sit out here and talk, or go inside and eat? The food is getting cold." Kelvin held up a brown paper bag, which appeared to contain Chinese take-out food.

Skyy gave him a fake smile before pulling into her driveway. She pressed the garage opener above her sun visor, and the garage door rose slowly. Skyy was a bit nervous, so when the garage door went down, she called Coco.

"Hey, diva."

"Coco, remember the dude Kelvin, the one that sent me flowers today? Why is he sitting in front of my house?!"

"So what's wrong with that?"

"I never told him where I lived. That's what's wrong."

"Oh. You need me to come over? I can come over before I go to the party if you don't feel comfortable."

Skyy bit her lip and thought about it for a minute. She really didn't want Coco to have to come all the way over her house for reinforcement; at least she didn't think she did.

"Hello?"

"I'm here, Coco. I was just thinking. I'll be okay. I guess I just wanted to let somebody know this guy was at my house in case I come up missing, floating down the James River in a suitcase."

"That's not funny, Skyy. Are you sure you don't want me to come over there?"

"No, I'm fine. He just caught me by surprise, that's all. Go ahead to your party and have fun. Call me later."

"I will."

Skyy hung up, grabbed her handbag, and looked around in her garage before she walked up the wooden steps to the door that led to her kitchen. A sequence of beeps sounded, and she entered her secret code into her alarm panel on the wall right beside the door. Once the beeps ended, Skyy turned on the lights in the kitchen. Her house, which shared the same earthtone colors as the salon, was not quite 2,000 square feet, but it was just enough room for Skyy. The floor plan was open and inviting, with nine-foot ceilings throughout. The kitchen was adorned with modern stainless steel appliances, granite countertops, and maple cabinets. The kitchen was connected to a formal dining room that was still empty since Skyy hadn't found any furniture she liked for the room yet. She'd only been in the house for four months, so she was still decorating.

Stepping down into the sunken living room, which was decorated with oversized suede-like crème-colored furniture, Skyy headed to the front door. Her cowboy boots thumped against the shiny, maple hardwood floors as she took strides. When she opened the door, Kelvin appeared with both hands full. He followed Skyy to the kitchen and put the bags on the breakfast bar.

"Nice place," Kelvin said, scanning the room.

"Kelvin, really, I wish you would've called first. Tonight is not a good night for me. I had a really bad day at work."

"I called you like four times. Didn't you get my messages?"

Skyy pulled her BlackBerry from her pocket and checked her missed call log. She noticed five calls from Kelvin, three missed calls from J, and two missed calls from Davin. She had ignored their calls because all she wanted to do was go home and be alone.

"I was busy today. Look, I appreciate you coming over with dinner and everything. Oh, and before I forget, thank you so much for the flowers. They are beautiful. But, I really want to be alone. How about a raincheck?"

Kelvin's smile turned to a frown. His demeanor instantly changed, and Skyy detected a certain coldness from him.

"You want me to leave?"

"Kelvin, look, it's not you. It's me. Today was probably one of the worst days of my life. I really want to take a long hot bath and go to bed. My feet hurt, my head hurts, and I wouldn't be good company tonight."

"What happened?"

"I don't want to talk about it. I just really need to be alone. Raincheck, please?"

"I came all the way over here to surprise you with good news, and you put me out?"

Skyy didn't care about any news, good or bad. All she wanted was for Kelvin to leave. She pulled her boots off and sat down on a beige and pewter barstool in front of the breakfast bar.

"So, aren't you going to ask me?"

"What is your good news, Kelvin?" she asked with agitation.

"My wife and I are separated. She took the kids and moved back to Raleigh." Kelvin said this excitingly, hoping to spark a positive reaction out of Skyy. Instead, he got the opposite.

"What do you mean separated?"

"I mean, we are no longer together. So now, you and I can be together."

"Is that what you think I want from you? Kelvin, you are way off, wayyyy off. I'm not looking for a relationship with you or anybody else."

"Oh, come on, Skyy. What woman doesn't want to take a relationship to the next level?"

"Excuse me? What relationship? We went out on what, two, three dates? Had one night of sex, and you're calling it a relationship? Kelvin, let me tell you a little something about me that you might've missed. I don't do commitments, to anybody. I fly solo at all times."

"Are you serious?"

"Kelvin, I don't do relationships. Period."

Kelvin had a look of confusion on his face. He thought Skyy wanted a commitment. What mistress couldn't wait for the day to hear those magic words, putting them one step closer to being the wife? Not Skyy.

"Look, let's go ahead and get this over and done with now. I'm not looking for a relationship, and I don't do single men for that very reason. So, if you are separated, then quite frankly, I can't see you anymore."

"What do you mean?"

"I mean, it, whatever *it* is, is done. I can't see you anymore, Kelvin. You're a nice guy and everything, but I'm not the woman for you."

Skyy stood up, facing Kelvin. She had to admit, he looked good and smelled even better. Still, he was too clingy and newly single, a recipe for disaster as far as Skyy was concerned. She tenderly rubbed his cheek before kissing it.

"I'm sorry."

Skyy waited for Kelvin to respond, but he didn't. She could tell he was upset with her. She stared into his eyes, the attribute Skyy admired the most. Kelvin brushed past her and proceeded to the front door. He didn't find it necessary to say anything since Skyy was dumping him. She'd basically said enough for both of them. Before exiting, he turned and looked at her one last time. Skyy gave him a concerned look, but it didn't mean much to Kelvin. He slammed the door behind him. Skyy listened for his engine to start before going to the door and locking the top lock. As if her day hadn't been bad enough, she had to end it on a sour note.

After taking a long, hot bubble bath in her Jacuzzi tub, Skyy threw on a pair of grey Victoria's Secret pajama pants and a matching grey tank top. She stood in front of the mirror in her oversized master bathroom and applied her favorite night serum after brushing her hair into a ponytail. The granite countertop, which was adorned with various high-end fragrances, such as Flowerbomb, Gucci, and Versace to name a few, took up an entire wall in her bathroom, as did the wall-sized mirror. The color scheme in the bathroom, which was mint green and chocolate brown, flowed into the bedroom. Her bedroom furniture was contemporary and sleek, in a dark tea finish. The headboard of the queen-sized sleigh bed was embellished with patches of leather in various shades of brown and tan. Her master bedroom, which was actually expanded by tearing down the wall that connected a second bedroom, was large enough to have an armoire, dresser, and a sitting area. The mint green and brown color scheme complemented the furniture, and Skyy didn't overindulge when she decorated with accessories from Pier One.

She fell back on her bed and stared up at the tray ceiling. Her heart was beating fast because she knew it was time for her to call Debi. She turned on her wall-mounted plasma TV, not to watch anything particular, but to provide some background noise for when she called her. She wished she didn't have to face this, but she knew if Debi was going to continue working in the salon, everything needed to be out in the open. She dialed Debi's number and waited for her to answer. Debi picked up on the second ring.

"Hello?"

"Hey."

"Hey."

There were a few seconds of uncomfortable silence before Skyy decided to speak up.

"Debi, we really need to talk."

"The way I see it, Skyy, you're the one that needs to do the talking."

"Well, yes, I agree. I owe you an explanation. Can I start by saying that none of this was intentional? I did not go behind your back and seek out your husband or anything like that. It was something that just happened one time. That's it."

"What do you mean it just happened? Sex doesn't just happen, Skyy."

"Listen, as much as I totally agree with you, I have to let you know that was the case in this situation. I was at the shop. It was raining. I was sleepy, so I fell asleep on the sofa. Eric woke me up when he started banging on the door. He was looking for you. He was drunk, Debi. He was distraught, crying, very upset over his relationship with you. One minute, I'm trying to console him, and the next minute, he's asking me to sleep with him."

"And you said yes? Why not tell him no and make him leave?"

"I did. I kept telling him he should leave. But, he just kept groping me and touching me, begging me for it. I tried to move his hands, tried to make him get up and leave, but he wouldn't. And I don't know. It sounds like I should've had more control than I did, but I didn't. He said you weren't having sex with him and he needed it bad."

"Ohh, so now it's my fault because I wouldn't sleep with him? So you decided to give him what he was missing at home, is that it?"

"Debi, it wasn't like that. Honestly, I tried. I really did, but he wouldn't stop."

"You know what, Skyy? I like how you're trying to push the blame on Eric. It's so typical of you. It's always someone else's fault. Never your fault."

"I didn't say I wasn't at fault, because I am to blame in this, too. I take full responsibility for my actions. I just wanted you to understand that I didn't pursue your husband. I didn't take what you told me in confidence and use it against you in any way. I needed you to understand that was not how it all happened."

Debi's silence was excruciating. Skyy didn't want Debi to hate her. She wanted her forgiveness.

"I'm really sorry, Debi. I never, ever meant to hurt you."

"Anything else?" Debi's tone was dry and patronizing.

"No, that's it, I guess. Do you think you can ever forgive me?"

"Today is not the day to ask me that. Maybe later, but right now, forgiveness is the furthest thing from my mind. I have to go." Debi disconnected without giving Skyy an opportunity to say anything else.

Skyy was glad she'd given Debi the details of how the encounter took place. Debi needed to know that Skyy didn't purposefully seek out Eric—that Eric threw himself on Skyy and it only happened once. To Skyy, that made a huge difference. The part about them having sex did not play as much of a role to her as the fact that he threw himself on her.

She propped herself up on her fluffy pillows and pointed the remote at the TV. Her BlackBerry vibrated on the nightstand. It was a text from Debi. 'Just to let you know, I'm going to another salon, effective immediately.' Second text, 'I'll go in tomorrow and get my stuff.' Third text, 'I can't work for a person I can't trust.'

So Debi was quitting. Skyy didn't really expect that. She thought maybe Debi would come in, keep her distance, and maybe not even speak to her for a few days. But, her leaving the shop altogether made Skyy a little sad. She wondered how Debi had found another salon to work in so fast. Furthermore, she didn't have the decency to give Skyy at least a two-week notice so Skyy could have the opportunity to find a new stylist. *Oh well,* Skyy thought. *Maybe this is for the best.*

As she read her messages, she realized she missed a text from Coco, which he'd sent while Skyy was taking a bath. He was checking to see if she was okay. Skyy sent him a text in response. 'I'm fine. Kelvin is gone. Debi is quitting. Call me 2morrow.'

Chapter 16

November came in like a thief in the night, blessing the city of Richmond with springlike days and wintery nights. It was truly Indian summer, as the old folks used to call it when the temperature outside didn't coincide with the season. Thanksgiving was two weeks away, and it was almost seventy-five degrees outside.

It was Sunday, and Skyy was returning from DC after having a rendezvous with J. He was in town for an album release party for a young rapper who was born and raised in DC. Closing the nightclub Platinum for the private party would've been difficult for anybody else, but of course, it wasn't for J. He invited Skyy to go to DC to attend the party with him, and she graciously obliged. The crowd was a bit too young for Skyy's taste; however, she didn't mind it, seeing as though she got to stay at the Four Seasons. And the constant VIP treatment didn't hurt either.

Getting away took her mind off of her problems, and she sure had a handful of them. First, there was Debi, who left that fateful day as promised, and her station was currently empty. Skyy needed a new stylist to fill Debi's chair, but unfortunately the 'Stylist Wanted' sign was still in the window. On top of that, Skyy had not heard from Debi, and all phone calls to her went unanswered. Then there was Kelvin, who was constantly calling Skyy asking for another chance. Skyy had started to rely on Coco for support whenever she felt like Kelvin may show up at her door. Since calling things off with him, he'd shown up unnannounced to plead his case. The whole scene made her very uncomfortable. After being caught by his wife at Fleming's, Kyle tried calling Skyy a few times, but she didn't think it would be wise to chance seeing him again. As long as his wife was out following him, they were at risk of being caught, and she couldn't take that chance. So, the only 'safe' men she had at the time were J and Davin. Since her time with J was sporadic, Skyy had begun spending more time with Davin, whenever his wife was out of town on business of course. Her love life was going dry, in a sense, because Kelvin took up the space that J left open. But, this was the risk she took in the adultery game she played with these men, so she would have to deal with it.

Skyy used her key to enter the salon, where Coco was busy cleaning his station and dancing to the loud music blaring from the speakers. He didn't notice Skyy; therefore, she startled him when she walked up behind him.

"Girl, you about to get a beatdown up in here, scaring me like that."

Skyy looked around for the remote before noticing it on Coco's station. She grabbed it and turned the music down.

"Good afternoon, Ms. Coco. How are you today?"

"I was fine until you came in here turning my Lil' Wayne down."

"You know I can't stand all of that, especially on a Sunday."

"So, how was the party? I'm still mad you didn't take me," Coco said, pouting like a five-year-old. He sprayed Lysol over the sofas, table, and everything else in the waiting area. The recent rise in the swine flu caused them to be cautious with keeping everything sanitized.

"It was okay. You would've enjoyed the party. I personally enjoyed the after-party." Skyy displayed a seductive smile.

"Ewwwww, you nasty. So, at what point in our friendship are you going to tell me who Mr. Music Mogul is? I mean, if everyone in his entourage knows about you, I should at least know about him."

Skyy grabbed the sponge from the bucket full of bleach and water and wrung it out so she could wipe down her station. "Coco, leave it alone. I'm not telling you who he is. You should be tired of asking me by now."

"I'm too nosey to be tired."

Skyy moved around the salon, wiping and scrubbing everything that might've been touched by someone with the swine Flu. There appeared to be an epidemic across the nation, with folks standing in lines for hours just to receive the HINI vaccine. Skyy didn't want to take any chances of it spreading in her salon.

"So, have you talked to Debi?" Skyy asked, trying to sound unconcerned.

Coco stopped what he was doing and looked over at her. He knew Skyy was still affected by Debi's departure and missed their friendship, even though Skyy would never admit it to him.

"Yeah, I talked to her Friday."

"Oh. How is she doing?"

"She's doing good. The brother-in-law asked to marry her. She's considering moving to North Carolina."

"Really? Well, I'm glad she's happy."

"Skyy, give her some time. She'll come around."

A knock at the door startled them. Since the blinds were closed, they couldn't see who it was. Skyy peeked out of the blinds and saw that it was Tiffany. She unlocked the door to let her in.

"Hey. Where's your key?" Skyy asked.

"Hey. I can't find it." Tiffany walked in hurriedly, as if she wanted to avoid eye contact with Skyy.

Skyy locked the door and followed behind her closely. Her chilly disposition told Skyy that there was a problem.

"Hey, what's wrong with you?" Coco asked, noticing how aloof Tiffany was.

Tiffany took off her coat and hung it on the coat rack. She sat her purse and keys in her chair, rolled up her sleeves, and grabbed the sponge from the bucket so she could wipe down her station. It was obvious she was in a bad mood and something was bothering her, which was becoming a norm with Tiffany lately.

"Tiffany?"

Tiffany scrubbed vigorously, trying hard to ignore them both. Without warning, bottles of fingernail polish hit the floor, sounding like the keys on a piano. Tiffany had violently knocked the polish from the station with her hands, swaying back and forth until everything that was on the station was now on the floor.

"What the f . . ."

"Coco!" Skyy exclaimed.

Tiffany broke into a high-pitched squeal, then took off running to the bathroom. Skyy and Coco stared at each other in shock, not sure who should take on the task of running behind Tiffany to check on her. When there was a knock at the salon's entrance, Skyy decided to head for the door, which left Coco in charge of checking on Tiffany. Skyy looked out of the miniblinds on the door and caught a glimpse of the private investigator who'd come by the salon a couple of months back. She almost wished she hadn't looked out of the blinds since it was obvious to him that she was in the salon, and she couldn't act as if she wasn't there. Reluctantly, she unlocked the door to let the private investigator in.

"Yes?" Skyy said dryly.

"How are you doing, Ms. Armfield? Remember me, Shamar, private investigator?" Shamar extended his hand to Skyy.

"I'm doing fine. Trying to figure out why you're here." Skyy stood directly in front of the door, making it hard for Shamar to come in further.

"Ms. Armfield, I really need to talk to you."

"I already told you, I'm not interested in talking to a private investigator."

"But, you don't understand. I was sent here from Baltimore. Someone in Baltimore has been trying to locate you."

Skyy could feel beads of perspiration forming on her back. Her chest was warm, her throat got tight, and her heart sunk to the pit of her stomach.

"Baltimore? There isn't anyone in Baltimore that needs to find me. I'm sorry you were sent all the way here for nothing, but I can't help you."

Shamar noticed how uncomfortable Skyy became once he said he was from Baltimore. It was obvious to him that Skyy was hiding something.

"For some reason, I don't believe that."

Skyy bowed her head, looking down at the floor. Shamar gently placed his hand on Skyy's chin and lifted her head so she was looking directly at him.

"Is there somewhere we can go to talk?" he asked her.

Skyy, who was obviously hiding something, didn't want to discuss anything while Coco and Tiffany were in the salon. Realizing that Shamar was from Baltimore, Skyy knew his finding her was not related to anyone's husband. More than likely, this was related to her past, a time Skyy had locked away in a private place for no one else but her.

"Listen, if you give me your card, I promise I will give you a call. We can't talk right now."

"I gave you a card the last time I was here."

"I threw it away. I'm sorry. I thought you were looking for me for . . . it doesn't matter."

Shamar reached into his pocket and handed Skyy his business card. He was beginning to think she had to be the person he had been trying to track down for almost a year. Her entire demeanor had changed once he divulged where he was from. Now all he needed to do was sit down with her, ask her some questions, and start putting the pieces together.

"I'm going to be waiting to hear from you. I really need to get my case closed. Promise me you will call?"

"Yes, I promise, but we have to talk in private." Skyy sounded like she'd been defeated.

Flashing pearly white teeth and a dimple in his right cheek, Shamar smiled at Skyy, hoping to soften the mood a bit.

"I'll be waiting to hear from you." Shamar let himself out and jumped into a rented Dodge Charger that was parked directly in front of the salon.

Skyy rubbed her forehead, feeling a bit of anxiety from just hearing someone say the word Baltimore. And to think there was actually someone in Baltimore who was trying to track her down. Skyy had been off, way off base.

Her stomach started doing somersaults, and then all of a sudden, she became nauseous. She didn't think she could make it to the bathroom, so she stepped outside and released right there on the concrete sidewalk. The brisk wind blew through the thin Ed Hardy t-shirt Skyy was wearing, but she didn't appear to be fazed by it. Her cheeks were flushed, and the space behind her ears was hot. Thankfully for her, Coco and Tiffany hadn't been around when Shamar mentioned Baltimore. No one, not even Coco, knew anything about Skyy's past. They definitely didn't have a clue about her time spent in Baltimore. Skyy had to make sure it stayed that way.

She stood outside for a few more minutes to get some fresh air and to get her head right. She leaned back on the glass window and let the wind encompass her, helping to cool her body temperature down. She tried to be still, hoping it would stop the circus going on in her stomach. Before she had an opportunity to go back inside, Coco poked his head outside.

"Hey, what are you doing?" he asked.

"Got a little sick to my stomach. Needed to get some fresh air. I think all that cleaning with bleach did it." Skyy told her friend a lie, which he fell for.

"Well, Tiffany is not doing so well. She has gotten herself into a little predicament."

"Lord have mercy. What is it?" Skyy seemed to forget about her stomach pain.

"She's pregnant by Trey, and honey, that ain't even the half of it," Coco said, over-exaggerating his words and trying to whisper at the same time.

He held his finger up to his lips, an indication that Skyy had to refrain from reacting. She and Coco would have to discuss it another time. It was obvious to Skyy that Tiffany had sworn Coco to secrecy, which lasted approximately seven minutes. Skyy held her pinky finger and thumb up to her ear, imitating a telephone, which meant Coco would need to call her when he got home later. Until then, Tiffany would be battling with her secret, just like Skyy seemed to be doing with her own.

Chapter 17

It was the fourth Thursday of November a.k.a. Thanksgiving. Skyy, who had no family to celebrate the holidays with, used the day off to deep clean her baseboards and hardwood floors and do laundry. Thanksgiving was just another day to her—no turkey, dressing, sweet potato pie, or cranberry sauce. One of the disadvantages of dating married men was that Skyy had to spend her holidays alone, while her men spent time with their wives and families. Sure, she'd been invited to several dinners by customers; even Coco invited her to dinner with his family. However, Skyy didn't want to be a charity case for anyone.

As full as Skyy felt her life was, she was actually very lonely. Growing up an only child, Skyy's mother was a single parent with a hefty drinking and drug problem. She only saw her father, who happened to be married, an average of once a week. The only time he would come around was long enough to go in her mother's room, where they would shut and lock the door while Skyy kept herself busy until they came out. Skyy would play with her dolls, read books, or do whatever to occupy her time. She could remember waiting patiently outside her mother's bedroom door for the moaning to end and the talking to begin. That meant her daddy would come out and see her, even if it was only for a few short minutes before he left. Sometimes, he would give her a treat before leaving or an occasional hug. By the time Skyy turned twelve, her mother had switched from alcohol to cocaine. Her father came around less and less, so Skyy went out searching for the love she wasn't getting at home. There was never a real connection between her and her father—the only thing she really knew about him was his name and where he worked. At the age of fourteen, Skyy became an orphan when her mother accidentally overdosed on painkillers and anxiety medication. Sky sought out her father to inform him of the death, hoping he would welcome her into his world, but he did just the

144

opposite, denying her refuge with his family. Skyy ended up living with her grandmother, only to be forced into foster care when her grandmother died. The remaining teenage years of Skyy's life were spent in a group home, where she would befriend no one. Forced to grow up fast, Skyy vowed to find love since her life had been without it, and when she turned seventeen, she thought that was exactly what she'd discovered.

Skyy jumped when she heard the doorbell chime. Since she wasn't expecting any company, she wondered who would be showing up at her door unannounced and uninvited. Skyy got up from her knees on the kitchen floor, pulled off her rubber gloves, and walked quietly to the front door. She figured if it was someone she didn't want to see, she could act like she wasn't home as long as they didn't hear her come to the door. She rose up on her tiptoes to peek out of the peephole. It was Kelvin. He was holding a white plastic bag in one hand and a bottle of wine in the other from what she could tell. The rumbling in Skyy's stomach sent a signal to her brain to make the words come out of her mouth.

"Who is it?"

"Kelvin."

Skyy bit her lip, hoping she was making the right decision by letting him in. Her first thought was how in the world he'd managed to get away from his family on Thanksgiving Day. There was no need in having a nice meal and bottle of wine go to waste, though, especially since Skyy was hungry and hadn't cooked anything.

She turned the deadbolt lock before opening the door for Kelvin. The collar on his black, leather motorcycle jacket was pulled up around his neck, shielding it from the cold air. Skyy didn't bother to fix herself up. Quite frankly, she was way beyond the stage of impressing Kelvin. All she really wanted was to get the most out of him, use him and then lose him. Tonight, she planned to use him for a free dinner and, if the wine did its job, some quickie sex. That was only if she wanted it, of course.

"Hi there. Happy Thanksgiving," Kelvin said, holding the bottle of Moscato wine up close to Skyy's face like it was a trophy.

"Hi, Kelvin. Same to you. What are you doing here? And how many times have I told you not to come over here unannounced?"

"Come on, give me a break. I miss you, Skyy, and I wanted to see you, that's all."

"What did I tell you the last time you were here? Huh?"

Kelvin shrugged his shoulders, appearing almost childlike.

"Kelvin, I told you, I don't deal with single men. It's just too much for me. Since you and your wife are separated, that officially makes you single."

"Wait. She's back home now. So, technically, I'm not single anymore."

Skyy squinted her eyes, trying to read Kelvin. Was he telling the truth? Or was he just trying to get back into Skyy's good graces by telling her a lie?

"Kelvin, come on now. It's Thanksgiving Day. If you were with your wife, there is no way in hell you would be standing on my porch with wine and, I'm assuming, dinner."

"Listen, we went to her mother's house in Charles City. Her mother doesn't care much for me, you know. So, to avoid having to be there all evening, I told her I had to work. So, here I am."

Skyy studied him. He looked good to her, that was for sure, and the drought she was currently in the midst of could sure use some interrupting. She decided to take a chance, only because she was hungry—and not just for food. Skyy hesitated before opening the door wide enough for Kelvin to come in.

"I knew you would be alone, so I decided to come over and give you some company."

"How did you know I would be alone?"

Kelvin stuttered. Skyy gave him an evil look before cracking a smile, easing the awkwardness Kelvin felt at that moment.

"Girl, you're crazy. I know you're crazy about me, too. You just want to play hard to get."

Skyy shut the door and followed behind Kelvin to the kitchen. For some reason, tonight, he seemed harmless to her. His eyes were softer, and there was something different about him. Skyy wasn't sure if she was making excuses for using Kelvin or if indeed there was something different. Kelvin placed the bag on the breakfast nook. He didn't even take off his coat before removing the Styrofoam containers from the bag. The aroma of turkey smothered in gravy and dressing filled the room quickly when he opened the container.

"Tah-dah," Kelvin said.

"Smells delicious. Who cooked this?" Skyy asked.

"Don't worry about who cooked it. You just go and wash your hands, sit down, and enjoy it."

Skyy had to admit, Kelvin was right on time with the Thanksgiving feast, and it didn't disappoint. He had all of the trimmings—homemade macaroni and cheese, collard greens smothered in hamhocks, turkey and dressing with a homemade buttered roll. Kelvin removed his jacket while Skyy went over to the sink to wash her hands. He pulled out one of the three matching barstools and took a seat. Skyy opted to sit at the tiny, wooden dinette set for two, which was strategically placed in front of a full-sized bay window. She bowed her head, closed her eyes, and said a quick prayer to herself before diving into her feast. Every decadent morsel satisfied her tastebuds in every way imaginable. Kelvin sat there and watched her, patiently awaiting her response.

"Well?" he finally said.

"Umph, umph, umph, this is delicious!" Skyy exclaimed.

"I knew you would like it." Kelvin smiled, proud of his decision to bring Skyy a Thanksgiving feast. He was sure this deed would score him major points with Skyy.

"Yes, it's so good. I haven't had food like this since I was a little girl." Skyy continued to consume her dinner. Then, when she was just about finished, she realized she hadn't offered Kelvin any. With her mouth full of food, she asked, "I'm sorry. You want some?"

"No, no, I'm good. Thanks, though."

Skyy took a bite from the roll before getting up to get something to drink from her refrigerator.

"You don't want any wine?" Kelvin asked.

"Yeah, I'll get some when I'm done eating. I need some water, though." She grabbed a bottle of purified drinking water from the refrigerator, twisted the cap off, and took several gulps before sitting back down at the table.

"Do you mind if I turn the TV on to watch the game?" Kelvin asked.

"No, go ahead. I'll be there in a minute," Skyy said, making reference to her living room.

She watched Kelvin stroll toward the living room, resembling Denzel in *American Gangsta*. His swagger stimulated her, and coupled with the scent of his Chrome cologne, between her legs throbbed. Since it had been a while for her, Kelvin would have to do.

Skyy closed the top on the Styrofoam container. Then she went to the cabinet next to the area over the stove and grabbed two Lenox crystal wine glasses. Before heading to the living room, she rummaged around in the kitchen drawer for a corkscrew. Kelvin had made himself comfortable on the sofa that faced the wall-mounted plasma TV. He seemed to be so engrossed with the men in tight pants and helmets, who were running around on the green turf tackling one another, that he didn't notice Skyy immediately. She sat down beside him, at which time he turned his attention to her. Seeing Skyy struggling with the bottle of wine and corkscrew, Kelvin took over.

"Let me do that for you."

Kelvin made opening the wine bottle look effortless as it made a popping sound. He poured two full glasses and handed one to Skyy. They clicked their glasses together before raising them to their lips. Aside from the light from the TV and the kitchen, the living room was dark, which helped to set the mood. Skyy, who was starting to feel the effect of the wine, decided she should go freshen up if she planned to let Kelvin finish feeding her appetite.

"I'll be right back. Don't move," she said seductively, while rubbing her hand across his shoulders.

Kelvin kept his eyes on Skyy until she disappeared into the bedroom. He took several fast gulps of his wine before pouring himself another glass. Knowing it would be his lucky night, a little smirk appeared on his face. He sat back on the sofa and tried to concentrate on the football game, but his mind was preoccupied with Skyy. He could hear the shower running, and the thought of her being butt naked covered in soap and water while washing herself made his nature rise.

Even though Skyy hadn't officially invited him to her bedroom, he didn't think it was off limits. So, Kelvin followed the muffled sound of the shower running until he reached the doorway of Skyy's bedroom. He stood there, examining the dimly-lit room, saving every facet of the room to his memory. Kelvin moved to Skyy's armoire, slowly opening and closing her drawers before reaching the one that held her undergarments. He lifted a pair of her lace thongs in the air, inspecting them carefully, before putting them to his face and sniffing them slowly. When he heard the water turn off, he closed the drawer and put the thongs in his pocket. Kicking off his shoes and removing his sweater, he laid back on the bed and waited for Skyy. When Skyy opened the bathroom door, she jumped when she saw him.

"Oh, Kelvin, you scared me." Skyy stood there for a moment, wrapped in an oversized, plush towel. There were still beads of water on her back and shoulders, and her hair was a bit damp.

"Mmph, come over here," Kelvin said.

Skyy looked around. "Did you bring the wine?"

"We don't need wine. Not yet. Come here."

Skyy held the corner of the towel, keeping it from falling while she walked toward Kelvin. When she was standing directly between his legs, he grabbed the towel from her hand and opened it slowly.

"Yeah, let me just look at you." He studied her body from head to toe before dropping the towel to the floor. He caressed her breasts, rolling her nipples between his fingers until they were hard. He pulled her closer so that one of her breasts was in his mouth. While sucking her breast, he massaged her butt, moving his fingers around its contour and in between her legs. Skyy pushed him back on the bed and climbed on top of him, grinding her naked body against his. She put her tongue in his mouth, and he flipped her over on her back so he could be on top.

"Can I get this or what?" Kelvin panted.

"Yeah, you can get it," Skyy whispered.

Kelvin pinned her arms down while planting kisses all over her body. Skyy groaned. He inhaled the smell of cherry blossom left behind by her Bath and Body Works shower gel. Taking his time, Kelvin wanted to make sure he did everything right to please her. It was also important for Skyy to remember this time since the first time she was too drunk to remember.

"Go ahead. Taste it. I know you want to."

Skyy gave Kelvin permission to explore her valley with his tongue, and he graciously obliged. He pushed her legs open wider, and using his fingers as his guide, he pushed back her vaginal lips and sucked her clitoris like a peppermint. Skyy could feel her juices starting to flow with every lick and suck.

"Come on," Skyy said, guiding Kelvin's head from her valley.

She reached over to her nightstand and grabbed a condom from the drawer, while Kelvin unbuckled his pants. She could see the bulge through his pants, and she knew he was ready. As he pulled down his pants, there was a loud thud from his belt buckle making contact with the floor. Skyy rolled the condom over his manhood carefully, ensuring its fit before lying back on the bed. Kelvin moved toward her and entered her slowly, grabbing the headboard for balance. Skyy took him inside of her with ease, and they rocked together. Kelvin's strokes started off slow at first, but all of a sudden, his thrusts became forceful and violent. Skyy tried to put some space between her and Kelvin, hoping it would cause him to slow down or at least ease up. Instead, he grabbed her by the hair and yanked it angrily.

"Whose is it? Huh, bitch? I said, whose is it?" he yelled repeatedly.

The pleasure she'd been feeling only minutes before was dissolving, and Kelvin was starting to hurt her. *Thump, thump, thump.* Over and over, her head hit the headboard from the force Kelvin was using. She tried to push him up again, but he was too strong.

"Kelvin!" Skyy yelled, but he ignored her, oblivious to anything around him. It was as if he was having an out-of-body experience. His eyes were open, but they were dark, almost evil. He mumbled to himself, while also screaming obscenities at Skyy.

"Kelvin!" Skyy shrieked again.

Thump, thump, thump. Between hitting her head on the headboard and Kelvin pulling her hair, Skyy was ready for it to be over.

"Kelvin, stop!" she yelled.

This time, Kelvin let go of her hair and put his hand around her neck. The air in Skyy's throat was slowly diminishing. Skyy could feel consciousness slipping away from her. She used the little bit of strength she had to pound her fists on Kelvin's chest. *Thump, thump, thump.* He wouldn't stop. Skyy's chest tightened, and the room seemed to get smaller. The fight behind her punches was weak, and she didn't have enough breath in her body to speak. *This is it,* she thought to herself, wondering how long it would be before anyone discovered her body. Just when she was about to close her eyes to defeat, Kelvin gave a forceful thrust, shuddered a bit like a fish out of water, then released his hand from her throat. He fell back on the bed beside Skyy, who was gasping for air by now. She sat up slowly, taking deep breaths to encourage her lungs to work properly.

"You motherfucker! Are you crazy? You almost killed me!" Skyy yelled, pounding her fist on Kelvin's chest.

Kelvin jumped up, appearing puzzled by Skyy's reaction. "What's wrong with you? Stop! Stop!" He tried to grab her arms, but she was swinging uncontrollably.

"You fucking asshole! Get the fuck out of my house! You almost killed me! Get out!"

Skyy moved away from Kelvin, closer to her nightstand and her BlackBerry. She had one hand on the phone and the other was rubbing her neck. It didn't matter to her that she was naked. All she wanted was for Kelvin to leave. He continued to stare at her with a look of confusion on his face.

"Skyy, what's wrong with you? Why are you upset?"

Skyy squinted her eyes and tilted her head a bit, not sure if Kelvin was serious or joking.

"Are you fucking kidding me? You just damn near rendered me unconscious, and you're asking me if I'm upset? Get out right now or I'm calling the police."

"But, Skyy, I don't ..."

"I said GET OUT!"

Kelvin hesitated at first, but realized Skyy meant business. He grabbed his clothes from the floor, pulling his pants on and putting on his shoes. Skyy was still standing by the nightstand, but by now, she'd pulled a portion of the sheet off the bed to cover herself. The numbers 9-1-1 were just a touch away on her BlackBerry. Carrying his shirt in his hand, Kelvin headed to the living room to get his coat.

"Skyy, I really ..."

"Kelvin, I swear, if you don't get out of here right now, the police are going to meet you at the door. Now, it would be very embarrassing to have one of your coworkers come over here. So, just get your shit and go. And don't bother coming back, you fucking lunatic!"

Kelvin turned and stared at Skyy. His eyes were different, almost the same eyes he had when he was on top of her nearly suffocating her to death. At first glance, Skyy thought he was going to leap over the bed and try to go for her throat again. But, instead, he disappeared to the living room. Skyy walked slowly to the bedroom door so she could be sure he was gone. There was a loud slam from the front door closing, immediately followed by a car engine roaring outside. Skyy ran to the living room and locked the top lock on her front door. Kelvin sat in his car for a couple of minutes before finally driving off. Out of paranoia, Skyy ran to the kitchen and checked her other door before dialing Coco's number. The sheet she'd been dragging from the bedroom was wrapped around her body. She pulled it firmly, trying to keep it from falling to the floor.

"Hello, diva."

"Oh my God, Coco, you have to come over here!"

"What's wrong?" he asked, hearing the panic in her voice.

"He, he tried to kill me."

"What are you talking about, Skyy?"

"Kelvin. He came over and brought me dinner and wine. Then, we were . . . then, he started choking me!" she screamed, hysterical and barely able to get her words out. "Now I'm scared he might come back. He's crazy, Coco. Please, can you come over here and stay with me?" Skyy was on the verge of tears, and Coco could hear desperation in her voice.

"Skyy, what in the world happened? Tell me the story, step by step."

"Coco, can you just come over? I can tell you everything when you get here."

When Skyy sniffled, Coco knew his friend was crying.

"I'll be there in fifteen minutes."

Chapter 18

Skyy sped through the city, trying to make it to Starbucks for her caffeine fix before heading to the salon. The December air was frigid, and the weather forecast called for snow. Skyy had a few early customers that she wanted to get in and out, and she would have to play it by ear with her afternoon customers. The sky was gray and cloudy, a sure sign that snow was coming. As if that wasn't enough, a flock of seagulls circled the parking lot as she pulled into Starbucks.

She wrapped her wool scarf around her neck before exiting the car. There was a line in Starbucks, as usual, so she waited patiently alongside the other caffeine addicts for her caramel brulee latte. There were about four people ahead of her in line, all of which couldn't seem to make up their minds on whether or not they wanted a muffin or some other savory pastry to go along with their coffee. Skyy checked her watch, noticing she only had about ten minutes before her first appointment was scheduled to arrive. She sighed heavily, realizing that whenever she was in a hurry, everyone else seemed lackadaisical. By the time she reached the register, she had her debit card in hand and was specific about her order so she could get her coffee and go. The coffee shop was crowded for an early Friday morning, when most people should be on their way to work or already at work by now. However, with Christmas only a week away, Skyy realized some of the people were probably on vacation for the holiday. She made a mental note to leave the house a few minutes early over the next few days, at least until the holiday was over.

Skyy pulled her car onto Cary Street, followed it up to the Boulevard, turned right on Broad Street, and found a parking space directly in front of the salon. This was her lucky day, or so she thought until she got close enough to notice the glass on the sidewalk from the broken window. There was now a big hole right in the middle of the window where Skyy's Hair and Nail Salon was once inscribed. The blinds hanging at the window swung back and forth from the cool air outside. Skyy looked in horror at the apparent act of vandalism, not sure if she should go inside and call the police or wait in her car and call them. She opted to make the call from her car, pulling her BlackBerry from her handbag.

"9-1-1, what is your emergency?"

"Hello, my place of business has been vandalized, and I need an officer to come over so I can file a report."

"One moment, please. Let me transfer you to the nonemergency line."

"But ..." Skyy tried to interrupt, but the operator was too quick for her.

As far as Skyy was concerned, this was an emergency. She didn't know if someone was actually inside the salon or what. What was more bizarre was the fact that her alarm wasn't going off. She listened to the hold music for a few seconds before the line was answered.

"Nonemergency hotline, how can I help you?" a woman answered.

"Yes, I need an officer at 109 East Broad Street. My salon has been vandalized, and I don't know if the person is still inside or not."

"Okay. I have a patrol car in the area now, and it should be en route."

"Thank you."

Skyy looked in her rearview mirror, noticing her customer was pulling up behind her. She got out at the same time so she could meet her on the sidewalk. Her customer exited the car with a look of disbelief on her face at the sight of the shattered window.

"Oh my goodness, Skyy, what happened?"

"I don't know. I haven't gone in yet. I'm waiting on the police to get here first."

"Dag, girl, who in the world did you piss off?"

Skyy shrugged her shoulders like she had no idea, but in her mind, she knew it had to be one person—Kelvin. His behavior the last time they were together warranted Skyy to give him the boot, which she'd done. However, Kelvin continued to pursue her. Over and over, he called apologizing for his behavior, asking for another chance. Skyy was convinced Kelvin was crazy, and she didn't want to have anything else to do with him.

"Come on. Let's get in the car until the police get here. It's cold as hell out here."

Skyy got back into the driver's seat of her car, while her customer climbed into the passenger's seat. The engine purred when she turned the ignition, providing them some heat while they waited.

"The police are supposed to be in the area, so hopefully, they will be here shortly," Skyy said.

"Really, Skyy, I can reschedule so you can take care of your business here. I truly understand." Her customer thought about the conditions she would have to endure for the sake of getting her hair done and catching pneumonia was not her idea of fun.

Skyy glanced over at the large hole in the window again. She didn't want to let her customer down, but it didn't make sense for her to do hair under these circumstances. If it were summertime, she might have considered it. However, with the temperature sitting right at forty degrees, she knew her customers wouldn't go for that.

"You're right, Mia. I'm sorry about all this. This is messed up because they're calling for snow tonight and tomorrow, so I don't want to tell you to come tomorrow if the weather is bad. How about this? If we get bad weather today and tomorrow, I will come in on Monday and take care of your hair. Is that cool?"

"Yeah, that works for me."

"Just give me a call tomorrow. Thanks again for understanding."

Skyy watched her customer exit the car before taking another sip of her coffee. A few minutes later, she noticed a car pulling up beside her in her peripheral vision. When she turned to see the police car, she felt relieved. The police officer pulled his car in front of Skyy's, taking his time to get out. Skyy made it to the curb, while the officer was still sitting in his car. What he was waiting for Skyy didn't know. He finally opened his car door, adjusting his police hat on his head before getting out. The officer had his gaze transfixed on the damage of the window for so long that Skyy had to say hello to get his attention.

"Oh, I'm sorry. I'm Officer Gaines."

155

"Skyy Armfield."

"You got some nasty damage there. Have you gone inside yet?"

"No, I was afraid to. I didn't know if whoever did this was still inside or what."

The officer reminded Skyy of the guy who played the psychopath in that movie with Jamie Foxx. He motioned for her to stay put before putting his hand on his gun and going toward the door. Realizing the door was locked, Skyy walked up behind him with the key. She put the key in the door, unlocked it, and stepped back so the officer could go in. She stuck her head inside once he made his way in, trying to scan the shop for further damage. There didn't appear to be any other damage other than the broken window and lots of glass. Slowly, Skyy eased inside as the officer checked the back of the salon, her office, and the restroom. The huge brick, which was the source of the damage, rested on the floor by the sofa in the waiting area. Skyy walked over to pick it up, but not before the officer yelled for her not to touch it.

"Don't touch that. I'm going to get it analyzed for fingerprints. Leave it there. I'll take it in a second." The officer pulled out his notepad and an ink pen. "Whoever it was is gone now. Do you have any idea who may have done this?"

"I think. Well, I don't want to get him into any trouble, but I really believe it was this guy named Kelvin."

"Ma'am, no offense, but getting him in trouble should be the last thing on your mind."

"It's not that. I mean, see . . ." Skyy fumbled over her words. She didn't know if telling this officer that Kelvin was also a police officer was a good idea or not.

"What is it, Ms. Armfield?"

"It's Kelvin. He's a police officer."

The officer's eyes got as big as lemons. Such an allegation could stir up unnecessary negative publicity for the City of Richmond that this officer didn't want any part of. He cleared his throat before speaking.

"A police officer? Are you sure? Do you know what precinct he works out of?"

"Well, no. He just said he worked for Henrico County as a police officer."

The officer let out a sigh of relief when he realized she was accusing one of Henrico County's finest and not one of the City of Richmond's finest.

"What is your relation to this person? And do you have a last name?"

"We were casual friends. I discontinued our friendship, and he wasn't too thrilled. His last name is Harris."

The officer scribbled on his pad. "Do you have an address, phone number, or any other information on Mr. Harris?"

"All I have is his cell phone number. Oh, and he drives a dark-colored Chevy Malibu, either dark blue or black. The last four numbers of his license plate are 4-9-2-1. I don't remember the letters, though."

"You remembered his license plate?"

"Well, I try to remember things like that when I meet a guy because you never know these days when you're single and out there meeting men."

The officer nodded in agreement. They both turned toward the front door when it opened and in bounced Coco.

"What the hell?" he exclaimed before noticing the officer standing with Skyy.

"Hey, Coco. Coco works here in the salon with me," she informed the police officer.

"Okay. I'm going to get an evidence kit from my car so I can collect the brick and take it back to the lab for fingerprints. I'll be back in a second."

Coco stood there motionless, staring at the gaping hole.

"I know, Coco. This is terrible."

"Terrible is not the word! First, I get two cancellations this morning, and now this? I'm not gonna make any money this weekend."

"I sure am glad you're concerned with my well-being," Skyy said sarcastically.

"You know what I mean. My two regulars are leaving early to go out of town for Christmas because of this snowstorm that's coming. Now I have to cancel the rest of my appointments for today because of this. Somebody, somewhere don't want Coco to get those pretty boots she's been asking Santa for." Coco sucked his teeth loudly.

"Coco, the world is not out to get you, honey. This is serious. I think Kelvin's crazy ass did this."

The officer entered, carrying a brown paper bag with a red seal and the word "EVIDENCE" printed across the front. He picked up the brick and placed it in the brown bag before sealing it. Skyy and Coco watched as he scribbled something on the front of the bag.

"Okay, I think this is all I need. I took some pictures of the damage in the front. Here's my card. If you think of anything else, give me a call. In the meantime, I will check out this lead and let you know what I find out."

"Thanks, Officer Gaines. I appreciate your help."

"Oh, by the way, there's a guy down the street who might be able to get that window boarded up for you until you can get it replaced." The officer scribbled a name and phone number down on a piece of his notebook paper, tore it off, and handed it to Skyy.

"Thank you so much."

"No problem. Have a good day. Make sure you get that window boarded up soon. You know snow is coming."

Skyy and Coco nodded and smiled politely as the officer left the salon. The cold draft from the window was sitting in the room like a block of ice.

"Coco, do me a favor. Can you call Tiff and tell her what happened? Need to at least try to catch her before she comes in."

"Ummm, excuse me, but I have to call my customers."

"Coco, can you just do that real quick so I can call this man about the window?"

He sucked his teeth and rolled his eyes before pulling his cell phone from his coat pocket. He tried Tiffany's cell phone number and her house number, but didn't get an answer. It was still early, so it was possible that Tiffany was still asleep. Coco left her a voicemail message and sent her a text explaining the situation at the salon. After leaving the message, he went over to Tiffany's station to see if her appointment calendar was somewhere in sight. There was a name scribbled beside 8:00 a.m., which meant Tiffany was supposed to be at work already.

"She has an early appointment. Let me try Niya to see if she has heard from her this morning," Coco said. He dialed Niya's cell. "Hey, Niya. Girllllll, you would not believe what is going on up in this shop this morning. Where's your cousin?" Coco listened for a few seconds before gasping loudly. "WHAT?!"

Skyy turned to stare at him, wondering what in the world could be wrong now. She continued to talk to the contractor that worked down the street, arranging for him to come to the salon to board the window up as soon as possible.

"You have got to be kidding! Uh-huh … uh-huh … uh-huh … oh my God!"

Finishing up her call, Skyy focused her attention on Coco's conversation. Coco put up his index finger, an indication for her to wait a moment and he would spill the story.

"Well, I'm so sorry to hear that. I knew Trey was no good. I can't believe Tiffany let herself get caught up." Coco raised his eyebrows, emphasizing his words so Skyy would understand the root cause of the situation was Trey.

"Keep me posted. I'll let her customers know she won't be in today. Talk to you later,"

Coco said, ending the call.

"What happened to Tiffany?"

"Girl, Ms. Tiffany got herself arrested by the FBI."

"WHAT?!" Skyy yelled.

"Yes, honey. Remember when she was here a couple of weeks ago and had that little meltdown? Well, she told me that she was in really deep with some sort of scam with Trey and couldn't get out."

"What type of scam?"

Coco tightened his scarf around his neck. It was so cold in the salon that it felt as if they were standing outside.

"The guy is coming to board up the window in about thirty minutes. Do you want to go in the office until he comes? We can keep the door open so we can hear him and any customers. Come on."

Skyy led the way to her office. Once inside, she sat in her office seat, while Coco sat in the chair closest to the door. He situated himself so he had full view of the front door.

"Did you lock the door?" Coco asked.

"Yeah, it's locked. Come on, tell me what happened."

"Well, Trey has been 'allegedly' running some sort of Medicaid scam with medical supplies."

"Huh?"

"You know the medical supply store on the Boulevard?"

"Hmmm, I don't think so."

"It's about two stores over from the beauty supply store. Anyway, Trey and Tiffany owned the store. They turned in all of these fake Medicaid claims and got money from the government for products they never actually delivered. The FBI has been investigating them for a couple of months and finally busted both of them this morning."

"Are you serious?"

"Yes, honey. Niya couldn't give me the whole story, but basically, Tiffany was hooked up with someone at the clinic where she got names and social security numbers of Medicaid participants. What they did was submit these bogus claims under these people's names and got big money. They never actually delivered any of the supplies they filed claims on."

"Coco, stop lying."

"I'm telling you what Niya just told me. I'm mad that I thought Trey was a street thug. That nigga has the nerve to be a white-collar thug. I'm scared of him." Coco twisted his neck overdramatically and crossed his arms.

Skyy looked at Coco in amazement, wondering how Tiffany let Trey pull her in as deep as he did. No wonder she had a hard time cutting ties with him. Not only did they have a son together, but they were in criminal matrimony, as well. Tiffany probably felt like there was no way out of it. Skyy shook her head in disappointment.

"Poor Tiffany. She's so young. Damn."

They sat there in silence, neither of them knowing what to say, probably a first for Coco. The knock on the door broke the awkward silence, and they both jumped up simultaneously.

"Who is it?" Skyy asked Coco.

"I don't know."

Skyy rushed past Coco, hoping it was the contractor. As she got closer to the door, she could see paint-stained dungarees and a plaid flannel lumberjack coat. Skyy unlocked the door and got a full view of the contractor, who had propped a large piece of plywood against the building and had a toolbox at his feet.

"Hi, I'm Jeff. Here to fix your window."

"Hi, Jeff. I'm Skyy. Nice to meet you. Do you need to come inside or will you be doing everything outside?"

"I'll need access to the inside, too."

"Okay, no problem. I'm a bit paranoid leaving the door unlocked. I need to go to my office, so if you need anything, just yell. Okay?"

"No problem." The contractor flashed a set of crooked, coffee-stained teeth. He smelled like he'd just finished a pack of Marlboro 100's right before coming into the salon.

Coco looked him up and down before returning to the office. He didn't bother speaking to the contractor, who seemed to ignore Coco just the same. The contractor started immediately with boarding up the window, and the hammering seemed to echo throughout the entire building.

"Coco, looks like it's just you and me. First, it was Debi, and now Tiffany. I can't afford to lose any more people." Uncertainty dripped from Skyy's words.

"Don't you worry about a thing. I'm not going anywhere. You got my word on that, sistah."

Skyy smiled at her friend. Throughout it all, Coco was always there for her, always had her back. Whether Skyy realized it or not, Coco was her everything—best friend, confidante, protector—all wrapped up in a pretty designer package. Without Coco, she wouldn't have anyone, and Skyy realized it at that moment. He never hesitated to drop what he was doing to come to Skyy's aid, and he would kill a rock over her. Skyy could feel tears welling up in her eyes.

"What's wrong?" Coco asked.

"You're always there for me. I love you so much, Coco, and you know that I don't do much loving. But, you? My heart is all yours."

Coco put his hand to his chest before walking over to hug Skyy. "Oh, Honey Bunches of Oats, I love you, too. You know that. What's with all the waterworks, though? That's so unlike you."

"I just feel like my life might be falling apart. For so long, I've been able to live my life and be the person I wanted to be. No boundaries, you know? But, it's like a black cloud has decided to follow me around. Bad karma or something."

"Chile, please. Listen, you and I, we are a lot alike. We don't let broken windows and empty booths put a damper on us. We sweep up the glass, put an ad on Craigslist, and keep it moving. You know what I'm saying?"

Skyy chuckled.

"I'm so serious, Skyy. All this is just a test. But, you're strong. Don't let this knock you down."

"Oh, Coco, I wish it were that simple. I play a good looking game, but trust me, I'm not as strong as you."

"Au contraire, mademoiselle. You *are* as strong as me. Any woman who has no family, living on borrowed companionship, struts through this world alone, but lets it all roll off her back like water on baby-oiled skin, has to have the strength of a bull. Skyy, you approach the world like it's your oyster, getting out of it what you want and only what you want."

"Okay. First, you speak French; then, you philosophize. You're something else, Coco."

"I know this."

They both laughed. The hammering in the front of the salon was not as loud now, which meant the contractor must have been doing some of his work outside.

"But, in all seriousness, Skyy, you're the woman I long to be in my next lifetime. I hope to have your courage and strength one day."

Skyy shook her head. "No, uh-uh. Don't put me on a pedestal. You have no idea what I am, who I am."

"I know enough."

"Yeah, well, if you knew it all, you would probably think differently."

Coco sat on the desk in an attempt to stay within arm's reach of Skyy. He was hoping she would finally open up about her silent past.

"Well, tell me then, Skyy. Tell me all about it."

Skyy hit the power button on her computer, ignoring him.

"We need to come up with a plan of action, Coco. I need to place an ad on Craigslist for a nail tech."

Coco watched as Skyy focused all of her attention on the computer. Just like that, she'd shut him out again.

Chapter 19

The year 2010 came in with a bang, and Skyy was more than happy that the holidays were officially over. The last few weeks had been pretty trying, and she'd been doing some soul searching. She was still looking for a nail technician, and Debi's chair was also still empty. January would be the first full month where she would only be pulling in Coco's booth rent. All remaining financial obligations were Skyy's responsibility.

It was Sunday, clean up day at the salon. While awaiting Coco's arrival, Skyy sat at her office desk, looking through the bills and clicking the computer keys. She went into her personal savings account and transferred some money to her business account, giving herself a little cushion. At this stage of the game, she was glad she did a good job of saving money, especially the money that J had been giving to her. She was sitting on a nice stack, which would help her out at least until she had her salon fully staffed again.

While continuing to pay her bills online, there was a loud knock at the salon door. Since it was early, she thought maybe Coco forgot his key. She made her way to the door, and as she got closer, she noticed the shadow of a police hat. Peeking through the blinds, she recognized the police officer who took her report when the salon was vandalized a couple of weeks back. Skyy unlocked the door for the officer.

"Good morning, Ms. Armfield. Remember me?"

"Yes, I do, Officer . . . ?"

"Gaines."

"Yes, Officer Gaines. Can I help you?"

"Can I come in and talk to you for a second?"

"Sure." Skyy opened the door wider, letting the officer in, and then locked the door behind him before taking a seat on the sofa in the waiting area.

The officer appeared a bit concerned and uneasy. He removed his hat and rubbed his fingers around the edges of it.

"What is it?" Skyy asked, noticing the officer's uneasiness.

"Well, I just wanted to come by to see if you got your window taken care of and to make sure you didn't have any more incidents."

Skyy looked at the officer. She could tell he was lying. "No, I haven't had any more problems. I got the window fixed a couple of days after it was broken. I appreciate your concern, though."

The officer looked down at his hat as if it was something foreign to him.

"Is there anything else?" Skyy asked.

"Actually, there is. I checked with the Henrico County police department, City of Richmond, as well as the Chesterfield County police department, and none of them have an officer by the name of Kelvin Harris. Are you sure this Kelvin person was a police officer?"

"That's what he told me. He said he worked for Henrico County as a police officer. He even went as far as to discuss some of his cases with me."

"Did you ever see him in uniform or in a patrol car?"

"No, I never saw him on the days that he worked. He only came around on his days off. His Chevy Malibu looked just like an off-duty police cruiser. And you checked Kelvin? Not Kevin, but Kel-vin, right?"

"Yes, I specifically asked them to check on a Kelvin Harris, just like you told me. I checked and double-checked, but came up empty. None of them knew of this person. Is it possible he could be using an alias or something?"

"At this point, Officer Gaines, anything is possible. This scares me, though. I mean, if he wasn't really an officer, then hell, he could've lied about his name, too."

"That's why I wanted to come over to tell you in person. I know you did the restraining order against him, but you should know if that isn't his real name, the restraining order is useless."

Skyy rubbed her temples. Even though she hadn't heard from Kelvin in weeks, it still made her nervous that she really didn't know who he was or what he was capable of doing. Skyy hid her fear behind a brave face.

"I appreciate your concern, and I thank you for all of your help. I guess he felt like he needed to lie to impress me. I haven't heard from him in almost a month, so I think it's safe to say he has moved on."

"Are you sure you're okay? Do you need me to keep an eye on this place for you? Our precinct is right around the street from here."

"I think I will be just fine. I'm sure he has the message now."

The officer placed his hat back on his head carefully. "Do you still have my number?"

"I sure do. It's on my desk." Skyy stood up to walk the officer to the door.

"Feel free to call me anytime if you notice anything suspicious." Before turning toward the door, the officer tipped his hat like someone from a 1940s western movie.

"I will. Thanks again for the information."

Skyy unlocked the door, letting the officer out. She immediately locked the door behind him before heading back to her office. Her stomach was in knots. Unbeknownst to the officer, Skyy felt very uneasy about Kelvin and his apparent lie. She knew Kelvin was a bit crazy, but now it appeared he was more psychotic than she thought.

Skyy looked at her BlackBerry, anticipating whether or not she should call J and accept his offer for a trip to Miami. Getting away from Richmond for a couple of days could do her a world of good. She dialed his number, looking at her watch to see what time it was. Noticing it was not quite ten o'clock on a Sunday morning meant it probably was not a good idea to call J right then. He was probably having breakfast with his kids and his wife.

She decided to send him a simple response to his text message from the night before. 'OK.' It was simple and discreet. She pressed send. Before she could put the BlackBerry down on the desk, it vibrated. J's quick reply made Skyy smile.

"Hello?"

"Hey, gurl. Wassup?"

"Nothing much. What's up with you?"

"On the way to the studio. Need to go and handle a little business today."

"Always working."

"Somebody gotta do it. So, you trying to meet me in Miami? I was trying to get you down there for the weekend."

"Oh. Well, maybe next time then."

"How about this weekend coming up?"

"That's okay. I was really trying to get away today. I have a lot going on up here, and I just needed a mental break."

"What's going on, gurl? Talk to me."

"Too much going on, J. My salon was vandalized, I had a guy stalking me, and I lost two of my employees. Major drama."

"Damn, gurl. Sounds like you need me right now."

"It's fine. I'll be alright."

"No. How about I come up there? You know, stay with you for a couple of days."

Skyy thought about it. Inviting J to stay with her for a couple of days could lead to him expecting to stay with her on more occasions. Even though J was a celebrity, he was also a man, a man who really wanted Skyy.

"You can't do that, J."

"Come on now. You know I can do whatever I want to do. I can be up there in no time. All you have to do is say the word."

Skyy thought long and hard. What she really wanted was a trip. Being holed up in her house for a couple of days was not her idea of a stress reliever. The only good thing that could come out of a visit from J would be a nice deposit into her bank account. That would come in handy, though, since the salon was understaffed.

J had never been to Skyy's house. Sure, he knew where she lived because he mailed her packages all the time, but she'd never invited him to stay with her at her place. They always met up in hotels. Keeping her home as her private domain was Skyy's way of not falling into the same trap she saw her mother in. Once you allowed a man access to your home, especially a married man, things somehow seemed unfair. They know everything about you at that point, while you, on the other hand, only have a name and a phone number. Kelvin had also taught Skyy a valuable lesson, even though she never officially invited him to her home. The difference with J was that he lived in Atlanta, so it wasn't like he could do a lot of unannounced visits. This rationale helped with Skyy's decision. As tough as she tried to be, the situation with Kelvin had her uneasy. So, having a constant male presence for a couple of days could help if Kelvin decided to stop by unexpectedly. Then again, she was also worried about Coco coming over and J's cover being blown. She battled with her decision and finally made a choice.

"Okay, you can come up for a visit."

"See, that's what I'm talkin' 'bout. Spendin' some time with my gurl. How about I come up tonight, stay this week, and then we can fly out to Miami on Friday?"

"All week?"

"Damn, Skyy, do you want me to come up there or not? One minute, you got a nigga thinkin' you wanna be with him. Then the next minute, you trippin' and shit."

"J, I want to spend time with you, but I don't want to send you the wrong message."

"Look, I'm coming up there, you gonna cook for me, treat me like a king, and I'm gonna treat you like a queen. We can play house for a minute. I can use a break."

"Play house? Oh hell naw! Never mind," Skyy joked.

"Gurl, you know you want me up there with you. I can hear it in your voice. Let me take care of a few things here first. I'll be up there around eleven tonight. I should be able to go unnoticed if I get there late. Have it ready for me."

"J, you do know I have to work while you're here, right?"

"Naw, you not working this week. Cancel all of your appointments. I got you straight."

"I can't just cancel all of my customers. Didn't you hear me say I'm short on employees as it is? I need to handle my business."

"Okay, okay, I'll let you work. I can do some work while you're working. That's cool. I gotta run. I'll call you right before I fly out."

"Do you need me to pick you up from the airport or anything?" Skyy asked.

"Naw, I'll get my assistant to arrange everything for me. I told you, all you have to do is have it ready for me. I'll see you later."

"Okay."

They ended their call, and Skyy felt some relief knowing J would be there for security. She didn't know if she would be able to put up with him for five days in the confines of her home, but seeing as though she would get a little cash and a nice weekend getaway out of the deal, she was willing to put forth the effort.

The sound of the front door opening captured Skyy's attention. The only person it could be was Coco, who was later than usual for Sunday cleanup duty.

"Diva!" he yelled.

"I'm back here. I'll be out there in a second."

Skyy stopped dead in her tracks when she saw Shamar, the private investigator, standing behind Coco. Immediately, she realized she never got around to calling him.

"Hello, Ms. Armfield. I'm still waiting on that phone call."

"Yes, Ms. Armfield, he's still waiting on that phone call," Coco mimicked.

"Coco, do you mind? I'm sorry . . . Shamar, right?"

"Yes. You promised me a call. I really need to talk to you."

"I know you do, and I'm so sorry I haven't called you yet."

"Well, what about now? Is now a good time to talk?"

Coco stood near his station pretending to be cleaning, but listening to Skyy and Shamar's conversation on the sly. Skyy looked over at him with her hands on her hips, realizing what he was doing.

"What?" Coco asked, knowing good and well why Skyy was staring at him.

"Shamar, let's go to my office." Skyy closed the door to her office and sat in the chair behind her desk. "Please have a seat."

Shamar unzipped his down-filled coat, removed his knit hat, and made himself comfortable in the chair. Skyy's chest tightened, scared of what Shamar wanted to know about her past, but anxious to get the questioning over and done with.

"So, you said before you had to ask me some questions. Ask away."

Shamar pulled a small notepad from his inside coat pocket, flipping several pages before reading.

"First off, I need to know if your real name is Skylar Armstrong."

"Yes, it is, but I changed my name a long time ago."

"Were you born in Baltimore, Maryland, on March 15, 1973?"

"Yes."

"Mother's name Sharon Armstrong?"

"Yes."

"Well, I think I have someone who wants to meet you."

"Look, Shamar. My mother died when I was fourteen. I was an only child. I don't know where my father is because, quite frankly, he wasn't around for me to know. My mother was an only child. So, no one else in Baltimore could possibly be looking for me."

"I'm not so sure about that."

"Well, I am. I answered your questions. What else do you need?"

"I need to bring my client to meet you."

"What client? Did you hear anything I've said to you?"

"Yes, and based on your answers, I'm pretty sure I have the right person."

"The right person for what? Shamar, really, I left Baltimore because I didn't want to be there. I wanted to get away from that life. I started my life over here almost twenty years ago and never looked back."

"You don't understand, Ms. Armstrong. I . . ."

"It's Ms. Armfield! Haven't you heard a word I've said?"

"Yes, but I'm pretty certain you would want to meet this person."

Skyy sighed heavily. Shamar refused to get it through his thick head that she did not want to go back to her past—period.

"Why? I just told you . . ."

"I know, I know, but this person has been looking for you and wants to see you."

Skyy's eyes got as big as melons. Could it be? It couldn't be.

"Is it my father?" Skyy asked.

"I'm sorry, I can't say. My client wants to disclose everything. My job was to track you down and confirm your identity. When can I bring him to see you?"

"Him? It must be my father."

Shamar smirked, but he still was not going to tell Skyy anything. "Like I told you before, my client wants to reveal his identity. When do you think I can bring him to meet you?"

Skyy thought long and hard. J would be at her house that night and staying through the week, so she wouldn't have any free time at home this week. That weekend they would be in Miami, so the weekend was shot, too.

"Well, this week is not good because I have company coming in from out of town tonight and staying until next week. What about next week?"

"Next week won't work. My client has an irregular work schedule. He works fourteen days straight, weekends included, before he gets a weekend off. Since you're not available this weekend, the next weekend he's off would be . . ." Shamar touched the screen on his BlackBerry, opening his calendar to check the date. "The weekend of February 13th. Oh wait, that's Valentine's Day weekend. I'm sure you have special plans that weekend."

Skyy chuckled at Shamar's obvious attempt to flirt with her.

"Actually, Shamar, I don't have any plans for Valentine's Day, but don't let me mess up *your* plans."

"Who said I have plans?"

"Come on, Shamar. A nice-looking brother like yourself, I'm sure you have a lady tucked away in Baltimore."

Shamar shook his head, flashing a boyish smile.

"Nobody?" Skyy asked.

"Nobody," he echoed.

"That's a shame." *A real shame,* Skyy thought to herself. *If only he was married, I could be his somebody.*

"So, do we want to set something up for Saturday, February 13th?"

"Sure. Let's plan to meet at . . . hmmmm, say seven o'clock? I should be finished working by then. Do you want to meet me here or somewhere else?" Skyy asked.

"We can meet here. Sure you won't stand me up again?" Shamar asked.

"You say that like we're having a date or something," Skyy responded.

"We can have a date. That's up to you."

Skyy stared at Shamar. His smooth chocolate skin enticed her, and his lips were inviting, especially when he smiled.

"I don't think so. I mean, how far could a date with me go? You live in Baltimore; I live here in Richmond. Besides, I'm sure you're looking for a nice woman to settle down with, someone to have your kids and grow old with. I'm not her."

"How do you know that?" Shamar stood up and moved closer to Skyy, taking a seat on the corner of her desk, bringing the scent of mint, lavender, orange blossom, and woods with him, compliments of his Jean Paul Gaultier cologne. The smell was alluring.

"Shamar, let's keep this strictly business. I'm not that girl. I promise you."

"We'll see about that. All it takes is for you to be still for a minute."

Not sure what he meant by his comment, Skyy gave him an odd look.

"Skyy, I've been trying to talk to you for months, but you haven't stayed still long enough to find out what life-changing information I have to share with you. Anything can happen to you and for you, if you'd just be still."

His tone was cunning, but Skyy knew this man was off limits to her. She couldn't give him what he wanted or what he needed. For a split second, she had a vision of their bodies intertwined, pulsating to a rhythm all their own. Yet, there was nothing she could do but dream of Shamar. He was a single man, too convenient, too needy, and definitely too clingy.

"I guess, but only if I allow it to happen. Well, I have you on my calendar for Saturday, February 13th at seven o'clock. Don't be late."

Skyy stood up, now looking directly into his eyes. She didn't know where the strong attraction resonated from, but there was something about him that made her heart flutter. They stared at each other in silence for what seemed to be an eternity, until Skyy finally turned away and headed for the door. The heat on the back of her neck was rising, and her hands were sweaty. This man actually made her nervous. Shamar walked behind her coolly, and before Skyy could open the door, his hand was already on the doorknob.

This caused his body to touch hers, and his breath moved across her neck.

"Let me get that for you," Shamar said.

Skyy purposefully leaned her body back into his as he opened the door. "Thank you," she said shyly.

"I'll see you soon. By the way, can I get your cell number? You know, to call you in case something comes up?"

Skyy already knew Shamar had the number to the salon, but she gave him her cell number anyway. Shamar created a contact for her in his BlackBerry while they stood there in the hallway. Then they shared another awkward stare for a few moments.

"Okay, take care." Shamar zipped up his coat and put his hat on his head, bracing for the bone-chilling temperature outside.

"You, too."

He walked ahead while Skyy stayed in the hallway. Her armpits were soaked, the back of her shirt was wet, and her ears burned. She waited for Shamar to exit before joining Coco in the front of the salon.

"Well, finally! What is the big secret with this private eye, or should I say private dick?"

"Coco! Watch your mouth!"

"What? You know that's what they used to call private detectives back in the day. You need to study your history."

Skyy shook her head, laughing at her friend. "You're crazy as hell. I'll tell you about it later."

Just like that, Coco was shut out again.

Chapter 20

The sun hid behind the clouds as light snow began to fall. Daylight was dissipating, leaving a grayish color in the atmosphere. The air was cold, and the wind moved the snow around wildly. Skyy was excited that the snow started in just enough time for her and Coco to finish their customers for the day. She was on her way to the store to make sure she had enough food stocked for her week with J since they wouldn't be able to go out in public together, at least not in Richmond. When she wasn't working, Skyy spent a lot of time cooking. It was the least she could do. J had done a lot for her financially, so it wouldn't hurt her to cook for him during his visit. Keeping up with him in the bedroom for a week would be a different story, though.

Skyy tightened her scarf around her neck in an attempt to keep the cold air out. She wished she had a hat with her because it was unbearably cold. The snowflakes were getting bigger. There was a winter warning in effect for the city and surrounding counties, and the weatherman had predicated up to ten inches of snow. Skyy forgot about that when she suggested J come and stay with her. The winter weather would result in numerous cancellations, especially from her customers. The parking lot at Krogers was packed with people scurrying about to stock up on bread and milk for the upcoming snowstorm. Skyy felt her BlackBerry vibrating in her coat pocket. She pulled in a parking space carefully before answering J's call.

"Hey."

"Hey, gurl. I have a problem. The company I normally use for my charted flights just called and said my two guys are stranded in DC. Apparently, there's a big snowstorm that hit up there today, and they can't get out."

"What? Oh no!" Skyy said.

"Yeah, so I probably won't be able to get there until tomorrow morning, unless Richmond gets hit. If that happens, then it will probably be later."

Skyy sighed heavily. She was looking forward to J coming to stay with her, especially after the news the police officer had shared with her earlier. For some reason, she had a bad feeling about being alone. Not that Kelvin had made any attempts to contact her recently, but the fact remained he wasn't the person that Skyy thought he was. In addition, since he had been lying about being an officer, there was no telling what else he was lying about.

"That's okay. I'll be at home. Just call me as soon as you're ready to fly out so I can be on the lookout for you."

The line beeped, alerting Skyy that she had another call coming in. She looked at the screen, noticing a 410 area code. Immediately, she knew who it was, and little butterflies fluttered in her stomach.

"J, I have to get this other line. It's one of my customers. Call me later tonight, okay?"

"Okay. Later." J hung up abruptly, a little pissed off that Skyy was dismissing him.

"Hello?" Skyy answered.

"Hey, Skyy. It's Shamar."

"Hi. What's up? You calling to reschedule already?" Skyy said.

"Ha! No. Actually, I was calling to see what you were doing. The weather is pretty bad in Maryland right now, so I decided to stay here in Richmond another night until the snowstorm passes over. So, are you still expecting company this evening?"

An instant smile appeared on Skyy's face. Shamar's timing couldn't be more perfect.

"Actually, there's been a change of plans. The weather sort of delayed my guest."

"Really? Well, I was wondering if we could do dinner. I mean, something quick before the weather gets too bad. My treat."

Skyy looked at the digital clock on her dashboard. It wasn't quite six o'clock yet. Her first instinct was to speed out of the parking lot to hurry home to meet Shamar. However, she knew she needed to stock up on food for when J would eventually arrive.

"I'm at the store now picking up a few things. I could just fix us something at my house, get us some wine. How does that sound?"

"Sounds great. What's your address?"

"7430 Winterstock Place. Do you need directions?"

"No, I can put it in my GPS. What time?"

"Let's say about 8:30. That'll give me enough time to get home, start dinner, and freshen up."

"Okay. I'll see you then."

Skyy turned off the engine and joined the throngs of people in the grocery store vying for food as if it was the last day on earth. Normally, Skyy would be agitated by it all, but for some reason, the thought of seeing Shamar again made her smile. J's delay was truly a blessing in disguise as far as she was concerned. Not that she planned to take things far with Shamar. She just wanted that feeling again, the feeling she had in the salon earlier that day. She couldn't really explain it, but she liked it. It was a safe feeling, and since J wouldn't be able to make it that evening, Shamar could provide her the protection she felt she needed.

Going over her mental grocery list, Skyy threw fresh vegetables and fruits in her basket from the produce section. She grabbed a couple of loaves of French bread from the bakery, deciding to prepare some sort of pasta dish with a tossed salad. Given her time restraints, it would be quick and easy. She wished she had time to make her famous homemade German chocolate cake, but since she didn't, she opted for the bakery version. Passing the aisle of tomato sauces and pastas, she grabbed a box of tortellini noodles, marina sauce, Alfredo sauce, and the other ingredients she needed for her cheesy tortellini bake. Up and down the aisles she went, throwing items into her basket for the week, but concentrating mainly on her dinner she would prepare for Shamar. On the wine aisle, Skyy selected several bottles of Moscato and took her time selecting a red wine for tonight's dinner. She opted for a bottle of 2008 Pinot Rose.

By the time she got through the line, the parking lot and her car were covered with snow. She couldn't wait to get home and out of the bad weather. The wipers moved the soft snow to the corners of the windshield. Skyy blew warm air into her fists to help warm her hands after loading the bags into the car. After searching through her tote, glove compartment, and even her coat pockets for her favorite Burberry gloves, she came up empty. Then she remembered leaving them in the pocket of her wool coat, which she wore during dinner with Davin a few days earlier. Once the car warmed up, she eased slowly from the parking lot, trying to make sure she had adequate traction under her tires to avoid slipping and sliding. Luckily for her, she lived only about ten minutes away, so she would be home in no time.

*   *   *

The garage door moved up slowly, and Skyy pulled her car inside. Even though the inside of the garage was cold, it was not half as cold as it was outside. It would be easier for her to unload her bags without having to fight against the elements. Several short, loud beeps sounded from the alarm system before Skyy entered her code to disarm it. She dropped a few bags on the kitchen table and then went back to the car to fill her arms up again. Since the garage was so cold, she decided to line up the bottles of wine against the wall, where the wine would stay at just the right temperature. She put the food that required refrigeration in the refrigerator, leaving the other items on the counter until she had a chance to take off her coat and put on her house slippers. She made sure she got her cell phone from her coat pocket and put it on the counter so she would hear it in case Shamar tried calling her.

Looking at the clock, it was just about seven, which meant she had an hour and a half to freshen up and have dinner ready. Grabbing a stainless steel pot, which hung conveniently from the rack above the kitchen island, Skyy filled it with water and turned the fire on the front eye of the range. While she waited for the water to boil, she decided to take a quick shower so she could take her time with the meal. Walking through her living room, she turned on her CD player, allowing Mary J Blige's "Stronger" to blast through the speakers. Entering each room, Skyy turned on the lights, bringing the house to life. She hummed to Mary J's voice, which provided her therapy for the situation at hand. Skyy was still a bit uneasy about Kelvin not being a police officer, and she thought about the time he appeared at her house unannounced. She wondered how he found out where she lived if he wasn't really an officer. Skyy tried to push the troubling thoughts from her mind and concentrate on her evening with Shamar.

The dual showerheads warmed up quickly, causing steam to fill the bathroom. Skyy undressed swiftly, placing her designer jeans in the hamper. While stepping into the shower, she pulled her hair up into a ponytail, letting a bit of water dampen her hair so she could brush it back easily when she got out. The corner shelves were filled with various Victoria's Secret body washes and body sponges. She decided to try her newest body wash, Secret Garden, allowing the smell of vanilla and coconut to permeate the air.

After washing vigorously in all the right places, Skyy grabbed an oversized towel to dry off. Wrapping the towel around her body, Skyy headed back to her bedroom and looked through her drawer for a Victoria's Secret cotton sleepshirt that she would throw on while she cooked. She would then get dressed when dinner was just about done. Before heading back to the kitchen, she sat on the edge of her bed, applying lotion to her legs and feet. As she squirted more lotion into her hands to rub on her arms, she was startled by the chime of the doorbell. The clock on her nightstand read 7:34 p.m. Shamar was an hour early. But, with the snowstorm cranking up, Skyy figured he wanted to get to her house before it got too bad. She slipped her feet into her fuzzy slippers and headed to the door. She would have to put him in the living room with a bottle of wine while she got dressed.

"I'm coming!" Skyy yelled, turning down the music on her way to the door. When she looked through the peephole, all she could see were red roses. *Wow, that was nice of him,* she thought to herself.

She unlocked the door and sheer terror filled her face. Before there was time to react, the impact of the vase smashing against her head was so hard that Skyy fell to the floor.

Chapter 21

Skyy gained consciousness. Feeling confused and dazed, she blinked several times in an effort to focus her eyes, but soon she realized she was taped to one of her brand-new chairs in the dining room. Kelvin was smacking her face, trying to help her come to. It took her a minute before she remembered being knocked over the head, caught off guard as she opened the door thinking it was Shamar with roses.

"Kelvin? What are you doing?"

"What am I doing? Oh, you know what I'm doing."

Kelvin pulled a .38 semi-automatic from his waistband. Skyy's eyes tripled in size at the sight of the gun. She knew Kelvin was upset with her, but she had no idea he was this upset. Nausea started to set in, and her chest tightened. On top of that, the knot on her forehead throbbed, and she had an intense headache.

"I came to get what's due to me. You owe me big time."

"Please, this is not right! Please don't do this!" Skyy shrieked.

Tears mixed with mascara streamed down her face, looking as if someone had thrown black watercolor paint on her. She squirmed a bit, trying to loosen her hands that were taped behind her. Her feet were duct-taped to the legs of an oversized dining room chair that belonged to the oversized oak table she had received as a gift. The tag, which was still attached to the brand-new Thomasville set, scratched her bare leg as she struggled for freedom. Ironically, Skyy had bigger worries than the tag on the chair.

"Don't do this? Don't do this? You started this! What made you think you could just play me like this? Huh? Huh? You think this is a joke? This is not a fucking joke!" Kelvin said, waving his .38 semi-automatic in Skyy's face.

"I'm sorry! I'm so sorry!" Skyy cried.

"You're not sorry. You're scared. If I didn't have this gun in my hand, you would be singing another tune. What was that you told me? Leave you the fuck alone? Was that it? You think you can go and put a restraining order on me?" He rubbed the barrel of the gun around the outline of Skyy's mouth. "You think you can leave me? You can't fuckin' leave me. You owe me. If I can't have you, nobody can."

"What do you want from me? I'm sorry. I'll do what you want me to do. Just please, please put the gun down, and let's talk about it."

"Oh no, you're not sorry, but it don't matter 'cause you fuckin' owe me. You don't care about me. You've never cared about me. Your whole life you've walked around like you're the shit, queen of the fuckin' world. But guess what? Tonight . . . tonight, you're gonna pay for everything. Everything!" he yelled.

Skyy wasn't sure what his plan was, but she was afraid. Kelvin didn't look the same. He had a sick, demented look about him. He reeked of alcohol, and the whites of his eyes were red. It was obvious to Skyy that Kelvin was drunk and high on something. Since she had been put on notice about him and the fact that he wasn't a police officer, she was even more terrified.

"Kelvin, please, we can talk about this. Tell me what you want me to do. Talk to me, please!"

Kelvin put the gun to Skyy's temple and leaned in closely so she could feel his breath on the side of her face. Skyy gasped loudly.

"Talk about this? Talk about this? There is nothing to talk about. You have ruined my life! My entire life has been ruined all because of you, you nasty, trifling bitch!"

"I don't understand what you want me to do. I will do anything, just please, put the gun down," Skyy sobbed, continuing to plead for her life.

Her arms were starting to hurt from being secured behind her, and her stomach ached from the anxiety she was feeling. Even though she'd broken things off with Kelvin, she had no idea it affected him this way. She was going over and over in her mind what she might've said or done to push him over the edge. Kelvin paced the floor erratically, mumbling to himself. Evidently, Skyy had underestimated Kelvin's mental state, and she feared for her life. She tried to stay quiet, but it was hard for her to contain her sobs. After about five minutes of pacing back and forth, Kelvin stopped in his tracks. He turned and looked at Skyy with a dark, evil stare. The look on his face was demonic and nothing like the handsome person Skyy had gotten to know.

"Skylar. I love Skylar. That's what he told my mother. Skylar. Skylar. Motherfucking Skylar!"

Skyy struggled for breath. She looked at Kelvin in horror. How did he know that was her name? Skyy had buried that name a long time ago.

"Kelvin, what are you talking about?" Skyy asked.

"Don't play stupid with me. I know who you are, Skylar Armstrong. But you don't know who I am, do you? Well, let me tell you who I am. On March 23, 1991, my life changed forever. My daddy came home and told my mother that he was leaving us. Know why? Because he loved Skylar, Skylar Armstrong."

"Kelvin, I don't . . ."

"Shut the fuck up and listen to me! You ruined my life! Because of you, my mother and my daddy are dead."

Skyy hung her head low. She sobbed uncontrollably because standing in front of her was a byproduct of the past that she had put way behind her and locked away. She always knew Kelvin's eyes looked very familiar to her, but she could never put her finger on it. The more she looked at him, the more she realized who he was. She never talked about her past to anyone. In fact, she had changed her name in an effort to get away from it. But, now, she was forced to revisit it along with its painful details.

"Kelvin, who are you?" Skyy asked the question, but she already knew. At least she thought she knew who it was, but she wanted him to tell her just to be sure.

"Is it coming to you? Huh? You putting the pieces together? Okay, let me give you some more. My daddy is, or should I say was, Chaz Donaldson Sr. Does that name ring a bell to you?"

"Oh my God . . . oh my God Jesus."

"Yeah, call on Him. You're going to be with Him soon," Kelvin said.

"Kelvin, I don't know what you want me to do. I didn't kill your parents. I, I didn't . . ."

Kelvin hit the right side of Skyy's face with the butt of his gun, and she shrieked loudly.

"Shut up! Shut the fuck up! You don't get to speak until I tell you to!"

Skyy's face throbbed like a toothache. She could feel it starting to swell.

"Because of you, Skylar, my daddy came home one day and told my mother that he didn't love her anymore. He said he was leaving us to be with you. But, my mother, she wouldn't let him leave. She told him if he left, she would kill herself right there in front of him. They argued. They fought. I stood in the shadows and watched them. They didn't know I was there. I was supposed to be next door at my friend's house. But, I came home to get my football. They never saw me there. They continued to argue. And then, then, the last words I heard my daddy say was 'I love Skylar'. That's what he said. I don't know where my mother got the gun from, but she aimed it at him and pulled the trigger. I watched my daddy fall to the ground right beside his suitcase. I stood there, frozen in my spot. I couldn't speak, couldn't move. She put the gun to her head and pulled the trigger. Just like that, they were both gone."

"Oh God, oh God, please! I'm so sorry. Please, oh God!" Skyy cried.

Kelvin whacked her across the face again. The sting intensified and Skyy screamed.

"Because of you, my life has been a living hell. My mother and father were the only family I had, did you know that? No siblings, no aunts or uncles, nobody. So guess what happened to me? They put me in a foster home where my foster father thought it would be good to put his dick in my mouth every night. By the time I was ten, he was fucking me in the ass. Nobody listened to me. I didn't have anywhere else to go. Can't you see? I've been fucked up all my life because of you. All of this happened because of you."

Skyy shook her head and continued to cry. It was all coming together for her. Kelvin was the little boy that was left an orphan eighteen years earlier because of the murder-suicide committed by his mother. At the time, Skyy a.k.a. Skylar was a seventeen-year-old high school junior who'd been having an affair with her high school English teacher, Mr. Donaldson, Kelvin's father. Skyy and Mr. Donaldson fell in love, or at least that's what they both thought it was, and Mr. Donaldson vowed to be with Skyy. However, Mr. Donaldson's wife refused to let him go. She meant what she said when she told him if she couldn't have him, nobody could. And with that sentiment, she blew his brains out right before blowing out her own. What Skyy didn't know was that Mr. Donaldson's eight-year-old son watched the whole thing happen. He carried that resentment around for eighteen years, vowing he would find Skyy and make her pay for destroying his family as well as his life.

"Kelvin . . ."

"Just call me C.J. Kelvin is the name that bastard foster father gave me. I prefer C.J."

"C.J., I am so sorry about what happened to your mother and father, but you cannot blame me. I was not there. I didn't pull the trigger."

Kelvin swung his arm across the breakfast bar, causing Skyy's grocery bags and oversized clear vase filled with marbles and fake foliage to fall to the ground. The sound of the marbles hitting the hardwood floor seemed to echo throughout the kitchen and dining room where they were. Kelvin had moved a chair from the formal dining room, which was adjacent to the kitchen, and had Skyy sitting in the area that connected the two rooms.

Skyy's face throbbed from the numerous hits she had endured over the past thirty minutes. She looked down at the front of her shirt and noticed her mouth was bleeding. Skyy was confident that Kelvin was going to kill her. There was no question about it. The whole relationship was a farce, all just a way for him to get close enough to her to gain her trust. Kelvin tracked her down and stalked her with the intent of getting revenge.

She watched as Kelvin unbuttoned his shirt and threw it on the floor. The gun was conveniently placed on the counter, only about two feet away from him. Not that Skyy had any sort of opportunity to reach it. She just felt a little relief when the gun wasn't in his hand. That feeling slowly subsided when Kelvin undid his belt and pants. Realizing that he was going to rape her, Skyy's breathing heightened.

"Kelvin, I mean C.J., can we talk about this first? I would never, ever want to hurt you. I understand why you hate me—truly, I do—but all this is not going to solve the problem. Why won't you let me help you? I understand growing up an orphan, having a horrible childhood. I really do. Why won't you let me help you?"

"Oh, you're gonna help me right now."

Kelvin pulled his limp penis from his pants while walking towards Skyy. She tried turning her head, but he grabbed her by her hair and forced himself into her mouth.

"Suck it!" he screamed, pushing Skyy's head back and forth.

Even though Skyy made very little effort, Kelvin's manhood grew as tears rolled down her face. By now, Kelvin had the gun in his right hand and Skyy's hair wrapped around his left hand at the top of her head, guiding it roughly back and forth.

"Yeah, that's right. Suck it, you filthy slut. Suck it!" Kelvin yelled.

Skyy tried hard to take all of him in her mouth since she had no control over the situation, but he was going so deep that Skyy was gagging and choking. Kelvin moaned in ecstasy. Skyy struggled to breathe. After what seemed to be an eternity to Skyy, Kelvin pulled his manhood from her mouth and then opened her legs. Skyy made it very convenient for Kelvin by not wearing any panties, a ritual she always practiced when she was relaxing around the house. Her oversized nightshirt gave him easy access. He pulled her body to the edge of the seat, and Skyy screamed from the pain it caused in her shoulders. Since her arms and feet were both restrained, the position was very uncomfortable for her. Just as Kelvin was about to drop his pants to his ankles, the doorbell chimed.

"HELP! HELP ME! HELP ME!" Skyy yelled at the top of her lungs.

Kelvin punched her in the face in an attempt to shut her up. He put his index finger to his lips, a silent demand for Skyy to shut up, and crept to the door to see who it was. Skyy sat there in fear, crying softly like a puppy. Shamar was on time, thank God, but there was nothing Skyy could do to get to the door.

"Skyy?" yelled Shamar on the other side of the door.

Kelvin turned and looked at Skyy, motioning for her not to say a word again.

"Skyy?" Shamar yelled again and then rang the doorbell.

Skyy watched Kelvin and thought to herself if she didn't yell to Shamar, Kelvin was going to brutalize her before killing her anyway.

So, she may as well take a chance at getting some help. With every ounce of strength, Skyy screamed at the top of her lungs.

"HELP ME PLEASE! HE'S KILLING ME! HE'S KILLING ME! CALL 9-1-1!"

The blow from Kelvin was so severe that Skyy and the chair toppled over and slid about three feet across the floor. He knelt down beside her and grabbed her.

"Didn't I tell you to shut the fuck up? Just for that, I'm going to make you suffer that much more. You make one more sound and I'm going to put a bullet between your eyes, you understand?"

"Fuck you! If you're gonna kill me, then kill me! I'm tired of this shit! Just do it and get it over with!" Skyy screamed.

She really didn't mean what she was saying, but hoped that Shamar could hear her. Kelvin sat the chair back upright and then grabbed Skyy from behind, covering her mouth with his hand.

"I know how to shut your ass up. This ain't over 'til I say it's over. And I ain't finished with you yet."

He held Skyy tightly until he assumed the person at the door was gone. When he let her go, he walked over to the door. The person was gone. Skyy started sobbing again. Kelvin cautiously peeked through the window before walking over to Skyy's CD player, which was nestled on a bookshelf in the living room. He turned the music up loud in an effort to drown out all other noise from inside the house. Mariah Carey's voice drifted through the speakers, singing about someone being obsessed with her. At that moment, the irony of the song hit them both.

"Kelvin, please, let me go. Please. I understand your pain. I know you're angry. But, this, this is not the answer. Please!"

Skyy tried to talk over the music, but Kelvin ignored her. He walked to the bar situated in the corner and popped the top off a bottle of Hennessy. He took four long gulps before setting the bottle down. He stared at Skyy from across the room, and from the angle where he stood, she saw Kelvin's father in his face.

"I loved him and he loved me. What do you think that did to me, huh? I lost someone that day, too, you know," Skyy yelled.

Kelvin appeared snakelike the way he moved towards Skyy. "Don't talk about my father! You don't have the right to talk about him!"

Another blow landed on Skyy's face.

"You know what? I'm ready to get this shit over with. I can't stand to even look at you anymore. Your ass is dying tonight, so I hope you're ready. Everything I ever went through, you're going through it tonight." Kelvin positioned Skyy on the edge of the chair.

"Kelvin, please! Please don't do this!"

Kelvin dropped his pants to the floor so he could force himself on her. He straddled her in the chair. Skyy screamed. The pain in her shoulders intensified, her face hurt, and now Kelvin was forcing himself inside her violently. The chair screeched across the hardwood floors with every thrust. Kelvin drove hard, pushing faster and faster, and Skyy closed her eyes, trying to imagine herself in another place. She started to pray quietly, realizing she was getting closer to the end of her life. *Where is Shamar? Didn't he hear me scream out for help? Oh please, let him come back,* she thought to herself.

The sound of the front door coming off of its hinges could barely be heard over the music. Skyy heard it first. Kelvin was too busy concentrating on reaching his climax to notice the two police officers standing at the door with their guns drawn.

"Hands up! Right now!" one of the officers yelled.

Kelvin stopped thrusting and stood up slowly. He pointed the gun at Skyy as he stood.

"Put the gun down now!" the other officer yelled.

At that moment, everything seemed to move in slow motion. Kelvin smirked at the officers before turning to Skyy.

"I'm gonna warn you one more time. Put the gun down!"

Kelvin pulled the trigger and the bullet hit Skyy with so much force, the chair fell back and hit the floor. The officers fired their weapons, letting off numerous rounds until they saw Kelvin's body drop. The officers ran over to them, one tending to Skyy and the other to Kelvin. Skyy was gasping for air after taking a bullet in the chest. Kelvin, on the other hand, was no longer breathing.

"This is Officer Morgan. I need an ambulance at 7430 Winterstock Place. I have a female with a gunshot wound to the chest and a male with multiple gunshot wounds. Male is DOA."

The female dispatcher confirmed the call, telling the officer that an ambulance was en route. The officers removed the tape from Skyy's arms and legs and positioned her flat on the floor. The blood in her mouth seemed to strangle her, and her body shook uncontrollably. Her skin looked ashen. Desperation was in her eyes, which were still open, pleading for the officers to save her life.

"Come on, sweetheart, hang in there. Don't die on us."

"Sir, I need you to step outside. Please, sir, do not come in," one of the officers yelled.

"Skyy! Skyy! Please hold on!"

That was the last voice Skyy heard before drifting into unconsciousness.

Chapter 22

It had been two days since the shooting, and Skyy had been in an induced coma ever since. When she was brought into the emergency room, she was coding so the doctors had to resuscitate her twice. They didn't want to jeopardize losing her again, which is why they decided to put her into a coma so she could be stabilized. After the first twenty-four hours, she started to take a turn for the worse, thanks to the bullet that punctured her lung when it entered her chest at almost point blank range and rested itself in her spine. Doctors performed surgery to remove the bullet and repair her lung, and they hoped her condition would improve. It was very important for them to remove the bullet from her spine because they were unsure of what type of damage it would cause. They really wouldn't know Skyy's fate until she came out of the coma.

Skyy opened her eyes slowly to the bright fluorescent lights in the ceiling. Her eyes scanned the room, moving from side to side, but she was having trouble moving her head because of the breathing tube in her mouth. Skyy moaned, trying to get someone's attention, but there was no one there. She was all alone in the hospital—no next of kin, husband, nobody there to care for her. Being alone made her sad. Even if there wasn't a tube in her mouth and she could talk, there was no one for her to call. Sure, she had Coco, but she never listed him as her next of kin, and since he wasn't family, the police wouldn't notify him in case of an emergency.

Teardrops rolled down her face, and she could feel the tears falling near her ears. Her brain was not quite computing the way it should, because for the life of her, she could not move. She could see around her, she could move her eyes, but her body was frozen. After about fifteen minutes of looking around the room, taking in every small detail—all of the monitors, an empty chair, a small nightstand, and a curtain which served as a partition—a short, dumpy,

187

red-headed woman entered wearing a hospital smock blazoned with Tweety Bird faces. The nurse got closer, realizing Skyy's eyes were open. Skyy's breathing became rapid, and the monitor beside her bed beeped loudly. The nurse leaned over Skyy and was directly in her face.

"Skyy, can you hear me? If you can hear me, blink your eyes two times."

Skyy blinked her eyes slowly.

"Good job, honey. We were all rooting for you to get through this, but don't rush. You need to heal. Are you feeling any pain? Blink once for yes, twice for no."

Skyy blinked her eyes once. Skyy was feeling both discomfort and pain. First and foremost, she really wanted them to remove the breathing tube from her mouth. The nurse fussed about, checking Skyy's blood pressure, heart rate, and other vitals. She had to ensure that Skyy's vitals were normal before removing her from the respirator. The nurse then carefully removed the medical tape from Skyy's face to loosen the plastic tube in Skyy's mouth.

"Now, this is going to be very uncomfortable for a few seconds until the entire tube comes up. Don't be alarmed."

She pulled at the breathing tube firmly but slowly, being careful not to harm Skyy. The tube seemed to be more than twelve inches long, at least to Skyy it did. When the tip of the tube was finally out of Skyy's mouth, she coughed uncontrollably and then moaned from the soreness left behind by the breathing tube.

"Let me get you some water, honey. I'll be right back." The nurse disappeared behind the curtain.

Skyy took this time to get reacquainted with herself. She moved her head from left to right, her senses all beginning to come alive. The sterile stench of the hospital filled her nostrils. Her mouth was dry, but when she tried to swallow, it hurt. Whoever was in charge of inserting her breathing tube did some slight damage to her throat. Skyy swallowed some more, then coughed. The nurse reappeared carrying a water pitcher and a plastic cup with small ice chips. She poured some water into the cup and handed it Skyy. The bed rose slowly. Skyy reached for the cup once the nurse put the remote for the bed on the table. The sudden movement caused excruciating pain in the middle of Skyy's chest. It felt as if a meteor had fallen from the sky and landed in her chest.

"Owww!" Skyy screamed.

"Easy, easy," the nurse said, taking the cup and putting it up to Skyy's lips.

Skyy leaned her head up to keep the water from drizzling down the front of her hospital gown. The water cooled the inside of her throat and felt good going down. She sipped cautiously, trying not to exert any unnecessary energy. Skyy leaned back against the pillow while at the same time exploring the large bandages on her chest, carefully locating the source of her pain. The area around the wound seemed to throb like a toothache, and the nurse realized this by the look on Skyy's face.

"Do you need something for the pain?" the nurse asked.

Skyy closed her eyes and nodded, moaning to herself. The nurse checked the IV bag hanging from the metal pole beside Skyy's bed. The notes on Skyy's chart indicated she was due for some more pain medicine.

"I'll be right back." The nurse disappeared again.

The light sound of rain hitting the window diverted Skyy's attention to the full-length window to her right. The raindrops seemed to fill up every available space on the window. It was evident they were not on the ground level because a few branches of a maple tree were visible, only an arm's length away. Skyy returned her attention to the door when the nurse came back with a silver tray, carrying a vial of medicine that she connected to Skyy's IV. Within a matter of seconds, Skyy began to feel relaxed and her eyelids got extremely heavy. Her body, on the other hand, got lighter and lighter.

*   *   *

The room was dimly lit with a light blue hue from the fluorescent light above the hospital bed. The rain sounded like it was pouring down the side of the building. Skyy focused her eyes, noticing the darkness through the window. She had no idea what time it was or what day it was; however, she knew she must've been out for a while since it was dark outside. The pain in her chest was not as intense, but it still hurt. Several muffled voices could be heard close by. Shadows of footsteps could be seen beneath the curtains. It appeared that she was in some sort of triage arrangement, possibly ICU. She could tell by the way the curtains separated each individual patient that they were in a huge room, which housed a nurse's station near the core of the room. Skyy must've been situated at the end of the room, because she was close to the door that had a huge red EXIT sign above it. Skyy wasn't sure how many other patients were in ICU besides her, but the nurses appeared to be busy shuffling around, opening and closing curtains.

Trying very hard not to create any additional pain, Skyy breathed slowly. The room appeared to be getting smaller, and panic suffocated her. Skyy reached over to the remote on the small table and pressed the red nurse's button. She was having a hard time breathing, and that along with her chest wound was causing her major distress. The curtain flew open, and a tall, copper-colored nurse with long, thin braids appeared. Her accent dripped with southern Mississippi charm.

"What's the matter, suga?" the nurse asked.

Skyy, who struggled to speak, tried to mouth to the nurse that she was having trouble breathing. The best she could do was gently tap her chest and gasp for air. The nurse got the message real quick. She grabbed an oxygen mask from the cluster of apparatuses near the curtain and wrapped the rubber strap behind Skyy's head.

"Take deep breaths. Slowly, slowly," she said.

Skyy took in the oxygen, and her breathing became normal again. The nurse turned on more lights before taking readings of Skyy's vital signs. She removed her stethoscope from around her neck after wrapping the plastic cuff around Skyy's upper arm to check her blood pressure. The sound of the plastic bulb being squeezed sounded like a tire on a bicycle being inflated. Once the cuff was as tight as it could get, the nurse pressed the stethoscope to Skyy's arm while slowly releasing the pressure of the cuff.

"One thirty over eighty. It's coming down a bit, though. Keep taking deep breaths, suga."

The nurse waited a few minutes and took another blood pressure reading. This time, she was satisfied.

"How is your breathing now? Is it better?"

Skyy nodded.

"Leave the oxygen on until I get back. I'm getting your doctor now."

Skyy watched her walk around the curtain to the nurse's station. She heard numerous voices before hearing her nurse page a doctor over the intercom. The thoughts inside of Skyy's head were jumbled, and she was having a hard time figuring out what was real and what was pretend. What happened to her? Did someone attack her? Or was she in a car accident? The EXIT door swung open, and a tall, olive-skinned man entered wearing a white lab coat.

"Ms. Armfield? Hello, my name is Dr. Banchek. I'm glad to see you are recovering so nicely." Dr. Banchek looked at Skyy's chart before removing her oxygen mask. "So, how are you doing?"

"Okay, I guess. I'm still trying to figure out what I'm doing here." Skyy struggled to speak, so her words came out slowly.

"You were brought in with a gunshot wound to your chest. The good thing is we got the bullet out, but it hit some vital parts. We had to repair your lung, and there was some spinal damage, as well."

Skyy was horrified by the news. Realizing her wound was a result of a gunshot slowly sunk in. However, her mind couldn't compute the actual event. She still couldn't remember the full details.

The doctor went to the foot of Skyy's hospital bed and pulled the covers back, displaying her feet. He removed an ink pen from his front pocket and rubbed it up and down the base of Skyy's foot. "Can you feel this?"

Skyy had a look of dismay on her face. She could see the doctor touching her foot, but she couldn't feel him doing it. Skyy shook her head slowly, tears forming in her eyes. Dr. Banchek tried her other foot. Nothing. He squeezed both ankles, then her calves. Skyy shook her head. By the time he reached her thigh, it was evident—Skyy was paralyzed from the waist down. Tears welled up in her eyes. The doctor took a deep breath before covering her feet with the blanket.

"I'm sorry, Ms. Armfield. I had a feeling the odds were stacked against you, but I didn't know for sure until now."

"Will I . . . Is it possible that . . ."

"It's too early to tell right now. It's only been four days, so we really need to see how your body heals, especially the injury to your spine. Let's just take one day at a time."

Skyy turned her head away from the doctor so he couldn't see her weep. The doctor stood there for several uncomfortable moments.

"I'm so sorry. But, things are still premature right now. Is there someone I can call for you? You really shouldn't be alone."

"There is no one," she sobbed.

"What about the guy who came in with you? He was very concerned with your well-being when you were brought in by the paramedics. He stayed here for several hours, waiting until you were stabilized."

Skyy turned slowly to face the doctor. She couldn't remember the events of that fateful night, so she had no idea who the doctor was talking about. Then she thought about her friend Coco. She wondered if he even knew what had happened to her.

"Did he say who he was?"

"Yes. I think he said his name was Mr. Wiggins."

Shamar. He was supposed to come over for dinner, but . . . Skyy thought long and hard. Still, the events that brought her to the hospital wouldn't come to her.

"He gave me his card. Asked if I would give him a call when you came to." The doctor felt around in the pocket of his white coat before pulling out a business card. The business card was familiar to her because she had been given it more than once. She took the card and placed it on the table beside her. The last thing she could remember was getting dinner ready for Shamar. After that, everything else was blank.

"Actually, I do have a friend that I can call. Can I get a phone?"

"Sure. I will have the nurse get a telephone in here for you." The doctor patted her feet again and proceeded to the nurse's station.

Skyy put her hands over her face and sobbed uncontrollably. Her life as she knew it was over. How could she do hair or run a business in a wheelchair? Being in a wheelchair meant she would need to be dependent on people to a certain extent. She'd always been independent. Now she was handicapped. Her house wasn't handicap accessible. All these things swarmed her at once. She put the oxygen mask over her face when she felt her chest tightening again. She sent signals from her brain to her legs, trying to command them to move, but nothing happened. Pinching and punching her legs proved hopeless. It was as if she was in a cruel dream that she couldn't wake up from.

The cool mist entered her nostrils in a moderate stream, and Skyy tried to relax so she could focus. Skyy needed to remember what happened to her, so she closed her eyes, thinking back to her last memory prior to waking up in the hospital. The first thing she remembered was hearing the doorbell, then seeing the roses. Her mind kept going blank after that. It must have been some sort of human traumatic reflex, because she couldn't remember anything after opening the door.

The nurse appeared carrying an old push-button telephone with a long cord hanging from it. The beige phone reminded Skyy of her childhood because she remembered having one exactly like it in the home she shared with her mother before she died. The nurse put the phone on the table, plugging it into the wall. Skyy moved the oxygen mask from her face.

"Here you go, honey. Press 9 to get an outside line." The nurse hesitated, giving Skyy an opportunity to ask her a question.

"Do you know?"

"Know what?"

"What happened to me? I can't seem to remember."

The nurse flashed a look of sympathy. She knew what the police had shared with the doctors and nurses who were all there when Skyy was brought in. She wasn't sure, though, if it would be a good idea to share it with Skky right now.

"Honey, why don't you call your family and try to get some rest. Don't worry yourself with the details right now."

"But I don't have any family."

"Well, I know you have some friends who are worried about you. Go ahead. Make a few calls. Get yourself some visitors. Things are always better when you have fam—well, friends close by."

Skyy pushed the incline button on her remote, causing the bed to prop her up. She looked at her legs, feeling like one of those department store dummies on the Old Navy commercials. She wiggled her midsection, hoping the feeling from her chest would miraculously make its way down to her legs. But, nothing changed. The nurse stood by, wishing she could be more supportive of Skyy. Instead, she did what she could by adjusting Skyy's pillows behind her back to make her comfortable.

"I know it's a bit uncomfortable in here, but the doctor is working on getting you moved to recovery. ICU is no fun, I know. We'll have you moved within the hour, okay?"

Skyy nodded. She didn't care about being moved to a recovery room. ICU, recovery room, none of that mattered because she would be paralyzed in whatever room they put her in. She picked up the receiver on the phone, but paused because Coco's number was on speed dial in her cell phone. Therefore, it took her a minute to remember his number. As instructed, she dialed 9 before dialing his number.

"Hello?"

"Coco?"

"This is. Who is this?"

"It's Skyy."

A loud gasp was heard on the other line. "OH MY GOD, SKYY! OH MY GOD! I have been worried sick about you! At first, I thought you went out of town for Valentine's weekend, but when you didn't show up for work yesterday, I went to your house. I saw yellow police tape and a sticker on your door like for a crime scene, and nobody would give me any information when I called the police because they said I wasn't your next of kin. I called the hospitals, but no one would tell me anything. What happened? Are you okay?"

Skyy sniffled. She couldn't force her mouth to say it.

"Skyy?"

"Coco, I need you to come to the hospital. I was shot."

"WHAT?!" Coco shrieked so loudly that he startled Skyy.

"Coco, I, I can't remember what happened, and nobody will tell me. All I know is that I was shot in the chest, and . . . and . . ." Skyy struggled with her words.

"And what, Skyy? You're killing me!"

"I'm paralyzed."

Dead silence.

"Hello?"

"I'm here, Skyy. I, I just don't know what to say. Where are you? What hospital?"

"MCV. I'm in ICU, the trauma unit, but they're trying to get me moved to a room soon."

"So why haven't you called sooner? I have been so worried."

"I was in a coma. I just came out of it today."

"I'm so sorry I wasn't there for you. I hate to think that you were all alone. But, I tried, honey. I really tried to find you. There was a little bit of it on the news, but they never revealed the woman's name, only the man that was shot and killed."

"What man?"

"The man they found in your house, I guess. I don't really know the whole story. All they said was that there was a shooting, a woman was critically injured, and a man died at the scene. Look, let me come there and talk to you in person. I'll be there in thirty minutes."

"Okay."

Skyy put the receiver on the antique phone, feeling a bit of comfort knowing that Coco made some sort of effort to find her. Then she started to think really hard about the man who was killed. Why couldn't she remember? The sound of the curtain being pulled back took Skyy out of her trance. A tall, redhead entered wearing a smock blazoned with Spongebob Squarepants. She looked young enough to actually watch the show.

"Hi, Ms. Armfield. So happy to see you are awake." Her southern drawl gave indication that she had to be from Mississippi or Alabama.

"Hi."

"I'm Robin. I was on duty when they brought you in. How are you feeling?"

"Besides the pain in my chest and the numbness in the lower half of my body, never better."

The nurse gave Skyy a peculiar look, not sure if she should pry or leave well enough alone. The other nurse had already given her a heads up on Skyy's condition. However, she didn't think Skyy was open to discuss it just yet.

"I'm sorry. If there is anything I can do for you, just let me know. I will be here until eleven tonight. Oh, before I forget. When you were brought in, there was this guy. He said he was a private investigator, a friend of yours. Anyway, he asked that we give him a call as soon as you came to. Do you want to give him a call? He gave the doctor his card, and he gave me one, as well. He was adamant that someone keep him informed of your status."

Skyy thought about Shamar, realizing their dinner never happened because of the unexpected chain of events. The nurse handed Skyy a carbon copy of the business card that the doctor had already given her. Shamar would have to wait, at least until she was moved to her recovery room. Just then, a revelation came to her.

"Wait a minute. Shamar came in after I was brought in?"

"Yes. I think he told the doctors that he followed behind the ambulance. Apparently, he was the one that called the police to your house."

"Really? I swear I don't remember any of that."

"I think you should give him a call. He was very concerned about you."

"I will. Thank you."

"I'll go and check on your room. Do you need anything right now?"

"My chest hurts a lot. Can you give me something for the pain?"

"Sure. I'll go and get you some medicine. What about food? Are you hungry?"

Skyy shook her head. "I am thirsty, though."

"I'll bring you some juice, too. Be right back."

Skyy looked at the slightly bent business card, reading over Shamar's name several times. It was obvious Shamar, the man who made her heart skip a beat, was also the man that saved her life.

Chapter 23

The sunlight from the window caused a glare on the TV screen that was mounted in the corner of the hospital room. For something as simple as closing the blinds in the window, Skyy had to press the nurse's button. This upset her. She was hoping the paralysis was temporary, and that as time progressed, she would regain the feeling in her legs. But, since being moved to a room, nothing else had changed.

Skyy rubbed her hand over the scar on her chest, wishing everything was all a dream. However, the bandages, stitches, and pain associated with the scar were very much real. The bed closest to the window was empty, neatly made with drab-colored hospital linen. The curtain that separated the two beds was pulled back against the wall, allowing the sunshine to envelope the room. Two outdated metal and faux leather sitting chairs sat against the wall beneath the TV, and there was an oversized metal and wood table near the window. The room reeked of alcohol, peroxide, and other hospital smells. There was a slight stench of bleach that seemed to seep through the bathroom walls into the room. The mixture of smells gave Skyy an instant headache.

The bed rose slowly as Skyy pressed the incline button on the bed remote. The knotty bedspread somehow got tangled under the bed, and as the bed rose up, the bedspread and Skyy's gown moved toward the floor, exposing a colostomy bag. Skyy looked down at it in horror, almost losing her breath at the sight. She tried reaching for the bedspread, hoping the quicker she could cover the colostomy bag it would go away. But, she couldn't reach it. Bending over to reach the bedspread felt like she was being held down by 500-pound weights. She tried with all her might, but fell back on the bed in defeat. Tears rolled down her cheeks. She was helpless. Crippled. Dependent. All of those summed up the person she had become. Reluctantly, she pressed the nurse's button for help. She continued to sob softly, shaking her head in denial. She pulled her hospital gown over the colostomy bag because she couldn't stand the sight of it. Muffled footsteps could be heard getting closer to the door before it sprang open and in bounced a bubbly, five-foot, two-inch, caramel-colored nurse with shoulder-length dreadlocks.

"Hi, Skyy. I'm Alicia. I will be one of your nurses during the evening shift until eleven tonight. How are you feeling?" Alicia asked, while checking Skyy's vitals.

Skyy shrugged her shoulders, not sure what she was feeling.

"Let me check your wound to see if your dressing needs to be changed."

Skyy obliged, giving Alicia approval to open her gown in the front. Alicia washed her hands in the bathroom and put on plastic gloves before carefully removing the medical tape, exposing stitches that looked like a small set of railroad tracks right between Skyy's breasts. She pressed the area around the stitches softly, trying to detect if there was any swelling. Before covering it with a clean dressing, Alicia swabbed the area with an antibiotic solution. Skyy closed her gown while Alicia threw her plastic gloves in the trash and rubbed her hands with antibacterial hand sanitizer.

"The wound is healing nicely. Now, the doctor wants to start you on a soft diet today. I can get dietary to bring up a tray now if you're hungry."

Skyy really didn't have an appetite, but thought it might make her feel better to eat something. Besides, it had been a few days since her body had any sort of nourishment, so it couldn't hurt at this point.

"What's the soft diet?" Skyy asked.

"Soup, applesauce, jello—soft foods like those. I'll order up a tray for you. You don't have to eat everything, but try to eat something. It will help you rebuild your strength. Do you need anything else while I'm in here?"

"Yes, can you close the blinds? And my blanket fell on the floor."

Alicia twisted the handle on the window blinds, and they began to close. Before adjusting the bedspread, she checked Skyy's colostomy bag to see if it was full.

"We will come in after you eat and do a sponge bath, get your bag changed, and a clean nightgown. If you want, you can wear your own sleepwear if you have some here."

"I don't have anything here."

"Maybe a family member can bring you some things now since you're out of ICU. It will make your stay a little easier if you had your own things."

Skyy offered up a fake smile. "Thanks."

"Your food should be up in about fifteen minutes or so. The doctor will be in to check on you soon. If you need anything, buzz me. Okay?"

"Okay. Thank you."

Alicia left the room, taking all of the energy with her. Skyy sulked, focusing her attention on Dr. Phil sitting on his makeshift stage while attempting to save someone's life. Skyy wished there was some way she could be on that stage, getting advice that could've changed her life somehow.

The sound of the door opening grabbed her attention. Five large 'Get Well Soon' mylar balloons floated to the ceiling. The balloons were attached to an oversized teddy bear that looked just as big as Coco. Skyy's eyes lit up at the sight of her friend. Behind Coco appeared Debi, who was holding a floral arrangement. Skyy put her hands up to her mouth, surprised to see Debi since it had been months since they'd spoken or seen each other. After what Skyy had done to her, Debi pushed it to the side to show concern for Skyy.

"Diva!" Coco yelled, having difficulty hugging Skyy with the balloons and the teddy bear in his hands.

Skyy reached up to embrace him and held on so tight that Coco almost lost his balance. Debi placed the floral arrangement on the table, then stood next to the bed while Coco and Skyy hugged. Debi and Skyy stared at each other, their eyes saying it all. Skyy mouthed 'I'm sorry' to Debi, who shook her head, held her finger to her mouth, and shushed Skyy silently. It was not the day for I'm sorry's. It was the day Debi came to show support for a woman that she once cared deeply about, a woman that used to be her best friend. Coco finally released his embrace and went over to the table so he could set down the teddy bear and balloons.

"How are you doing?" Debi asked.

Skyy just shook her head. Her lips quivered and she burst into tears.

"Oh, Skyy, don't cry. It'll be alright. Shhhh, don't cry," Coco said.

Coco sat on one side of the bed, and Debi lowered the silver handrail so she could sit on the other side of Skyy. They wrapped her in a group hug and let her sob uncontrollably.

"I'm crippled, y'all. I can't walk. What am I gonna do? I don't know what I'm gonna do. I can't live like this. I can't ..."

"Skyy, don't talk like that. It's gonna be okay. One day at a time, you hear me? We're here for you, to help you. Just take it one day at a time."

They stayed in their group hug for several minutes, allowing Skyy to grieve for the life she used to have. Debi rubbed her back, trying to help ease her pain.

"It's okay. It's okay. Let it all out." Debi grabbed a tissue from the table and handed it to Skyy.

Skyy wiped her puffy, swollen eyes. Normally always the talkative spirit, Skyy was at a loss for words.

"The first order of business is this hair. Ewwww!" Coco said, and they all laughed.

"Is that all you can say to me? I almost died, and the only thing you can think of is my hair?"

"Honey, you and I both know that hair is definitely a life or death situation," replied Coco.

"Debi, how are you doing?" Skyy asked.

"I'm fine. I need to be asking you how you're doing."

"I don't have an answer for how I'm doing. I bet you think I got what I deserved, huh?"

"Skyy, what happened to you, I wouldn't wish on my worst enemy. I was upset with you, but I would never wish you dead."

"I need your forgiveness right now, Debi. I don't have anything going for me right now. I laid here in this hospital for two days in a coma, all alone. Nobody here with me, concerned about me. How could I have possibly thought I was living a full life? Not one person was here with me."

"But, Skyy, we're here now. I'm here now," Coco said.

"Coco, you don't understand. If something happened to you, they would contact your next of kin—your mother, sister, somebody would be there for you when you woke up. Same thing with you, Debi. But, me? I had nobody. I was all alone. Dying here all alone. It was just, just sad." Skyy bowed her head, trying to keep the tears from falling again.

"Skyy, you survived a gunshot wound to your chest. You're still alive. Don't you think your life was sparred for a reason?"

"My life was sparred? Is that what you think? I was left alive as half of a person. I can't walk. This is punishment."

"Skyy, don't talk like that. It will get better."

"How, Coco? How will this get better? I can't run my business in a wheelchair. I can't do hair in a wheelchair."

"I know it seems like this is the end for you, but you can't give up on life. Being in a wheelchair is not the end of your life. Sure, your life will change, but it won't end."

Skyy didn't want to hear positive words of encouragement from her friends. Not today. Maybe after some time had passed and she had come to terms with her situation, but not today.

"I'm sorry you two. I shouldn't take my frustration out on you. All you did was come to help me. I'm sorry."

"Skyy, I love you. You're my best friend. If there was anything I could do, anything to change this, I would. I hate seeing you this way. You're my girl, one of the strongest women I know. You can pull through this. I know you can." Coco rubbed Skyy's arm. He wished there was something he could do to ease his friend's pain, but this was something Skyy would have to conquer. He would be there to help her, only when she was ready to be helped.

All of them turned to the door as it opened, watching a young woman from dietary roll in a food cart.

"Soft diet tray?" she asked, before placing the tray on the versatile tray attached to the bed. Debi moved out of her way to allow the tray to be moved closer to Skyy.

"Thank you," Skyy said politely.

The girl wheeled her cart out of the room, mumbling "you're welcome" under her breath. The three of them looked at each other, each finding the young woman's hair weave repugnant and dreadful.

"Okay, I really should've given her one of my cards," Debi said.

"Hell, I felt like dragging her ass downtown with me. There ought to be a law against such foolishness. That was just plain foolishness," Coco said in his best Neicy Nash imitation.

"You know what's so frustrating right now? I can't even remember what happened to me." Skyy removed the cover from her food and inspected the chicken broth, cherry Jell-O, and applesauce. None of it appealed to her, so she covered it back up.

"You don't remember anything?" Coco asked.

Skyy shook her head. Coco grabbed his Louis Vuitton messenger bag from the table and searched through it until he found a comb.

"Maybe that's best," Debi said.

Coco stood above Skyy, running the comb through her hair. Skyy closed her eyes.

"That feels good," she said.

The door opened again, and a police officer entered. Coco and Debi froze, not sure if they needed to leave the room or stay with Skyy for moral support.

"Good afternoon. I'd like to speak to Ms. Armfield, if you don't mind."

Debi and Coco looked at each other, then looked at Skyy for direction.

"Can they stay? They're my friends."

"I'd prefer to talk to you alone, at least until we officially close your case."

"You mean this isn't over? He's still out there? Am I still in danger?!" Skyy shrieked, her eyes getting as big as golf balls.

"No, please calm down. Unofficially, it's over. I just need to get a statement from you, make sure everything is documented so the file can be completed and closed out. That's all."

"I would really like it if my friends stayed in here. I need them here."

The officer sighed heavily. He figured it couldn't hurt anything at this point.

"Okay, that's fine."

The notebook he pulled from his pocket reminded Skyy of the officer that came to her salon that day. That day. It was still a little fuzzy, all jumbled up in her brain, but somehow, she remembered that officer and his notebook.

"Before we begin, how are you feeling? You getting along okay?"

Skyy shook her head no. "I don't want to talk about that right now, though. Let's just get this over with."

"I understand from your doctor that you were having a problem remembering what happened, is that correct?"

"Yes."

"I was one of the first officers on the scene. Me and my partner took down the suspect, a Mr. Chaz Donaldson. What was your relationship to Mr. Donaldson?"

For a moment, the only thing that registered in Skyy's brain was the name—Chaz Donaldson. She shook her head for a moment, trying to figure out why the officer was asking her about Chaz since he had died almost twenty years ago.

"I don't understand. Why are you asking me about Chaz? Chaz died in 1991. What does that have to do with me?"

The officer gave Skyy a peculiar look before flipping through his small notebook. Debi and Coco were trying to figure out who they were talking about.

"Chaz Donaldson Jr . . . Oh wait, he also goes by Kelvin Harris. What was your relationship to him?"

"Kelvin? Yeah, okay." Skyy thought long and hard, then she remembered. Kelvin came to her door with the flowers. She thought it was Shamar. Kelvin tormented her, beat her, and attacked her all in the name of his father, Chaz Donaldson Sr., the man that Skyy had dreams of building a life with. The only man that Skyy had ever truly loved and who Skyy believed loved her back. The love she lost. It was all coming back to her. Kelvin had a vendetta to settle with Skyy. He blamed her for his parents' deaths. 'I love Skylar Armstrong'—she remembered Kelvin screaming those words at her. Raping her, hitting her, ultimately shooting her. Her swollen, red eyes teared up again. The event started to replay in her head and it was painful.

"Skyy, you okay?" Coco asked.

She nodded, putting her hands over her face. "I remember. I remember." Her voice was muffled behind her hands. Her shoulders moved up and down erratically, so much so that Debi wrapped her arms around Skyy real tight.

"It's okay, Skyy. It's okay. Officer, maybe do this another time?" Debi asked.

Coco moved in front of the officer, almost like a lion protecting one of his cubs.

"I'm sorry. I realize how upsetting this must be, but I really need to know what she remembers. We need to put this story together."

"She'll still be here tomorrow. Give her some time."

The officer, standing below Coco's stance, gave Skyy the time she needed. The trauma of the event was hitting her full force like a freight train, so she needed time to relive the entire event. Coco followed the officer to the door, almost like he was his escort. Skyy's muffled sobs sounded like a wounded puppy. Debi and Coco let her cry in silence. Kelvin took so much more from Skyy than the use of her legs. Her life as she once knew it was gone forever. The only sound in the room besides Skyy's soft cries was the voice of the local news anchor on the TV. Coco looked around for the remote so he could change the channel in an effort to evade the news story about Skyy. He went through several channels before stopping at a judge show.

"Can I get something for you, diva?"

"Coco, what am I gonna do? I don't know what I'm supposed to do now. I mean, where do I go from here?"

"Skyy, come on now."

"Come on? I can't even wash my own ass! I can't get up and go to the fucking bathroom! I have a plastic bag hooked to my bladder so I don't pee on myself. I may as well put on some Depends!" she yelled.

"Skyy, you can get through this. I know you can. You're a strong woman."

"Stop saying that! I'm not strong! I'm mean and evil, and God is punishing me for hurting people. All my adult life, I have been self-centered and egotistical. I never cared about anybody but myself. I'm getting it all back. I'm so sorry! Debi, please forgive me," Skyy sobbed again.

Chapter 24

Skyy stirred a bit in the darkness before realizing she'd fallen asleep. Coco and Debi left hours earlier, but not before summoning a nurse to the room to give Skyy something to calm her down. Whatever the nurse gave Skyy put her out quickly, and the last thing she remembered was apologizing to Debi.

The light from beneath the door illuminated the room, and the only sound that could be heard was the ticking of the clock that hung on the wall. Skyy moved her hand slowly across the bed, feeling for the television remote, hoping she hadn't knocked it to the floor. She turned on the TV, squinting her eyes to adjust to the light. It was almost nine o'clock, and she noticed she had on a different hospital gown. Apparently, the nurses had given her a sponge bath while she was out cold. She hoped like hell those nurses didn't do anything to violate her. Not that she would be able to tell since everything below her waist was paralyzed. She reached for the bed remote so she could raise the bed to prop herself up.

There was a knock on the door, then the doctor entered. He flipped the light switch, catching Skyy off guard, and her reflex caused her to cover her face with her hand.

"Ms. Armfield? I'm sorry. Were you still sleeping? I heard the TV, so I thought . . ."

"It's okay. I'm up."

"Are you feeling a little better?" the doctor asked with his strong Indian accent.

Skyy touched the scar on her chest, still feeling the soreness and pain it produced. "This scar hurts really bad."

"I'll have the nurse give you something for the pain. Have you noticed any change in the paralysis at all?"

Skyy shook her head.

"It's still pretty early on. Because your injury was spinal, it's possible that the nerves can rebuild themselves and you will regain the feeling in your legs again. Don't give up hope, though."

Skyy tried to hold back the tears as the doctor went on with numerous medical terms that she didn't recognize, all leading back to the fact that nothing was certain for her at this point. Halfway through his spill, the nurse from the earlier part of the day entered. She tried not to interrupt the doctor while taking Skyy's vitals.

"If there's anything you need, I'll be here until midnight. But, feel free to have one of the nurses call me if you have any problems. Okay?"

"Thank you, Dr. Banchek."

The doctor looked toward the nurse, wondering why she was standing at the door like she was waiting on him for something.

"Do you need something, Alicia?" he asked.

"Oh, no. I have to check Skyy's scar. I was just waiting for you to finish talking to her."

The doctor nodded, gave Skyy a friendly pat on her shoulder, and left the room.

"Did you have a good nap, sweetie?" the nurse asked.

"I guess."

"Your friends were really worried about you."

"Where did they go?"

"They left after we gave you a sedative. But, don't worry. They said they will be back tomorrow. One of your friends wanted to go to your house to get some of your things, but he needs to get approval from the police first. I called the officer that came in earlier, but he hasn't called me back yet."

Alicia closed Skyy's hospital gown after changing the dressing on her wound.

"It looks good. Do you need anything? Oh, before I forget. There were two gentlemen here about an hour ago to see you. When I told them you had been given a sedative, they said they would go and grab some dinner and come back. I believe they were from out of town or something."

"Did he say what his name was? Was his name Shamar?"

"There were two of them. I think one of them was named Shamar, if I'm not mistaken. They should be on their way back up here soon. I told them that visiting hours are normally over at eight, but he said they were family members from out of town. So, that's fine."

Skyy could feel her breathing quicken. Shamar and his 'client', who Skyy was convinced it was her father.

"Can I get a washcloth or something to wash my face? And a comb or something for my hair? What about a toothbrush? I need to freshen up."

"Sure. We gave you a sponge bath earlier. Let me get your washcloth."

Alicia disappeared to the bathroom, and Skyy could hear her running the water in the sink. After a couple of minutes, Alicia returned with a washcloth, a small bowl filled with water, a toothbrush, and toothpaste. Steam rose from the washcloth, indicating the water must've been piping hot. Alicia handed the washcloth to Skyy, who placed the entire washcloth over her face, letting the steam open her pores. She took her time going into the crevices of her eyes and lips, hoping to clear away all evidence of sleep. Alicia poured some of the water from the bowl to a cup.

"Here, you can use the bowl and cup to brush your teeth. Rinse with the cup of water, brush using the bowl."

Skyy brushed her teeth, using the technique instructed by Alicia. She washed her face again before handing everything to Alicia to take back to the bathroom. Sadness overcame her with the thought of not being able to walk to the bathroom and do such simple tasks on her own. Alicia reappeared from the bathroom with a small hospital-issued haircomb.

"I know this isn't much, but hopefully, it will do for now."

Skyy chuckled at the small comb, hoping she would be able to get it through her hair. Luckily for her, Coco had tamed her hair some earlier that day, so it wasn't so bad.

"The last thing I need is some lotion."

Alicia disappeared to the bathroom again, returning with a small bottle of generic hand lotion. The lotion felt more like water pouring into her hands than the thick body lotions Skyy was accustomed to. Reluctantly, she rubbed some of it on her face, yearning for some sort of scent, but there was none. Even though her lips were extremely dry, Skyy figured it would be a long shot asking the nurse for Vaseline. So, she tried rubbing some of the cheap lotion on her lips instead.

"What else?" Alicia asked.

"I think that's about it."

"You have your buzzer, so if you need anything else, let me know. Do you want to leave the light on?" Alicia asked.

"Yes, may as well." Skyy watched the way Alicia's golden dreadlocks swayed from side to side when she walked away.

The thought of Shamar seeing her like this was heartbreaking. Meeting the mystery person in this state was even more depressing. Still, Skyy tried to put on a brave face. She could no longer run—literally. Nervous energy took over, and she found herself patting her fingers and hands on the handrails. She looked up at the huge clock on the wall, which reminded her of the clock she had in her fourth grade class. The second hand ticked loudly, about as volubly as her heart was beating in her chest.

Skyy tried to remember the man she saw maybe once or twice a week that disappeared to her mother's room for hours at a time. His face was indistinct to her, and as crazy as it sounded, she couldn't recollect what he looked like. At any rate, Skyy was eager to finally see him after all this time.

The knock on the door interrupted Skyy's thoughts, and her heart started to beat faster. When the door didn't open right away, Skyy knew it was Shamar.

"Come in," she said nervously.

Shamar poked his head into the room first before opening the door wider. He looked to the person behind him, giving him a nod of approval before entering. His silence indicated he was beyond words. Just seeing Skyy there like that disturbed him; she could see it in his face. The person behind him appeared slowly, but it wasn't Skyy's father. She knew this because this person didn't look old enough to have a driver's license, let alone be her father. Shamar had to pull the young man into the hospital room further because he appeared to be hesitant. He didn't look at Skyy right away, but when he finally looked up at her, she noticed his eyes. The large, round eyes with extensive eyelashes were identical to Kelvin's and Chaz's eyes. His short stature and sandy-colored, wavy hair made her feel as if she were looking in a mirror. Like a baseball being hit by a bat, the blow struck Skyy immensely.

"Skyy, I have someone who wants to meet you. Skyy, this is Dominique. Dominique, this is Skyy, your mother."

Skyy hung her head low, shaking it over and over again. A small purr-like sound came from her. Never in a million years did she think he would find her. The adoption was supposed to be sealed. No one knew about the baby, not even Chaz before he was murdered. Skyy was going to tell him that she was pregnant when they ran away together. However, his wife put an end to his life and their future together. Since Skyy was only seventeen and on her own, with nowhere to go, she thought it would be best to put her baby up for adoption. The day she handed him over to the woman from the adoption agency was the day her life as Skylar ended and her life as Skyy began. She looked at Dominique, a little piece of her and Chaz all mixed up in one package. Even though he shared his father's eyes, everything else was a carbon copy of Skyy. There was no way she could deny him.

"Dominique?" Skyy echoed.

He nodded his head, his eyes filling with tears. Skyy reached out her hand to him. Dominique moved toward Skyy slowly, appearing childlike. However, based on her quick calculations, Skyy knew that at age twenty, he was hardly a child. Shamar stood back cautiously, letting Skyy and Dominique have their moment together. When Dominique was beside Skyy, she grabbed his hand.

"How? Why?" she cried.

"Please don't cry. I didn't come to cause you any more pain. I just wanted to meet you."

"But why? Didn't you have a good family? They told me that a nice, stable, Christian family was adopting you. I wanted to be sure of that so you would never feel like you missed out on anything, especially me."

"I did have a good family. My mother and father were wonderful parents. But, I lost them both in a car accident last year. They never told me that I was adopted. I found out when I collected their documents from a safe deposit box. They were going to tell me when I turned twenty-one. They had a letter all typed up and everything. That's just how my parents were. Very well organized, had everything all planned. I went to the agency to find out who you were and just sort of went from there."

"I'm so sorry about your parents."

Shamar slipped out of the room unnoticed.

"Thanks. Ever since I found out that I was adopted, I've dreamed of meeting you. I always knew there was something missing. My whole life, I just felt like a piece of me was missing."

"Didn't they show you love? I specifically requested a home full of love."

"Yes, they showered me with love. They were great, the best parents anyone could ever have, but I never felt like—how can I say it, like I fit with them. There wasn't a resemblance. People always told me that my whole life. Then there were just certain times when I would feel so alone, and I wasn't sure why. They tried very hard, probably overcompensated because they knew I was adopted, but I always felt like something was missing."

Skyy selected her words carefully, because her reality was that she had locked Dominique and all memories related to him away a long time ago. She never thought she would ever see him again.

"That's sweet, Dominique, but you have to know that I . . ."

"I didn't come here to cause you any trouble, Skyy. I just wanted to meet my real mother, that's it. You don't owe me any explanations of when and why. I don't want to take you back to any of that right now. Shamar told me what happened to you, so I'm just happy that you survived your ordeal and I got a chance to meet you."

Tears rolled down Skyy's cheeks. Dominique wiped them away.

"No, I don't deserve this. I don't deserve you being nice to me. I've been horrible to everyone. I was horrible to you. I was horrible to my own friend, and now, because of it, I'm stuck in this bed and can't use my legs."

"You weren't horrible to me. Why are you saying that?"

"I gave you away. I abandoned you for selfish reasons. Always about me. I couldn't take care of you? Hmph! I didn't even try. All I could think about is how a baby would put a damper on my life if I did it by myself. God is truly punishing me. Here you stand, after everything that has happened, a reminder of my selfishness once again."

Skyy sobbed. Dominique sat on the edge of the bed, wrapped his arms around her, and hugged her tight. Skyy let all of her pain out, allowing her tears to run down the back of Dominique's The North Face down coat.

"Skyy, listen to me. A year ago, I thought God was punishing me by taking the only two people away from me that loved me unconditionally. But, when I found the letter and the adoption papers, I realized the accident was just that—an accident—and God was letting me know that I still existed. I'm still here. My parents took care of me and made sure I had the best life possible. But, you? You gave me life. I have to move on with my life, just as you have to move on with yours."

"But, things are so different for me now. How am I supposed to move on?" Skyy said.

"Look at my life. Things are different for me now, too. I'm still trying to figure out how to do it without being able to pick up the phone and call my dad. I miss Sunday dinners with homemade peach cobbler and sweet tea. My mom was the best cook. Even when I decided to move out on my own after I graduated from high school and got a job, I never missed Sunday dinner with my family. I regret not going to college, because that's what my dad wanted. I regret not telling my mom how much I loved her peach cobbler." Dominique's eyes watered.

Skyy felt awful. Again, she was thinking about herself. Dominique was still grieving, and he didn't have anyone to share his grief. All of his life, he had felt alone, despite growing up with a family. Skyy knew how it felt to be lonely even if you weren't truly alone, because she had felt the same way growing up in her mother's house an only child. The difference was her mother would put her on the back burner for a couple hours of companionship from a man who didn't even take the time to buy her a card for her birthday. Dominique felt a void in his life, as did Skyy. Now, here they were, face to face, trying to figure out how to fill that void.

Skyy rubbed his hand. "I know how to make homemade peach cobbler. I don't know if it can top your mom's, but I can make you some, if you'd like." Skyy didn't really know how to respond to Dominique. She just wanted to say something to ease his pain. For once, she was thinking about somebody else besides herself.

"I'd like that."

Chapter 25

"Mobility, mobility, mobility," Skyy said to herself repeatedly with each stride her feet made as they glided slowly across the belt of the treadmill. With assistance from the nurse, she held on to the steel rails for support. Her legs felt like lead, and she moved them as if she were a robot. Since being released from the hospital two months ago and beginning rehab soon after, Skyy had made tremendous progress toward being mobile again. As tough as the journey had been, she was determined to regain her independence by walking. However, she was still incapacitated and needed a wheelchair to get around.

Dominique walked in, trying not to disturb Skyy's physical therapy session. He pulled the door closed behind him quietly and stood there, watching Skyy tackle her greatest feat yet. Beads of sweat were forming on her forehead, and her hair looked unkept, but she still looked beautiful to Dominique. He gave up life as he knew it by moving in with Skyy to help her. Initially, it all began as a temporary move, but as time went on and Skyy realized how dependent she'd become, Dominique volunteered to stay with her. Sure, there were home healthcare nurses that came to check on her during the day, but when they weren't there, she was alone.

Coco had been spending his time running the salon in Skyy's absence, taking on her customers as well as his own. So, he didn't have much time to spend with Skyy. She understood, though. That was one less thing Skyy had to worry about as she went through recovery. In the meantime, Dominique jumped in like her savior, spending time and making sure Skyy's house was wheelchair accessible by adding a ramp to the front porch, widening the doorways inside the house, and lowering the vanity in her spare bathroom. He figured eventually Skyy would walk again. So, it didn't make sense to make major changes to her master bathroom, especially since it was her favorite room in the house.

Dominique decided to take a leave of absence from his job working as a customer service representative for a credit card company to help Skyy. After taking a month leave when his parents died and then taking leave to tend to Skyy, he was sure they would let him go if he stayed out much longer, but he didn't care. Spending time getting to know Skyy was his number one priority. Besides, working in customer service had taken its toll on him seeing as though his lifelong dream was to own his own business, particularly a jazz club. Since he received a hefty insurance payment from his parents' deaths, he really didn't need to work. He only took on the job to keep his mind occupied. His plan was to eventually enroll in college to get his degree in business, then take some of his insurance money and open a jazz club. Unbeknownst to Skyy, Dominique was a talented saxophone player who could also play the piano and the trumpet. She knew that jazz music was his favorite, but she had no idea that he played. Growing up an only child, Dominique never took a liking to sports like most of his friends. Instead, he would spend countless hours practicing his instruments and studying music.

Dominique watched Skyy lift her feet, which appeared to be broken at the ankles. He could see the tension in her face from her effort with each pace she took.

"I can't, can't . . . I can't do it," she panted, struggling.

"Come on, you can do it. Just three more minutes," the nurse said empathetically.

The muscles in Skyy's upper arm protruded slightly, an indication that she was putting most of her weight on her arms. The five-minute walk felt more like five hours to Skyy, but she knew she had to push on so she could rebuild her strength.

Dominique took a seat in a chair that was meant to be used for massage therapy. He tried to go unnoticed, but the unintentional kick to the five-pound weight on the floor startled Skyy and her nurse. They both turned to look in his direction.

"Sorry," Dominique said, looking a bit embarrassed.

Skyy smiled at her son. Not caring much about her appearance, she was now concentrating on completing her five minutes of physical therapy on the treadmill without whining or complaining. Dominique had that affect on her. He gave her the will to work harder just by his presence. Over the past two months, Dominique

213

had been her rock. Instead of viewing her shooting as an accident that left her helpless, Dominique convinced her to view it as a second chance at life. Skyy was beginning to view the precise time that Dominique came into her life as an act of faith. No longer feeling sorry for herself, Skyy was hopeful that God had given her another chance to do things differently, and she intended to fight hard to go back to a life of independence.

The nurse helped Skyy to her wheelchair, which was sitting right beside the treadmill. Dominique walked over to help get her situated comfortably in her chair.

"Same time next week?" Skyy asked the nurse.

"Yep, I will be right here. See you two then."

The nurse didn't wait for them to leave the room. Instead, she disappeared to the offices situated at the opposite end of the physical therapy room.

"How's it going, handsome?" Skyy asked.

"Just fine, beautiful," Dominique replied.

They turned to face each other, then burst into laughter. They were both still amazed at the strong resemblance they shared, so their private joke was to always compliment each other's looks.

Dominique used his foot to unlock the wheelchair before turning it around and wheeling Skyy to the door. He stopped before exiting the room so he could grab her coat and purse from a coat hook.

"Here you go." Dominique guided Skyy into her coat, carefully pulling it around her back and over her shoulders comfortably. He attempted to wrap her scarf around her neck before Skyy grabbed it from him.

"I can do it," Skyy snapped. She hated feeling helpless.

"Sorry," Dominique said, putting his hands in the air like he was being placed under arrest.

Skyy looked at him, feeling bad because she realized he was only trying to help her. She sighed.

"Hey, don't be sorry. I'm sorry. All you are doing, all you have done, I know it's just to help me. I appreciate everything you do for me, Dominique."

His face lit up like a child on Christmas Day. As much as Skyy wanted to please him, he wanted to please her, too. They were still in that probationary period of their relationship—both were still cautious about how they should handle each other. There were twenty years of catching up that they had to do. Sure, it would take time, but they both took their time, easing into the relationship carefully.

They headed to the elevator, riding it to the lobby of the north building at the Medical College of Virginia. The oversized lobby was a flurry of activity with a mixture of doctors, nurses, patients, and visitors bustling amongst each other. In the center of the lobby was a customer service desk and in front of that was an escalator. MCV, the number one hospital in the city for treating trauma patients, was an enormous hospital that housed numerous buildings and clinics. Dominique and Skyy had gotten used to their weekly trip to rehab. However, it was obvious to them that there were some people there who were lost. Dominique moved Skyy close to the door and then used his foot to lock the wheelchair.

"Be right back," he said before heading outside to get his car.

Skyy looked around, trying to see if anyone was looking at her. She still felt self-conscious about being in the wheelchair and always felt uneasy whenever Dominique left her alone. The revolving door pushed in the cool March air. The door moved constantly while Skyy sat beside it, catching everyone's attention. She tried to pretend not to see the little girl standing at the customer service desk staring at her. It was natural for young children to stare, but she still hated it. She wished she could just go home and hide, but she had to leave physical therapy to go to her counseling session. It made things much easier for Skyy to get all of her appointments taken care of on the same day since it was so much trouble getting her in and out of Dominique's Ford Explorer.

Dominique reappeared through the revolving door. He unlocked the wheelchair and went toward the non-revolving glass door. A young man with sagging pants and an oversized hoodie sweatshirt rushed ahead of them without holding the door for Dominique.

"Asshole," Dominique said under his breath.

The young security guard who'd been standing at the receptionist desk walked over to hold the door for Dominique. With lust in his eyes, he smiled at Skyy, probably not caring that she was in a wheelchair.

"Thanks," they both said.

The March wind took them off guard. The flapping of the American flag hitting the flagpole high above them vibrated loudly, sounding more like someone hitting their fork against a champagne glass. After Dominique opened the passenger door to his truck, Skyy put one arm around his neck and helped to push herself up with the other hand. Dominique, small in stature, struggled with Skyy, but was able to twist both their bodies around and get her in the passenger seat. Skyy pulled the door shut and watched Dominique fold the wheelchair. Once the wheelchair was collapsed, Dominique put it in the cargo area in the back of his SUV. He then got in and started the engine. The percussion and horns blared so loudly that it startled Skyy.

"Sorry about that," Dominique said, turning the volume down.

"Who is this you're listening to?" Skyy asked.

"Wynton Marsalis. He's my favorite musician."

"Ah, okay. This is nice." Skyy bobbed her head to the music and enjoyed the ride.

Absorbed by the music, Dominique drove cautiously, like Skyy was a breakable China doll. Unconsciously, his mouth movement mimicked the sound of a trumpet, something Skyy had become accustomed to since Dominique had began taking her to her appointments.

They coasted up Broad Street, immediately passing the state buildings, the new theater, and a shell of the former downtown, including the old Thalhimers and Miller and Rhoads buildings. Erected in their place were pricey condominiums and parking lots that catered to the traffic from the copious Richmond Convention Center. Only a stone's throw away from the convention center were a few stores that had managed to stay open, thanks to traffic fueled by public transportation. Crossing over Belvidere into Virginia Commonwealth University territory, the scene on Broad Street was completely different. The brick storefronts, restaurants, and even student housing all carried a different flair than the decrepit look of old downtown Broad Street. College students carrying books and wearing backpacks scurried about, creating college memories that would last forever.

"See what you're missing, Dominique? See how wonderful college life is?" Skyy teased, while they passed the throngs of students on Broad Street.

"I still have time. There is always time for college." Reflecting on the countless conversations he shared with his parents about attending college, Dominique looked sad. Since going to college was one of the things his parents wanted most for him, he felt as if he had let them down.

They drove the rest of the way in silence, with only the sounds of jazz music filling the air until they reached a short set of single-level office buildings hidden behind the Taco Bell on Libby and Broad Streets. They entered the parking lot slowly, easing toward building number three. Today's counseling session was going to be different. Since seeing the therapist, Skyy had been attending the meetings alone, while Dominique waited for her in the waiting room. This session, Dominique would be joining her. The counselor thought it was time to talk about her childhood, and Skyy suggested that Dominique join her. It was a way for Skyy to finally allow someone in. Besides, it would give her an opportunity to answer questions Dominique had about his biological father.

As hard as it would be to tell her story, it would be a relief to get it off her chest. Kelvin reopened a chapter in her life once left sealed away. It all resurfaced that fatal night. While waiting for Dominique to unload the wheelchair, Skyy pulled down the visor's mirror to check her hair. Still a bit out of place, she smoothed her hands over it in an attempt to tidy her ponytail. She applied some MAC lip gloss to her lips and let her natural beauty be her guide. She looked down at her Ed Hardy t-shirt and matching Ed Hardy sweatpants. Since she couldn't feel her legs, she didn't know one of her pants legs was up near her knee. She pulled it down to her ankle. The door to the SUV flung open, and Dominique pushed the wheelchair as close to Skyy as he possibly could.

"Here we go again. Hold on. Let me get my strength up for this one," Dominique said, flexing imaginary muscles.

Skyy chuckled at his dry humor. Dominique used all of his strength to get Skyy into her chair. A soft groan came from his mouth. Skyy used her arms as a guide into the chair.

"I am not that heavy," she said.

217

"That's what you think," he joked, and she slapped his arm playfully.

Dominique wheeled Skyy up the wheelchair accessible ramp to the glass door. The lobby area was small and uninviting. The lighting was dim, with the sun providing most of the light through the glass door and windows. A couple of ficus plants bordered a few leather-covered benches that lined the gray walls. There was no receptionist, and the lobby was uncomfortably quiet. It appeared that most of the suites may have been empty in this particular building.

They checked all the names on the board until they saw 'Dr. Frank Powell—Suite 129'. Directly in front of them was suite 125. So, they moved past four doors until they reached Suite 129. Skyy could feel her heartbeat racing. Nervousness started to set in. She took a deep breath as Dominique opened the door to the small, cramped waiting area of Dr. Powell's office. The room was so small that there were only four chairs, two on each side of the wall. A small coffee table littered with old *Time* magazines took up the center of the waiting area, which was clad with wall-to-wall, outdated, mustard yellow, shag carpet. To the right of the room was a glass partition separating Dr. Powell's secretary from the rest of the room. She rose from her seat and pulled the glass window open when Skyy and Dominique entered.

"Hi, Ms. Armfield. Let me get you to sign in," the forty-something receptionist said, while handing Skyy a clipboard.

Dominique smiled at the receptionist, saying hello with a quick nod before grabbing the clipboard for Skyy.

"I'll let Dr. Powell know that you're here." The receptionist disappeared through a door on her side of the partition that led to Dr. Powell's office.

Dominique tried his best to maneuver the wheelchair around the cramped office, but ended up leaving the chair in the middle of the floor next to the table.

"You ready?" Dominique asked Skyy.

She hunched her shoulders.

"If you're not comfortable with me going in with you today, I can wait. I told you before, I'm not in a rush," Dominique said.

"No, today is the day. Everything you ever wanted to know and then some. You promise not to judge, right?" Skyy asked.

"This is not about judging. This is about learning and knowing."

"I know, Dominique, but I just don't want you to ... I don't know. I don't want to disappoint. You've been so forgiving and loving up to this point. I don't want anything to change that."

"I have searched for you for over a year. Don't you think I've thought about all of the different scenarios I could've been faced with when I found you? I have lived my childhood. I had two wonderful, loving parents that I could never, ever replace. All I ask of you is that you tell me the truth. I just need to know where I come from, that's all. I promise not to judge you."

The door that led to Dr. Powell's office opened, and a teenage girl appeared just as the secretary made her way back into her office on the other side of the partition. The teenage girl stopped at the window, and the secretary scribbled a date and time on a small appointment card and handed it to her.

"See you back here in two weeks," the secretary said. The teenage girl left the office quickly without glancing at Skyy or Dominique. "You two can go on back to Dr. Powell's office."

Dominique opened the door, propped it open, and backed the wheelchair through. Dr. Powell's office was directly across from the waiting room. The same hideous shag carpet from the waiting room covered the floors in Dr. Powell's office. His office appeared to have more space than the waiting room, with several chairs, a black leather sofa, and a huge desk. Two huge dry erase boards hung on the walls, and there was also a flip chart in the middle of the floor with two chairs on each side of it. Two windows provided a view of some woods and a privacy fence which separated the office park from the residential area. Dr. Powell, a tall, thin, dark-skinned man with mixed gray hair and thick glasses, stood when they entered the room. He had been sitting in one of the chairs next to the flip chart.

"Skyy, how are you? And you must be Dominique," he said, reaching to shake hands with him.

"Hi. Yes, I'm Dominique."

"Glad to finally meet you. Please, take a seat."

Dr. Powell pointed to the chair on the other side of the flip chart, and Skyy awkwardly moved the wheels on her wheelchair so she was situated next to Dominique. She still struggled a bit with manually handling the wheelchair independently.

Dr. Powell opened his manila folder, wrote something on the front of it, then took out his legal pad.

"Dominique, before we begin, let me first give you a quick overview of how these sessions normally work. I usually ask Skyy questions, often times open-ended questions, and I look to her to do most of the talking. My job is to remain neutral and to trigger dialogue, with hopes that the client will somehow come to conclusions of their own. Today, Skyy has decided to share some details of her childhood. I will give you a piece of paper, and you can write down any questions you want to ask her during question and answer time." Dr. Powell tore off a couple sheets of paper from his legal pad and handed them, along with a pencil, to Dominique. "Do you have any questions?"

Dominique shook his head no.

"Good. Let's get started. Skyy, tell me about your mother. What was the thing you remember the most about her?" Dr. Powell asked.

"Hmmm. My mother and I didn't really have a relationship like I saw on television or like the kids at my school had with their mothers. She wasn't the affectionate type. No hugs, no kisses. She never told me that she loved me, but I know she did. She showed her love in other ways. Her thing was to cook and bake. I remember the time we spent baking homemade peanut butter cookies, apple pies, and all sorts of cobblers. Her homemade carrot cake was better than any I've ever tasted. The time we spent in the kitchen was probably when we bonded the most. But, that didn't happen every day, only on Saturdays and Sundays."

"Why Saturdays and Sundays?"

"Those were the days when my father would come over. She would wake up early on Saturday mornings, sometimes as early as five a.m., and clean the house. By the time I was up, she was preparing a big dinner for him. Homemade lasagna, chicken Florentine, shrimp Alfredo with fresh homemade Alfredo sauce. My mom could cook anything from scratch. And, of course, there would be dessert. I remember how she would always take a bubble bath before he came, and I would sit on the edge of her bed and watch her put on her make-up and rub this Egyptian musk body oil all over her body. Sometimes she would let me put some on. I loved the way it smelled. By the time she was finished dressing, she would force me out of her room so she could 'freshen up', as she would say. That was my cue to get my Barbie dolls and other toys and sit on the floor directly in front of the floor model color TV. I had the TV all to myself. I watched cartoon after cartoon."

"Did your mother work?"

"No, she always told me she was too ill to work. Monday through Friday, she would get me up for school. I can remember getting cereal before catching the bus, then coming home from school and she would always be in the bed. The only time my mother really got out of the bed was on Saturday and Sunday."

"What about in the evenings? Did you cook with her then?"

"No. She would always fix something quick for dinner when I came home from school—fish sticks or ravioli from the can, stuff like that. However, when the weekend rolled around, she came to life. Every now and then, there would be leftovers from the weekend that I would have during the week. But, for the most part, Mom didn't come alive until the weekend."

Dr. Powell scribbled some notes on his legal pad, as did Dominique.

"Tell me about your father. What is the thing you remember most about him?"

"He was married. That's about all I remember about him."

"How would you explain your relationship with him?"

"I didn't have a relationship with him. I saw him once or twice a week for maybe fifteen, twenty minutes, long enough for him to come out of my mother's bedroom to eat his dinner. He would sit at the dining room table while my mother waited on him, and I stayed on the floor in front of the TV, pretty much invisible to him. He didn't talk to me. The only time he had any conversation was with my mom."

"How long did this go on?"

"It went on consistently until I was about twelve. That's when his visits became fewer, and finally, it would be months before my mother and I would see him. She'd started going through her weekend ritual only to be stood up by him. The less we saw of him,

221

the more my mother drank. Then one day, I came home from school and the paramedics were there. They wouldn't let me in the house. My grandmother was standing in the driveway crying, and I kept asking her to tell me what was wrong, but she couldn't. She just kept shaking her head. Grandma said she drank herself to death. I think she died of a broken heart. I went to stay with my grandmother until she died when I was sixteen. Cancer. I had nowhere else to go then. My mother was an only child, and I didn't have any aunts or uncles. So, I was moved into a group home."

"Let's step back a minute. The relationship between you and your mother, were you happy with it?"

Skyy thought about the question for a minute before answering. She looked over at Dominique and tears welled up in her eyes.

"No. I resented her for always putting me last. I never felt like she loved me the way she loved him, but I know for a fact that I loved her more than he did."

"Why do you feel as if she put you last?"

"The only time my mother functioned was when she was getting ready for him on the weekends. She was a zombie during the week, could barely get out of bed. But, on the weekends, she had this strength to pull it all together. She never had the strength for me. When I wanted to try out for gymnastics, she told me I couldn't because she couldn't pick me up after school. I never, ever stayed after school for basketball games or any extracurricular activities in middle school. As sad as I was when she passed away, I felt relieved in a way because staying with Grandma gave me a new lease on life, but that was shortlived."

"When your mother passed away, did you ever see your father again?"

Skyy bowed her head with sadness. "No. I haven't seen him since the funeral. I thought when Dominique had the private investigator looking for me that my father was actually looking for me."

"How do you feel about your father now?"

"I don't. All he is to me is a name. I can barely remember his face." Skyy picked at the embellishment on her sweatpants.

Dr. Powell wrote down a few notes, while Dominique sat quietly.

"Let's fast forward to high school. After your grandmother passed away and you were living in a group home, you had no family left. Tell me about that time in your life."

"I try not to think about a lot of it because most of it was no fun. Secondhand clothes, kids teased me a lot. The only thing I had going for me was my looks. So, the boys liked me, but the girls hated me. I had a hard time fitting in. I guess it had a lot to do with me spending so much time alone as a child. It didn't do a lot for me socially, that's for sure. Then I met Chaz, and that all changed."

"Who is Chaz?"

"Dominique's father."

Dominique perked up when he realized this was the part of the story he had the most interest.

"Tell me how your life changed when you met Chaz."

Skyy took a deep breath and swallowed. As much as she loved Chaz, she knew his chapter in her life would be the most difficult to discuss.

"He was the only one during that time that treated me special and showed me love. My mother was gone, my grandmother was gone, and I had a father who didn't think enough to take me in when I needed him. Chaz was just so sweet and caring, and he always told me how much he loved me. Keep in mind, I never had anyone tell me they loved me, ever. But, Chaz did."

"Okay, so you finally meet someone that shows you affection you missed out on as a child. He filled a tremendous void for you. So what happened between you and Chaz?"

Skyy put both hands over her face and wept silently.

"You're doing great, Skyy," Dominique said.

Skyy thought about him and realized she needed to find the strength to purge this information for Dominique's sake.

"I met Chaz my freshman year. He was my English teacher. He tutored me because I had so much trouble with English. When my grandmother died my sophomore year and I was moved to the group home, I remember these two girls told everyone in school that I lived in a boarding house with the retards and how I was a retard, too. This particular day, they were following me through school being really cruel, so I ran into the bathroom and missed my bus. Chaz was still in his classroom. I asked him for a ride home, and that's how it all started. I was so upset that day. He took me to the mall, we got ice cream, and he told me how pretty I was and how those girls were just jealous of me. He even bought me a pair of Used jeans. I loved those jeans. From then on, our relationship blossomed. He treated me so nice. Always bought me things, gave me money, and took me places.

"He was the first man who ever showed me any love. And I loved him back. We agreed that when I graduated from high school, we would be together for good. He was going to leave his wife, and we were going to move to Florida and start our life together. However, during my junior year, I got pregnant. The group home where I lived found out and they put me out. I had nowhere to go. I never got a chance to even tell Chaz about the baby. The only thing I told him was that I was homeless, and he told me not to worry about a thing. He told me to meet him at the train station that evening with my bags packed and he would take care of everything. But, he never showed up. I waited and waited and waited. Then I saw it on the news in the lobby of the train station. She killed him and then killed herself."

"Who?"

"His wife. It seems she was not willing to let him go so easily. Murder-Suicide. I had no money. Nowhere to go. I was pregnant and had nobody. Nobody. I found a women's shelter in downtown Baltimore that hooked me up with an adoption agency. They found a family for the baby that paid me enough money to leave Baltimore for good, so that's what I did. I had the baby, got on a train to Richmond, Virginia, and never looked back. I worked two fast food jobs at first and made enough to afford an efficiency apartment on Chamberlyne Avenue. Went back to school and got my GED, then went to cosmetology school. I worked in a small salon on Brookland Park Boulevard until I got certified, then moved to the Hair Cuttery on Brook Road. Worked there for a few years, built up my clientele, then I opened my own salon. Everything in my life was perfect. And then, out of nowhere, Chaz's son entered my life, wanting revenge for his parents' deaths."

By now, Skyy had nonstop tears rolling down her cheeks, and Dominique's eyes were red. He was trying hard to be strong, but it wasn't working. Dr. Powell sat motionless, taking in every word.

"Skyy, at any point during your relationship with your teacher, did you think the relationship was inappropriate?"

Skyy hunched her shoulders. "I mean, I know it doesn't sound good now, and as an adult, I realize what happened between me and him was wrong. But, I loved him, and he loved me. I never felt about anyone the way I felt for him. When he died, I just came to the realization that I couldn't love anyone because they would eventually be taken away from me."

"Is that why you gave your baby up for adoption?"

"My life was hopeless. Nobody to love me, nowhere to go. I couldn't get attached to anybody else. I had to let him go, too. Save myself the pain. Everyone that I ever loved left me. My mother, my grandmother, Chaz—all gone. I vowed to never, ever fall in love with anyone else. I guess that's why, as an adult, I've only dated married men. I don't want anyone to love me. I don't want the letdown."

Skyy sat there with her face in her hands, shaking her head. It was hard for her to put her emotions on the table this way, but she had to admit, she felt as if a load had been lifted.

"Skyy, I don't know if you realize it or not, but you have based your entire life around your relationship with your father. Your teacher was the father figure you longed for your whole life, but he took advantage of it. He crossed the line with you, having a relationship with one of his students. You have to stop going through life living in fear of committing to your feelings. Stop expecting the worse. Everybody deserves the best. But, you have to expect the best. Don't close yourself inside yourself. You have a son who has shown you that he is willing to love you the way you deserve to be loved. However, you have to be willing to love him back without fear of losing him. Dominique, do you have any questions? I saw you taking some notes."

"I did at first, but it's not important now."

"Are you sure?"

"Positive."

Skyy couldn't tell from his tone whether he was upset with her or not. He had a solemn look on his face. Then again, what could she expect? This was a lot to absorb at once, especially as it pertained to his biological mother and father.

"Can I say one thing?" Skyy said. "I just wanted Dominique to know that the person I was before the shooting is not the person I became after the shooting. If there's any conciliation, Dominique has taught me how to be unselfish when it comes to love. I'm not afraid anymore."

Dominique reached over and squeezed Skyy's hand.

"It was nice to peel the layers back today, Skyy. We're going to keep working on getting to the core. The aftermatch of the shooting will dwindle away with time, but what we accomplished today will be with you forever. Remember that."

Epilogue—Four months later

The summer heat was so thick it felt as if Coco was wearing a wool coat in the middle of July. Today, his clientele would be light since it was the fourth of July holiday weekend and many of his customers would be celebrating by attending cookouts, fish frys, and maybe even going to the beach. Hairdos would take a backseat this weekend.

Coco unlocked the door to the salon and felt a bit of relief when the cool air hit his face. Even at seven in the morning, the humidity was unbearable. He turned off the alarm and locked the door behind him. Since Skyy had been away, Coco had kept things pretty much the same with hopes that Skyy would be returning soon. He still held on to hope that Skyy would go back to her old self, so he continued to work with her customers, insisting it was only temporary until Skyy returned. He pulled out his BlackBerry to check his calendar. Only six appointments scheduled, which was very light for Coco. He didn't mind. It would give him an opportunity to get out of the salon early on a Saturday for a change. He was actually looking forward to leaving early so he could go to his mother's house for a family cookout, followed by a night of clubbing at Richmond's newest gay nightclub called Sensations.

The salon telephone rang, causing Coco to stir around to find the cordless phone that was missing from its base. He hated when Shauna, the newest stylist in the salon, didn't put the phone back on the cradle. For one, it didn't allow the phone an opportunity to charge, and two, it made it difficult to find when needed. Coco was still trying to break her in, even though she'd been at the salon for three months now. The only good things were that she paid her booth rent on time, and she had a hefty clientele.

Coco found the cordless phone on the sofa in the waiting area, and by the time he reached it, the person had hung up. His

BlackBerry vibrated next, which meant someone was trying to get in touch with him.

"Hello?" he answered.

"Well, good morning, diva. Are you going to come and get me or what?" Skyy asked.

"Hey, Honey Bunches of Oats. I'll be right out."

Coco put the cordless phone on its base and went to the door, peeking out of the blinds. He spotted Dominique's SUV parked directly in front of the salon, and Skyy's wheelchair was already on the sidewalk. Coco went out to assist Dominique with Skyy.

"Good morning, sunshine! Hi, Dominique," Coco sang.

"Hey, wassup, C," Dominique said, trying to sound hard. He had a difficult time calling Coco by his name, feeling a bit homophobic by doing so.

Coco leaned down and kissed Skyy on the cheek before taking control of the wheelchair.

"What time, gorgeous?" Dominique asked.

"Say about three, handsome," Coco responded.

"I was talking to Skyy," Dominique said.

Skyy and Coco laughed.

"See you later," Dominique said before getting back into his SUV.

Coco and Skyy watched him drive off before going into the salon.

"Okay, so this ensemble is cute. What is this, Ed Hardy? I like. You look cute," Coco said, referencing Skyy's cotton tank top and cropped sweatpants with matching Ed Hardy sneakers. Coco struggled to get the wheelchair in the salon, seeing as though the salon was not wheelchair accessible.

"Coco, stop trying to butter my muffin."

"Butter your muffin? W-T-F?"

"Dominique said his mother used to say that to him all the time. You know, when he was trying to con her about something. She would always say he was trying to butter her muffin."

"Oh okay. Corny, but anywayyyy. How are you doing? Still going to physical therapy?"

"Of course. Physical therapy, mental therapy, you name it and I'm doing it. I've actually been moving around the house using a walker. I'll be on my feet soon. I know it."

Coco moved the wheelchair to the shampoo bowl. "Yes, I know you will, too. So, Dominique has been the perfect little son, huh? I tell you, that boy is delicious."

"Coco, stop talking about Dominique like that. He likes girls. I told you he has a girlfriend back home."

"Sure, he does, at least for now. Just wait."

Skyy hit Coco's arm playfully. "Don't talk about my son like that," she said in a protective tone.

"Awww, how cute. Look at you sounding all Mufasa like."

"You so stupid," Skyy said.

"Okay, time for muscles. Come on. Let me get you into this chair," Coco told her.

He moved the wheelchair so that it was facing the shampoo bowl, then he lifted Skyy to the shampoo chair. Skyy used her arms to situate her body comfortably in the chair as Coco slung the wrinkles from the plastic cape before wrapping it in front of her.

"So what are we doing? Just a wash and roller set? Better yet, when was the last time you got a relaxer? Ewwww!"

"Shut up, Coco. I haven't had a relaxer in over a year. I've just been getting Dominique's girlfriend to wash and blow dry it for me. Then I wear it up in a ponytail. Very simple. You know I can go a while without a relaxer anyway. Just wash it and give me a good conditioner, please. It's not like I have any plans to go anywhere."

"Speaking of plans, have you talked to any of your men friends lately?"

"Please. J has been trying to come up here to visit because he doesn't believe I'm paralyzed. He knows I was shot because he saw the crime scene tape at my house when he came to visit the day after the shooting. But, he thinks I'm lying about being paralyzed to avoid seeing him. I mean, why would I lie about something like that? Kyle, well it didn't take much to get rid of him. He acted concerned after hearing about everything on the news. I think he wanted to be sure it was me. I haven't heard from him since. And Davin, well, we talk from time to time, but that's about it."

"Damn, girl. Why won't you let J come and see you?"

"For what? Our relationship was based on one thing, and that *thing* is something I am not concerned with right now. Let's get off of that. Let's talk about you and how things have been going here since I've been gone. Everything appears to be in order. Glad to see you haven't redecorated," Skyy joked.

"I don't envy you being the lady in charge because handling the business is tough work. But, I think I have it all under control," Coco said.

"How is the new girl coming along?"

"Great clientele, but she is still young and a bit immature. I'm working on her, though. She's serious about her customers, so at least I don't have to worry about her coming in late and all that. Still can't find a nail tech, though. Tiffany called the other day. I still can't believe that girl is in jail."

"I know. Fed time at that. Her mom is taking care of the kids, right?"

"Yeah, girl. The new baby looks just like her son. I feel sorry for those kids, having to grow up without their mother at such a young age."

"Well, maybe she will get some time off for good behavior or something. I don't know. I just wish she would've talked to us before getting into that mess with Trey."

Coco held Skyy's head back in the sink once the water level was comfortable. Vigorously, he soaked her hair with the water before applying shampoo. Skyy closed her eyes because getting her hair washed was relaxing, but she also wanted to keep from getting soapy water splashed in her face.

"I talked to Debi last week. She calls me at least once a week to check on me. She said she likes North Carolina."

"Yeah? Can we call her a ho since she's marrying her ex-husband's brother?" Coco asked.

"Coco, mind your business."

"I'm just saying."

"Saying what? The girl found love. That's all that matters. Who cares that it's her brother-in-law."

Coco stopped shampooing Skyy's hair, causing Skyy to open her eyes. His hands were still in her hair, soap and all.

"What?" she said.

"Did you hear what you just said? Brother-in-law! That's just downright trashy, Jerry Springer shit."

"Does it matter that she dated him first before she dated Eric?"

"Either way you shuffle it around and pour it on the table, it's wrong."

"I'm just glad she's happy, and even happier that she forgave me."

"Mmm-hmmm," Coco said dramatically.

"Come on, Coco, that happened last year. Give me a break."

"What? I didn't say a word."

Coco rinsed the soap from Skyy's hair after washing it several times. He then applied some conditioner to it and combed it through before putting a plastic cap on her head.

"Okay, over to the dryers."

Skyy grabbed Coco's hand as he was about to lift her from the chair. "Coco, before your other customers get here, I need to tell you something."

He stopped in his tracks and turned to face Skyy. "What's wrong?"

"I just want you to know how much I love you and appreciate you for being my friend."

"Uh-oh, here we go again. Skyy, you already told me all this. Don't start with the mushy stuff."

"I know, but you don't understand. I really, really appreciate everything. You jumped in and took care of my business when I couldn't. You came through and helped take care of me when I couldn't take care of myself. You're like my family, the only family really besides Dominique. I realize that for as long as we've known each other, I never let you in, but you never let that stop you from being a true friend to me. I want you to know I'm not saying all of this because of everything that you've done. I'm saying it because you're my friend and I love you."

A small tear rolled down Skyy's cheek. The moment that Coco had worked hard to create, only to be blocked by Skyy's unwillingness to share, was finally right there between them. Coco leaned over and hugged Skyy tight.

"I love you, too, Skyy. I think if the tables were turned, you would do the same for me, right?" he asked.

"It's funny, because eight months ago, I probably would've given you a different answer. It took for me to become paralyzed to realize the most important things in my life. All the designer clothes, shoes, handbags, jewelry—none of that stuff is important to me anymore. I realize now that putting other people's feelings before mine is what's important. I have a totally different outlook on life. I made a promise to myself that when I walk again, and I will walk again, I won't be the person I used to be. That's the old Skyy. The new Skyy has learned how to love. Not just love myself, but to love and respect those around me, especially my friends."

Coco nodded his head. There really wasn't much that he could say, but he was happy. He was happy because his friend was finally happy, truly happy. And underneath it all, she finally got it.

About the Author

LaKesa Cox is the author of *After the Storm* and *Water in my Eyes*. She is also a contributor in *Nikki Turner Presents: Street Chronicles—Girls in the Game* and *Street Chronicles—A Woman's Work*. She lives in a suburb of Richmond, Virginia with her family and is currently working on her fourth novel.